PRAISE FOR DIRK KURBJUW

'*Fear* shifts our moral codes. It makes us sympathetic to violent revenge, accessories to murder. Do we want the victim to survive? No, we don't. Long after I had put this book down I still didn't. A great achievement.'
Herman Koch, bestselling author of *The Dinner*

'A smart, psychologically complex and morally acute fable of modern German society decked out in the garb of an intricate thriller.'
Sydney Morning Herald

'An unnerving portrait of how close many of us can come to committing unspeakable acts of violence—often motivated by a fear of violence itself.'
Lifted Brow

'Dirk Kurbjuweit exposes the evil lurking just below the surface of civilised life.'
Stern

'Gripping, suspenseful and unbelievably dark…As a thriller, *Fear* more than holds its own against the competition.'
Die Welt

'High-voltage and multi-layered.'
Frankfurter Neue Presse

'A subtle and engrossing psychological thriller that gives an intelligent, carefully considered response to the question of how much our liberal values are worth when we feel our lives are threatened.'
Brigitte

Dirk Kurbjuweit lives in Berlin and is a journalist at *Der Spiegel*. He has received numerous awards for his writing, including the Egon Erwin Kisch Prize for journalism, and is the author of nine critically acclaimed novels, many of which have been adapted for film, television, theatre and radio. *Fear*, *Twins* and *The Missing* are the first of his works to be translated into English.

Imogen Taylor is a translator who has lived in Berlin since 2001. Her translations include *Promise Me You'll Shoot Yourself* by Florian Huber, *Fear* and *Twins* by Dirk Kurbjuweit and *The Truth and Other Lies* by Sasha Arango.

The Missing

DIRK KURBJUWEIT

Translated from the German by Imogen Taylor

t

TEXT PUBLISHING MELBOURNE AUSTRALIA

textpublishing.com.au

The Text Publishing Company
Swann House, 22 William Street, Melbourne Victoria 3000, Australia

The Text Publishing Company (UK) Ltd
130 Wood Street, London EC2V 6DL, United Kingdom

Originally published in German in 2020 as *Haarmann. Kriminalroman*, by Penguin Verlag, a division of Verlagsgruppe Random House GmbH, München, Germany
Published in Australia and New Zealand by The Text Publishing Company, 2021

Cover design by Chong W. H.
Cover image from Wikimedia Commons
Page design by Rachel Aitken
Typeset by J&M Typesetting

Printed and bound in Australia by Griffin Press, an accredited ISO/NZS 14001:2004 Environmental Management System printer

ISBN: 9781922330444 (paperback)
ISBN: 9781925923858 (ebook)

A catalogue record for this book is available from the National Library of Australia.

GOETHE INSTITUT The translation of this work was supported by a grant from the Goethe-Institut.

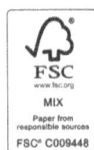

FSC
www.fsc.org
MIX
Paper from
responsible sources
FSC® C009448

This book is printed on paper certified against the Forest Stewardship Council® Standards. Griffin Press holds FSC chain-of-custody certification SGS-COC-005088. FSC promotes environmentally responsible, socially beneficial and economically viable management of the world's forests.

The Missing

1

He'd been walking along the road for an hour, but there was still no sign of dawn and, despite his fear of being seen, he longed for light. So far he hadn't met a soul—only a motor car had passed him, coming the other way, and he'd hidden behind a tree. The driver was staring ahead, the passenger asleep, his head pressed against the window. The boy waited until the noise of the car had faded, then he stepped out from behind the tree and carried on walking. He looked at his watch. It was half past five and the train left at five past six; he ought to catch it. Just as long as no one caught him first. He looked about him. Take it easy, he told himself. Why would anyone follow you? Why would anyone try to find you? Mother and Father were still asleep; they'd get up at six to wake him at a quarter past. Those were their times.

It was really his father's watch, not his, but it was all he'd taken. The money was his own; he'd been putting it aside. There wasn't a lot left, but it would get him to Bremerhaven. He'd send the watch to his father as soon as he arrived; he'd made up his mind to that. 'You'll get your watch back,' he'd written in his letter of farewell. 'I've only borrowed it.' And: 'We'll see each other again some day, I promise.' That was all. He couldn't tell them where he was going, and the other thing would come out soon enough. It might even be a comfort to them.

A sudden crash made him start—a thundering and snorting— and he dropped his suitcase and froze, not knowing what had happened. Then a shadow flitted past and a deer crossed the road. Two deer. Lord, what a fright he'd had. They ran into the field, slowed to a walk—and then stopped and turned and looked at him. Silly creatures. His heart steadied, he picked up his suitcase and went on his way.

A faint light on the horizon, a yellow shimmer, and already he was coming to the edge of the small town. Two men on horseback drew near from behind at a leisurely pace, clearly not looking for anyone. They said good morning and passed by. He was hungry; he'd set off without breakfast or coffee. When he reached the town it was a quarter to six and he went into a bakery and bought three rolls. One of these he ate at once, going along; the others would have to last him until Hanover. He'd have some time there between trains and would treat himself to a bit of hot lunch—a sausage, some potato salad. The people he saw paid him no attention; they were hurrying to work, to market. He was afraid all the same—afraid of being recognised, talked to. But he needn't have worried. He got to the station at five to six, bought a ticket and boarded the train to Hanover.

———

Late in the evening, long after Müller had gone home and the corridors of police headquarters had fallen silent, Robert Lahnstein went down to the archives. He often worked late into the night and, with the chief's permission, he'd had a set of keys made for himself.

The light switch clacked. Lahnstein saw rows of shelves filled with files, fat ones and thin ones. The air felt greasy, soaked with the stench of manila and yellowing paper, the reek of the past.

What he wanted were new files, unthumbed, not yet yellowed. He went up and down the rows, beginning on his knees at the lower shelves and gradually straightening himself until he was craning his neck to make out the writing on the spines. On the front side of the shelves he worked through the files from right to left; around the back, from left to right. His knees were soon aching, his neck stiff. The dust made him cough.

Here was a new-looking file. He pulled it out, opened it. A murderer—own wife and kids. Lahnstein put it back and kept going. Two hours later he found what he was looking for: an empty folder, unused, the cardboard still shiny. It was filed under the letter J, but that didn't mean a thing; they'd probably switched the files so that no one would know which was missing. His guess was that it hadn't been moved far, maybe from somewhere between G and M.

He locked up the archives, fetched his hat and coat and set off for home on foot, making his usual detour past the theatre where the prostitutes loitered, most of them boys, or 'dolly boys', as they were known. They stepped out from the shadows of the trees and hooked their arms through his; sometimes one of them grabbed his crotch. He'd swipe the cheeky hand away and hiss, 'Be careful,' meaning it both ways, and the boys would laugh. He watched the other men from the corner of his eye, to see if any of them were acting oddly, but the only odd thing about them was that they were all doing their damndest not to attract attention. He lived in hope of a hunch, a lucky break.

Soon after midnight he reached his lodging house, a big flat with three rooms for rent. Lahnstein was the only lodger at present. He slipped off his shoes—house rules— and stepped over undulating parquet into his room. In bed he lay awake for an hour, waiting for sleep, afraid of the too-familiar dream.

He had to keep his eye on the sun because he knew they'd come that way, take him by surprise, invisible against the light until they were almost upon him. He looked into the glare; he looked ahead and then down. He saw farmers tilling their fields, cattle grazing, a motor car on a country road, villages, farms, people by a river.

The sun, focus on the sun. Nothing there. He listened. The steady throb of the engine, the roar of the wind, the usual sounds. All in order.

He turned to glance at the back seat where Lissy was sitting with August on her lap. Lissy shouted something, but he couldn't hear her. She waved, gesticulated. He looked at the sun again—still nothing. He looked down through the small bomb bay and saw a church tower, houses, a pond—all calm and tranquil. But now the engine was stuttering, the propeller rotating more and more slowly.

They were floating, drifting; the plane was dropping, though not fast. Lahnstein glanced back from time to time. August had gone to sleep, clasped tight in Lissy's arms. Looking ahead again, Lahnstein scanned the countryside for somewhere to land—a flat meadow, a road that wasn't lined with trees. But there were only rocks and mountains, rivers winding through gorges, rugged, barren country.

There was nothing for it but a crash landing. But it never came; he always woke before they hit the ground or were wrecked on a mountain. He woke feeling that he was still flying, and yet already he could see the room where he was sleeping, the foot of the bed, the little window, the crooked cupboard, the hooks on the wall where his things hung. He was awake but plummeting towards earth. That was the worst moment.

Then it was over and he lay motionless in bed; he had survived. The clock on his bedside table said half past six. Lahnstein preferred it when the dream struck in the middle of the night; then he could go back to sleep and recover. This way, he had to start the new day with the falling, plummeting feeling. He wondered what the day would bring. Another missing boy?

The last had been reported missing on 27 October 1924; two other reports had been filed on the twenty-fifth and the twelfth. One boy had disappeared in September, one in August. A lull in July, one boy in June, two in May, another lull in April, another boy in March. The first, Fritz Franke, had gone missing on 12 February 1923. The names were firmly imprinted on Lahnstein's mind; he knew them all.

There was no rhythm. He had studied the intervals, added and averaged, grouped and regrouped, drawn lines and arrows—but it was hopeless; there was no pattern. The longest interval between crimes—if crimes they were—was a good two months, between 20 March and 23 May; the shortest was two days, at the end of October. Ten boys in total, aged between thirteen and eighteen—most commonly sixteen. Heinz Brinkmann was the last so far, thirteen years old. The ages, too, had kept Lahnstein occupied; he'd fiddled around for hours, trying to correlate each boy's age with the date he'd gone missing. But there was no pattern there either. And there were no corpses, no clues of any kind.

He got up, swaying slightly, not yet properly landed. What if it was over? If no more boys went missing? There would still be ten cases for him to solve. His hope was that the next case would provide him with a clue, a corpse, something to start from. Horrific thought, but there it was. He needed another case. He needed a dead boy, a murder. That was what he was waiting for, though he told himself it was impossible, out of the question. He wasn't like that, was he? He hoped not.

Listening at the door and hearing nothing, he stepped out into the passage and staggered to the lavatory in his pyjamas. As there was no evidence of the nature of the crimes, his imagination was free to wander. Lahnstein couldn't help himself; he saw everything—carnage, bloodlust. When he woke like today, feeling thin-skinned and vulnerable, he was thirteen-year-old Heinz Brinkmann in the last minutes of his life, skinned alive, screaming and screaming. On other days, he was the murderer, knife in hand. But why a knife? They knew nothing, not a thing.

Were they even dealing with murder? In his moments of optimism, Lahnstein had his doubts. Boys that age often ran away—to America or to join the Foreign Legion. So many were disappointed because the war had come to an end before they'd had a chance to be drafted. They went looking for wars of their own—took themselves off to Strasbourg, got themselves recruited, went to fight in the jungle or the desert. It was a possibility, anyway.

Lahnstein stopped to listen again before returning to his room. Not a sound. But when he opened the lavatory door, he found himself staring into his landlady's boozy face. She'd been lying in wait for him.

'All well?'

'Yes.'

'Caught the murderer yet?'

'Getting there.'

She stood before him in her grey house dress and grey slippers, barring the way to his room. He pushed past her. As he put his hand on the door handle, she said something behind him.

'They've found human flesh.'

He wheeled round.

'Where?'

'Walterscheidt's Inn.'

'How do you know it was human?'

'There was a man there who'd lived in Africa and knew the taste. Said he could tell for sure. Spat it out, he did.'

'Can I speak to this man?'

'I don't know him. He left pretty sharpish, he was that disgusted.'

It was always the same: panic-mongering, rumours, never anything solid. Everyone had heard things; nobody knew anything for certain.

'Why would anyone sell human flesh?' he asked the landlady.

She lowered her voice. 'To make ends meet, keep the prices down. The government's behind it, the powers that be.'

Nonsense.

He went into his room and stood at the washbasin, steady on his feet at last. His little plane had landed or crashed or whatever—at any rate, it had left the air and returned him to earth. He had a cursory wash and shave, staring into pale-blue eyes. His face was narrow, his nose and ears delicate rather than distinctive (which he didn't like), his forehead high (which he did, rather). He had pale skin and a mole to the right of his nose.

In the cafe Lahnstein glanced at the morning papers. Was there a new case? No, everyone was still writing hysterically about Hitler: the coup in Munich, the march on the beer hall—a putsch with Ludendorff, of all people. It had failed; Hitler was in custody. Thank God, thought Lahnstein; they'd have ended up blaming him for the coup, because he couldn't solve the murders. The whole country was nervous. Or was it just him? Calm down, he told himself.

He withdrew into a corner of the cafe with a regional newspaper and ordered coffee and a bun. Then he scanned the local pages for police reports. Brawls, thefts, seized smuggled goods, a case of rape. He'd heard about the rape the day before. The offender had been led past his office, a fifty-year-old who'd lain in wait for a neighbour in the cellar. The neighbour was forty-one and a woman—nothing to do with the missing boys. But he'd have a look at the interrogation transcripts all the same. He leafed back to the front of the paper and read about the attempted putsch. Hermann Göring had escaped. Lahnstein had met him once on an airfield. He was said to be an ace. Now he was a wanted man.

Lahnstein put on his hat, paid the bill and went out into the wind and rain, his coat collar turned up. Clutching his hat to his head, he hurried through alleys, past little houses that stood shrunken and slumped like very old people, leaning against one another, as if to prop each other up. Half timbered, paint peeling, windowpanes patched with cardboard or tarnished and murky. A rolling, dipping landscape of cobblestones. Horses' hooves, clicking sedately, goods carts, the occasional motor car, furious hooting. You were faster on foot in this crush, and fastest of all were the newsboys. Loudest, too. *Putsch in Munich, Hitler in Gaol*. No missing boy today though. Take care, Lahnstein thought, you're just the age. So far none of the victims had been newsboys. Most of them were workers or tradesmen, still apprentices. He wondered about that. Why were there no rich kids and so few grammar-school boys?

Were they one-seven-fivers—offenders against Section 175, guilty of 'acts of indecency'? Probably.

There was a crush on the narrow bridge over the Leine and the whiff of poor hygiene—one bath a week, if that; old clothes, rarely changed. It was unpleasant, but Lahnstein was forbearing. The age of hyperinflation was not the age of cleanliness. People were too poor to buy new clothes, too distracted to keep clean, always trying to get rid of old money and lay hands on new, always busy watching the prices, trading and bartering. Clothes were swapped for food. You could smell it. Lahnstein was no stranger to the difficulties. His own coat was riddled with holes, but it was never the moment to replace it. The value of money was beginning to steady; he would wait.

A man rammed into his shoulder; Lahnstein had been lost in thought and hadn't seen him coming. Turning around, he saw a coat that swept the floor, a narrow back, an empty sleeve. He considered going after the man and confronting him, but thought better of it. *Somme*, the man would yell, *Verdun*, *Eisack*. Those magic words explained everything, excused everything. It was the same at headquarters.

He hurried on, more attentive now. Matches, scarves, socks, cigarettes, vases, knives—these were the wares offered to him, held out to him on the short walk, sometimes wordlessly, with only a look of entreaty. Since the war, they had become a nation of hawkers. First heroes, now hawkers, he thought bitterly. He bought nothing, not even cigarettes. His stocks were low, but he wanted to call in at the tobacconist's that evening. Was it because of the woman who ran the shop? He felt slightly ashamed at the thought, because Lissy was still in the plane. He saw the sea, the wind, the sluggish propeller. Sometimes Lissy looked as if she wanted to wave but was too weak to raise her arm. August was still asleep.

A horse pissed on the road next to him and the strong stream splashed up from the cobbles onto his feet. The rain had smeared horseshit all over the place. The closer Lahnstein came to headquarters, the more afraid he grew. He didn't want to find a boy's parents waiting for him—or, worse still, a widow who was missing her son, the spitting image of his dad. Then again, that was precisely what he wanted.

All was quiet at headquarters. Relieved, Lahnstein hurried past the reception clerks; they returned his good morning tepidly, barely civilly, but there was no mention of waiting visitors. There was no one upstairs either; the office was empty. Elated, disappointed, Lahnstein went to the lavatory, took a wad of paper and rubbed his shoes till they were clean, then polished them with spit till he was satisfied with the shine. Back in the office, he sat down at his desk. He ought to have reached straight for a file or the telephone, but he missed the moment and was sucked down into his eddying thoughts.

August. Lissy. He thought of the goodbyes at the station in Salzburg after their fortnight together in a guesthouse on Lake Irr. Lissy had relatives in the village. He had three weeks' leave. August was six months old. It was a wet summer, but they walked around the lake every day, the mountains behind them when they set off, and in full view as they neared the end of their walk. That way they gave themselves something to look forward to, and the last stretch seemed less of a slog. They both loved the mountains. One day they went to Fuschl, another to Lake Wolfgang. August lay in his pram, and when he cried Lahnstein took him out and carried him a little way. Sometimes they sat down in a meadow and Lissy nursed him while Lahnstein lay on his back, staring up at the confounded sky.

They went to see Lissy's brother, who was a farmer. Lahnstein took August into the shed to show him the animals, but a bellowing cow startled the child and it took a quarter of an hour to calm him.

From the farm they walked up a mountain, where Lissy's brother said there was a beautiful chapel. Pushing the pram was hard work; Lahnstein made steam-engine noises and Lissy laughed. In the evenings they sat on the bed with the baby between them, happy when they saw a new expression cross his face, a shift of features that seemed deliberate rather than random. They were eager for progress, development. August had only to smile and Lahnstein was lapped by the warm, milky comfort of a new emotion. It was a good antidote to the war, the shooting, the military hospital; all those things were blotted out until Lahnstein woke in the middle of the night and they rushed back and engulfed him. Another twelve days, he'd think, another eight, another six.

'You're always looking up at the sky,' Lissy said.

It was true; he scanned the clouds, observing the light, gauging the weather like a pilot. Was it good flying weather— and if so, for whom?

'Stay down here with us,' Lissy said, taking his hands. They didn't quarrel on this holiday, although the room was small and August cried a lot. Sometimes Lahnstein wished he were far away, up in the sky where the Sopwith Camels were waiting for him—but wasn't that horribly disloyal to his family? He felt shame at putting the hateful war before his wife and son, just because they were sometimes hard work. The thoughts passed.

Lissy talked a great deal about the future, as if they'd already put the present behind them. A bigger flat, three or four children, his police career, the money they could expect to come into, the little house they'd buy—for her, these things were certainties, facts from tomorrow's world. She smiled all the time. Sometimes a Sopwith came flying out of the sun and Lahnstein fired and fired until he realised that Lissy was holding his clenched hands. 'Shh,' she said, 'shh.' She made the same gentle hushing sounds to soothe August when he fretted.

They both wept on the last evening. August was asleep and they lay intertwined and promised to see each other again at Christmas. It was only September; Lahnstein tried to work out how many combat missions he'd have flown by then, but the number was too high to bear thinking about. He stopped counting and said nothing to Lissy, but he was trembling; she must have known what was going through his head. The word 'fear', the greatest taboo of all, rumbled at the back of his mind and he longed for the relief of saying it, but knew it was impossible. It wasn't a word you spoke out loud.

They didn't make love as they had most other nights. They woke when August woke at two, and again at half past four. Lissy nursed him and Lahnstein soaked up their contentment, toying with the thought of staying on—hiding out in the mountains until the present gave way to the future. But that wouldn't give him the life Lissy was looking for either; he'd only end up on the run or in gaol or before a firing squad. When Lissy and the baby were asleep again, he lay on the bed, his arms under his head, looking out at the almost full moon. He heard a splash that might have been a leaping fish in the lake. At half past five they got up; they'd ordered a cab in Salzburg to collect them and drive them back to the station. On the platform they stood at the carriage door—a last embrace, a kiss on August's forehead. Then Lahnstein stood at the window and waved till his arm ached. Lissy waved back, holding August in the air. That was the last image he had of them, but it wasn't a picture that found its way into his dreams.

The door started open, making Lahnstein jump, and Müller came in, Lahnstein's subordinate.

'Morning,' Müller called out, loud and brisk as a soldier.

Lahnstein turned to him, feigning alertness. 'Morning,' he said dully.

Müller was short and stocky with a knobbly nose and blue-grey eyes; his hair and goatee were white, though he was only in his early thirties, a little younger than Lahnstein. Tannenberg and then Verdun. After the war, his career had taken off; he'd been in charge of the case until Lahnstein arrived, but with no clues and a growing number of missing boys, he'd dropped to second-in-command.

Slipping off his coat, Müller unlocked his desk drawer and took out his gun. He sat down, pulled out the magazine, clattered the cartridges onto his desk and then put them in again.

'Is it possible,' Lahnstein asked, 'that there's a file or two missing from the archives?'

'Don't know,' said Müller. 'I haven't missed one yet.'

'There's at least one gap and it doesn't strike me as being very old.'

'What have you been rummaging around in the archives for?'

'Had a bit of a recce yesterday. Don't want to overlook anything.'

Müller shrugged. 'Haven't been in the archives for years,' he said. 'I always have the files brought up to me.'

'There was an empty file,' Lahnstein said.

'Won't be empty long. Not the way things are going.'

'But why would anyone put a file on the shelf with nothing inside?'

'No idea. You tell me.'

'To cover up the removal of another file.'

There was a knock at the door. Lahnstein jumped again. Müller noticed and smiled.

'Maybe it's the missing file,' he said. Then, jerking his head the other way, he called out sharply, 'Come in.'

Lahnstein stared at the door.

A clerk came in, followed by a middle-aged couple. Was this Number Eleven, Lahnstein wondered, at once resigned and hopeful. He didn't like this numbering business, but all his colleagues referred to the boys by their numbers and the habit was catching.

'The lady and gentleman would like to report a missing person,' the clerk said.

'A boy?' Müller asked.

'Our Adolf,' the woman said.

She was, Lahnstein guessed, in her late thirties, though since the war and the years of hunger and Spanish flu, he was often far off the mark when it came to putting an age to people, especially simple working people like these. The woman was wearing a coat full of holes over a long dress; the man, a coarse, battered suit of black cloth sprinkled with pale specks. (Sawdust, Lahnstein realised; he was a carpenter.) They both wore heavy shoes and they were both gaunt and skinny; the man was a head and a bit taller than his wife. His face was broad; hers was pinched. There was fear in their eyes. The woman was carrying a cloth bag.

Lahnstein signalled to the clerk to draw up two chairs to his desk and asked the couple to sit down. Müller came around the side of his own desk and leant against it. Lahnstein laid out a pad of paper and took up a pen.

'Your names, please.'

'Jakop Hannappel.'

A Rhenish accent.

'You're from Cologne?'

'Düsseldorf.'

Lahnstein glanced at the woman.

'Marie.'

'Also Hannappel?'

'I'm his wife.'

Lahnstein addressed the man again. 'You're a carpenter?'

'Yes.'

'How old is your son?'

'Fifteen.'

'Born on 28 April 1908,' Mrs Hannappel said. 'Only a minute or two after midnight.'

'How long has he been missing?'

'Haven't heard from him for a week. Usually had a letter every other day. Last thing he sent was a parcel of sausage, for Martinmas.'

'Why sausage?'

Shrugs.

'Your son sent the parcel of sausage? Or could it have been someone else?'

'It was Adolf,' the woman said. 'It was his writing.'

She gave a sob.

'We don't have much,' the man said.

'He wanted to do us a kindness.'

'And what,' Lahnstein asked, 'was in this parcel of sausage?'

'Sausage.'

Müller grinned. Too late, Lahnstein realised that his ridiculous question would soon be all over headquarters. The Sausage Question.

'I know that,' he said. 'I meant, what kind?'

'Liver sausage, boiled sausage, blood sausage,' the woman said.

'Is there anything suspicious about it?'

'No,' the man said, 'it's tasty.'

'You've already had some?'

'We had some of the blood sausage.'

'I see.'

'We brought the liver sausage down to the station,' Mrs Hannappel said. 'We didn't know how long a wait we'd have.'

'Stopped off at Döbbert's on the way for half a loaf to have with it,' her husband added.

Lahnstein leant back in his chair. 'All right,' he said. 'Let's start at the beginning. Tell us about your boy.'

'He had tubercular peritonitis earlier this year.'

'Did a spell in the sanatorium at Watersloh.'

'But he's better now,' the woman said. 'If he's alive.'

She gave another sob.

'Does he have work?' Lahnstein asked.

'He'd started an apprenticeship with head-dairyman Rudolf Dehne on Widow Sürmann's farm,' Mr Hannappel said. 'In Linsborn near Lippstadt. He was learning to be a cowherd.'

'Why not a carpenter?'

'He started out apprenticed to a carpenter,' the man said sadly. 'But after the TB, they said that carpentry was too hard for the boy; he'd be better in the country doing something less taxing.'

'He's a good boy,' Mrs Hannappel put in. 'Hard-working, decent. And good to his mum and dad.'

'Hence the parcel of sausage,' Müller piped up from the back of the room. Lahnstein avoided his eye, afraid of the contempt he might see.

'Do you think,' he said, 'we could have a piece of that liver sausage?'

The two of them stared at him in astonishment.

'A piece of our liver sausage?' Mrs Hannappel asked.

'Just a sliver.'

She looked at her husband.

'We don't want to eat it,' Lahnstein said. 'We want to have it analysed.'

'It's good sausage,' Mr Hannappel said.

'I don't doubt that. Even so, if you wouldn't mind...'

The woman rummaged in her bag and pulled out a greasy package from which she unpacked a ring of sausage. Her husband produced a short knife from his trouser pocket and she scanned the cluttered desk for a free space. Lahnstein pushed a notebook to one side. Mrs Hannappel spread out the paper and placed the ring of sausage in the middle. Mr Hannappel got up and cut through it at one end. Then he marked off a thick slice with the knife and looked enquiringly at Lahnstein.

'Half of that'll do,' Lahnstein said.

The man sawed off a small piece and held it out to him.

'Wrap it up, please,' Lahnstein said.

Mrs Hannappel tore off a corner of paper and wrapped it up. The rest of the ring she packed in the remaining paper and stowed in her bag.

'Piece of bread to go with it?' she asked.

'No bread, thanks,' Lahnstein said. Müller hadn't stopped grinning the whole time.

Inspector Sausage, Lahnstein thought, that's what they'll call me.

'All right,' he said, 'let me ask you some more questions. Your son's apprenticed to a dairyman on a farm belonging to

Widow—' He looked at his notes. 'Sürmann.'

'Not anymore,' Mr Hannappel said.

'But he only started in October.'

'Widow Sürmann wouldn't keep him.'

'Why not?'

He looked at his wife.

'She said he's a good boy, but...'

'But what?'

Silence. A strong smell of liver sausage.

'He had a gun,' Mr Hannappel said.

'A gun?'

'Widow Sürmann said that only Communists have guns,' Mrs Hannappel explained.

'Did you know your son had a gun?' Lahnstein asked.

'We've never seen him with one,' she said.

'Maybe it's not true, what she said,' Mr Hannappel suggested.

'Though she's a good, capable woman,' his wife said. 'Her husband didn't come back from the war.'

'And is your Adolf a Communist?'

The man looked nonplussed.

'Red flags?'

'What? In his room? No.'

'Books by Karl Marx?'

Now they both looked confused.

'Is it possible that your son has taken off to Russia, to the Soviet Union?' Müller asked. 'To join the other Communists?'

'Why would he do that?'

'To fetch orders for the revolution.'

'What revolution?'

They looked terrified.

'It's all right,' Lahnstein said. 'It's just that we have to consider every possibility.'

'So many boys have gone missing,' Mrs Hannappel said. 'We're afraid for our son. Will you find him? He was last seen here in Hanover.'

'How do you know that?'

'He came here to ask for a job at Wenger's dairyman's office in Ballhofstrasse.'

'Did he ever show up there?'

'No.'

'So you don't know whether or not he got to Hanover?'

'No, it's true, we don't.'

'Has your son been acting unusual in any way lately?'

'Oh no, he's been the same as ever.'

'Same as ever,' Mr Hannappel echoed.

'There's something else I must ask you,' Lahnstein said. 'Please don't take offence. It's a routine question.'

Müller raised his eyebrows. The Hannappels sat up in their seats like pupils waiting to be questioned by a fierce examiner. They eyed Lahnstein attentively, submissively.

'Does Adolf have a girl?' he asked.

'Oh,' the woman said with relief. 'No, he's too young for that and he's a good boy.'

'Is he...friendly with a boy?'

'Of course,' Mr Hannappel said. 'Erwin, Kurt and quite a few others. He's a popular boy, is our Adolf.'

'What I mean,' Lahnstein said cautiously, 'is...is he *fond* of Erwin or Kurt?'

'Oh yes,' Mrs Hannappel said, 'I should say so'.

Lahnstein looked at the floor and asked, 'Does that mean, do you think, that they might sometimes have...kissed?'

There was no reply. He looked up into perplexed faces. Müller signalled to him to stop.

'Kissed?' the woman asked. 'Boys?'

'Are you talking smut?' Mr Hannappel asked menacingly. He rose from his chair; his wife got up too.

'Calm down,' Müller said, stepping forward. 'Inspector Lahnstein didn't mean it like that. We have to investigate every avenue, but evidently your Adolf wasn't involved in anything of that nature. You've made that quite plain. And now, if you would give us a description of your son, we could let you go home.'

'We've brought a photograph,' the boy's mother said. She pulled it out of her bag and handed it to Müller.

'Very good,' Müller said. 'Do you know what your son was last wearing?'

'He had a lovely pair of brown breeches,' she said. 'He wouldn't wear anything else. Them and a pair of box calf boots, a blue jersey and braces. He had his trunk with him.'

'Made it himself,' Mr Hannappel said. 'In my workshop. He was...he *is* so talented. A crying shame he can't become a carpenter.'

'Took the spirit level too.'

'Maybe he's hoping to be a carpenter after all. Maybe that's why he ran off with the spirit level—so he can be a carpenter though he's been told he can't.'

'Because of the TB,' Mrs Hannappel said. 'He's only been

out of the sanatorium since September.'

'Maybe he's in America,' her husband added. 'They're short of carpenters over there.'

'Thank you very much,' said Müller and gave them both his hand. 'You can leave your address with the clerk on your way out. We'll be in touch.'

'Will you find him?'

'I'm optimistic. You've given us a lot to go on.'

Lahnstein rose and held out his hand to Mrs Hannappel. She stared at him as if he were a reprobate. Mr Hannappel turned abruptly and made straight for the door without even deigning to look at him.

'Didn't know you were so keen on liver sausage,' Müller said, when they were gone.

'Very funny.'

'Thanks. But what are you going to do with it?'

'Get Schackwitz to analyse it.'

'You think the boy wanted to poison his parents? They seem to have survived the blood sausage.'

'I've heard rumours that there's human flesh on the market.'

Müller looked at him in astonishment. Then he burst out laughing.

Lahnstein opened the notebook on his desk and stared angrily at the pages.

'I'm sorry,' Müller said, stifling laughter, 'but I wouldn't have thought you'd fall for that nonsense.'

'So you've heard the rumours too?'

'They've been around long enough—at least since the end

of the war, when meat was short. People said the Frogs and Brits got all the beef and pork, and the Germans had to eat human flesh. A lot of rot.'

'I don't believe it either,' Lahnstein said, embarrassed, 'but I'd like Schackwitz to have a look at the sausage all the same. May I see the photo?'

He saw a serious, broad-faced boy who took after his father—a tired-looking boy, caught off his guard by the camera, his face frozen between expressions, eyes half shut, mouth crooked.

'Interesting about the gun,' he said, 'and that the woman should think he's a Communist.'

'Yes, that is interesting, but can a child be a Communist?'

Of course he could—certainly a boy of fifteen. Three years ago, Lahnstein had seen young Communists throwing stones; he'd seen them with rifles at the Ruhr uprising. He'd seen a boy shot dead at a demonstration, red flag in hand.

'Maybe it's a response to the coup in Munich,' he said.

'But the other boys went missing before the coup.'

'I know,' Lahnstein said. 'But we don't know that it was always the same offender. We don't even know that there are crimes behind these cases. Whereas here, with Adolf Hannappel, we have a clue, a lead. Maybe the boy did have a gun; maybe he really was a Communist. It's getting harder and harder to separate politics from violence in this country. Do you know how many National Socialists there are in Hanover?'

'A few hundred.'

'You're not one of them, by any chance—if you don't mind my asking?'

'Absolutely not.'

Lahnstein believed him. Müller may not have been a democrat—no chance of that—but he was more likely a monarchist than a Nazi.

'Still,' said Müller, 'it's a starting point.'

'You think my theory's plausible?'

'There may be something in it.'

'That's the first time you haven't disagreed with me,' Lahnstein said.

He was in good spirits; he had a lead in the direction he'd been leaning for a while. The one-seven-fiver scene was a distinct possibility, but it was a hunch that had so far led nowhere. Wasn't there a chance that this series of murders—if murders they were—was in some way a product of the times, a consequence of the war and its aftermath? For four years, they had lived in a vast abattoir; every day for four years they had slaughtered and watched others slaughter. What were eleven murders compared with a machine-gun salvo, or a command to fire a barrage of shells, or a load of bombs dropped from an airship? Germany was home to millions of experienced mass murderers. Lahnstein had to find the one who'd carried on, unable to kick the four-year daily habit.

The trouble was, he thought bitterly, that he wasn't one of them; he'd only brought down two planes, one double seater and one single seater—three dead in all, if no one had survived. This was a cause of some chagrin to Lahnstein. There was no such thing as killing too many people, but it was certainly possible to have killed too few.

So many men had been soldiers that war service was not sufficient qualification for his list of suspects; it would have gone on forever. Looking for something more, Lahnstein had made it one of his first tasks in Hanover to scan the reports on the Leipzig war crimes trials, searching for men who had butchered Belgian civilians or executed prisoners without orders. He'd hoped to find someone from Hanover, but no one seemed to fit the bill.

Politics was another possible motive—the brutalised politics that were a consequence of the war. Revolution, counter-revolution, murder. Liebknecht, Luxemburg, Eisner, Landauer, Erzberger, Rathenau, the attempted coup in Munich.

'Aren't almost all the missing boys workers or tradesmen?' he asked Müller.

'Yes.'

'Maybe they were all Communists.'

'There's nothing in the files to suggest it. Not that that means anything.'

'These Hitler people are great enemies of the Communists, aren't they?'

'I believe they are.'

'Will you find me as many men as you can muster?' he asked Müller.

'Certainly.'

'And please look into that missing file.'

Five policemen assembled in the office.

'Only five?' Lahnstein asked.

'Versailles,' Müller said.

Whenever there was a lack of men—and there was a permanent lack of men—the peace treaty was to blame. Besides imposing military restrictions, the Allies had set limits on police numbers, presumably supposing that it was but a small step from armed policeman to soldier. Then again, Müller might be using the word *Versailles* as an excuse. Lahnstein had yet to fathom the intricacies of headquarters and Müller seemed disinclined to enlighten him.

Lahnstein cadged a cigarette off him and told the men about the Adolf Hannappel case and his suspicion that the boy had been killed or kidnapped by Hitler's men.

'They're just a bunch of lunatics,' one of the policemen said.

'Never mind that,' Lahnstein said. He assigned each of them their duties, leaving himself the task of questioning Widow Sürmann.

'The Nazis are demonstrating in Hanover next week,' another policeman said.

'Why?'

'Because of this business in Munich. Because Hitler's in custody.'

'We must be there,' Lahnstein said, and dismissed the men.

That evening he stood for a moment outside the tobacconist's. He got as far as putting his hand on the door handle, but then he withdrew it and bought five cigarettes from one of the boys on the street.

'Go home now,' he told the boy. 'It's dark.'

—

It was seven in the evening when he woke. Why had he slept so long? He'd only wanted a little lie-down, a bit of a rest. The sheets were clammy—had he been sweating? No, autumn had come, that was all; it wouldn't be dry in his room for months now, with the damp from the rain and the nearby river. It was dark and he felt like going out, felt like company—Cafe Köpcke, and then maybe on to the station. First, though, he had to tidy things up, do some cleaning—there were still bloodstains on the floorboards. This wasn't a good place for his kind of work; he'd have to look for new lodgings. But the rent here was cheap and business wasn't good. Prices were falling.

A tiled room—that was what he needed, like in a proper butcher's. A quick mop around would be enough then. The boards were a hell of a job to scrub and the blood stuck in the cracks. Ought he to get up? He lingered in bed a few moments longer. The clothes business was another worry. Demand was down; there were more new goods in the shops. People were better off, too—not a lot, but in his line of trade you noticed the difference at once. He threw off the covers and went to the back window. The lamps were lit in the houses opposite and there was a crescent moon—enough light to see by, but not enough to be recognised.

He filled a bucket with water and scouring powder, got down on his knees and started to scrub, working swiftly, deftly, routinely. Dörchen was coming in to clean today—didn't want her seeing the blood. She'd already peached on him once. Could have been worse, mind. Girl had been a fool, but nothing had come of it; he'd forgiven her. Human flesh? What a daft question. Horsemeat, he'd told the halfwit policeman, people are greedy for horsemeat—he had his sources. Maybe the officer himself could be tempted…Well, yes, now that he asked…

The floor was clean—or as clean as it got; some stains never washed out. He put on his shoes, opened the door of the little cubby hole, took out the bucket, covered it with a towel, pulled on his greasy hat and left the flat, head down, walking fast. A beast of work, like so many. He hurried past the row of houses to the small park that backed onto the River Leine. By day children played there, and he sometimes saw a pair of sweethearts, but they were always too engrossed in each other to care about a man with a bucket. He walked to the riverbank and, after listening for a moment to the babble of water, he pulled back the towel and threw the bones into the Leine—idly, like someone feeding ducks. When the bucket was empty, he knelt down and rinsed it until all the blood was gone and his hands were cold. Then, satisfied, he returned home to freshen up and change. The evening could begin.

2

The wind in Dunedin came from the South Pole—the boy knew that; Craig had told him. Icy cold, slap-in-the-face wind. He'd stored the expression away. He couldn't remember why Craig had come to the village, but it must have been soon after the war. A New Zealander, a man from the antipodes—he'd stayed a few days, put up at the vicarage. Funny German he spoke, the sentences all back-to-front, but he had a way with words. Slap-in-the-face wind. The vicar brought him into class and he told them about Dunedin, a seaside city on the South Island of New Zealand, so close to the Antarctic that people had been able to watch the race between Scott and Amundsen through binoculars. The class went very quiet when Craig said that. They'd been secretly smirking at this strange man and then wham! Scott versus Amundsen. He'd actually seen them. The kids believed Craig until he grinned and told them it was a thousand miles to the South Pole from Dunedin—though the bit about the wind was true. And there were penguins—that was true too. Ever since then, the boy had felt this yearning, and when he needed somewhere to run to, he knew it had to be Dunedin.

Third class was full of people—journeymen, peasant women, mothers with babies—but apart from the rattle of the carriage and the occasional whistle of the engine, all was quiet, and luckily there was no one he knew. He looked at his watch: Hanover was still two hours away. Once he got there, he'd have to be careful; Mother and Father might have telegraphed a missing-persons report to Hanover. They'd be missing him by now, that was for sure. He wondered what they were thinking and rubbed his eyes to stop the tears; he mustn't, for goodness' sake, cry. He glanced around surreptitiously, but no one was taking any notice of him.

It wasn't his fault that the carpentry workshop where he was apprenticed had been commissioned to make the new church pews. Each morning he'd hurried up the little hill to the church and set to with the journeyman, ripping out the warped, rotting wood of the old pews and kneelers and helping the master to put in new ones. It took them several days and soon Monika, the vicar's daughter, was coming to watch every afternoon. She was the youngest of six and about his age, almost seventeen.

The engine whistled and braked abruptly, sending half the passengers flying through the carriage into each other's arms. Somebody screamed; babies started to cry. The boy was thrown off his wooden bench and landed in a heap on an old man's lap. He began to gather himself up. All around him, people were struggling to their feet, rubbing their aching limbs and apologising awkwardly, especially the men who had found themselves flung onto women. The train had stopped in the middle of nowhere. Nothing but fields of cows for miles.

—

'May I trouble you for a moment, sir? I'm Number Three's mother.'

Lahnstein was on his way up to the office, deep in thought; he hadn't noticed the woman.

Rapidly he ran through the list in his head.

Number One: Fritz Franke, born on 31 October 1906, missing since 12 February 1923, schoolboy, son of a publican.

Number Two: Wilhelm Schulze, born on 31 August 1906, missing since 20 March 1923, clerk's apprentice.

Number Three: Richard Schiefer, born on 7 August 1907, missing since 23 May 1923, pupil at Bismarck Grammar.

'Mrs Schiefer?'

'Yes, that's the name I go by outside this building.'

She gave him a bitter smile—a fairly large, stout woman of about forty with a round face and dark-brown hair. Her coat and boots were dark brown too, the boots new and shiny.

'You've numbered the boys, haven't you?' she said. 'I remember. I'm glad it doesn't mean you've forgotten their names.'

She held out her hand and Lahnstein shook it briefly.

'Lahnstein,' he said.

'You're the new man. That's why I want to talk to you.'

Number Three's parents had a reputation for being a nuisance. They had placed a wanted ad in the papers and hired a detective to find their son—without success.

'You mustn't think,' Lahnstein said, 'that the boys are mere numbers for us.'

She made to wave this aside, but stopped.

'Oh, but they are' she said, 'and it bothers me. Shall I tell you why?'

'By all means.'

'May I buy you a cup of coffee in the cafe across the road?'

'We can have a cup of coffee in the office.'

'I should like to speak to you in private—without Inspector Müller.'

It was of course sad, she said, to know that your poor missing boy was a mere number to people.

Lahnstein shook his head and she reached a hand across the cafe table and placed it on his arm.

'I know you don't see it like that. But the others do.'

She was wearing a black dress under her coat. There was another thing, she said. It was bad enough being the mother of a missing number, but it was even worse that her son was on this list—one victim among many, part of a series. It meant that the case of Richard Schiefer was being treated just like all the other missing-boy cases; the police were hunting for a serial killer, someone who had murdered them all. In fact, they weren't even searching properly because they'd got it into their heads that the boys had emigrated or joined the Foreign Legion—but quite apart from that, it was a grave mistake to treat them *en bloc* like this; it was preventing Richard's case from being solved.

'My son is not part of the series,' she said.

'What makes you so sure?'

She spoke of the other boys' backgrounds, or what she knew of them from the papers. They were the sons of tradesmen and workers—hoi polloi and, in some cases, layabouts; dubious, shady characters. She couldn't say what had happened to those boys, but she was quite clear about what had not happened to Richard.

'Richard did not run away,' she said vehemently. 'Not to America and not to join the Foreign Legion. He'd no reason.'

She said he'd been happy both at home and at school, a good scholar—an excellent scholar, in fact, only the best marks.

'Especially in chemistry, of course,' she said with a wry smile.

It was chemistry he'd wanted to study, like his father; his mind had been set on it. She and her husband prepared medicines—they had a chemist's shop—but Richard was going to invent medicines; there were still so many illnesses without a cure—plenty of scope for a gifted young man, especially in Germany—just think of all those German chemists, the best in the world: Fischer, Baeyer, Buchner, Ostwald, Wallach, Willstätter, Haber, Nernst—Nobel laureates, every manjack of them—and one day they would be joined by Richard Schiefer—first a job at IG Farben, then the Nobel Prize in Chemistry. She looked blissful, as if her dreams had already come true.

'With prospects like those, a boy doesn't run away to America or go off to fight. He would have married, he'd have had children, grandchildren.'

She's going to cry, Lahnstein thought, but she didn't.

'And now he's on a list with all those other boys—most of

them ne'er-do-wells, if you ask me.'

'That's not for me to judge,' Lahnstein said.

'Of course it isn't, I'm sorry. But it doesn't matter what happened to the other boys. I want to know what happened to my son. Would you like to hear my theory?'

'Very much.'

'Murder and robbery. He was wearing an expensive watch, a present from his grandfather. He was wearing good clothes. You know what that means in this day and age.'

'Absolutely.'

'I knew you'd agree. But no one's following it up. Just because robbery's unlikely in the other cases, the police are wasting this opportunity of solving my son's death.'

Lahnstein recalled an entry in Schiefer's file. According to the private detective, Richard had been seen at the station talking to an old-clothes man by the name of Franz Hörmann. The police had been unable to trace anyone of that name.

'Are you thinking of Franz Hörmann?' Lahnstein asked.

'Him or another. I don't know. That's up to the police to find out. But they do nothing. That man Müller is extremely disobliging. *We're doing what we can, we're doing what we can.* But what *are* you doing? That's what I want to know. Maybe *you* can tell me.'

'Your robbery theory is very helpful to me,' Lahnstein said. 'I'll take care of things, I promise.'

Her face brightened a little, but immediately darkened again. As he could probably imagine, she said, it wasn't the first time she had heard that.

He nodded.

'I don't want to promise too much.'

'Just a moment ago you said, *I promise.*'

'I'll take care of things.'

'I sometimes see him,' she said. 'If a boy passes me, about his age and height, I turn to look, because I think it might be him. Or if I see a brown ulster—he was wearing a brown ulster the day he was murdered.'

'We don't know that he was murdered.'

'For me, he was,' she said matter-of-factly. 'He didn't run away, so he must have been murdered.'

She looked at him with faint disapproval. A woman who is used to being right, Lahnstein thought.

'Is he political?'

'What do you mean?'

'Did he…does he have sympathies for a political party? The Communists, say?'

'God forbid. He had other things in his head, more important things. Certainly not the Communists.'

'I must be getting back to work,' Lahnstein said. 'I have a meeting.'

'Solve this case, please, Inspector, find his corpse—we shall know no peace until you do. And think about robbery, it's the only explanation. The other boys are a different matter. Not that we have anything against these people; I wouldn't want you thinking that. They come to us in the chemist's when they're in trouble and believe me, we don't stint them.'

Back at headquarters, Lahnstein thought of an old dream of his youth, a dream of flying that had begun in Berlin on a visit to his uncle—or perhaps it would be more accurate to say on a visit to his cousin Wilma. Word had got about that Orville Wright was in town with his flying machine. He'd taken it apart in America, packed it up in boxes, and sent it over the Atlantic on a ship, all the way to Berlin. Now it had arrived and Wright was going to fly over Tempelhof Airfield and set a new record. Lahnstein had to go; he took his cousin with him.

Until then, Wilma had been in charge. She had shown him the big city—Potsdamer Platz, the Brandenburg Gate, the palace where the Kaiser lived; she had taken him to Wannsee and to the lakes at Krumme Lanke. Wilma was rather forward, not as mild and charming as Lahnstein remembered her. Perhaps she had changed a great deal in the last two years, or perhaps he had idealised her for the sake of his fantasies. Either way, she was good company on those walks around Berlin—educated, intelligent, and assertive enough to forge a path through the crowds and find tables in apparently full cafes. She was sixteen to Lahnstein's eighteen and had a high forehead and pigtails.

They were surprised at how busy it was; the underground to Tempelhof was packed and people were pouring onto the airfield in their thousands to see the famous American— one of the brothers who had pioneered motorised flight. Eight minutes in the air, ten minutes—Lahnstein had read the reports in the papers with rapt excitement, staring at the grainy photograph. You couldn't see much of the machine, but it was in the air; it was flying. To think that was possible. Zeppelins had been around for a while, but they were so big and unwieldy that there was little joy in watching them. It wasn't man flying when the Zeppelin flew; it was a monstrous contraption.

Earlier in his visit to Berlin, Lahnstein had seen an airship piloted by Count Zeppelin himself at the Kaiser's invitation. Orville Wright was already in town and stood on the dais beside the Kaiser as the count made his giant cigar bob a kind of curtsy. Lahnstein was not impressed. The filigree flying machines of the Wright Brothers, with their narrow wings and thin struts, made man akin to birds, but the zeppelin was a cumbersome intruder that had strayed into the wrong element.

Since reading the newspaper reports, Lahnstein had been plagued by a yearning he couldn't shake. He had to get up there too—to glide through the sky like a seagull, a crane, a buzzard.

People thronged on the airfield, more than a hundred thousand. Lahnstein was disappointed not to get closer to the plane. All he could make out with any clarity was the pyramid-shaped wooden tower which he knew housed the construction that would catapult the machine into the air. The plane itself was only dimly visible, clinging to the ground beside the tower, surrounded by a scattering of tiny people. He was afraid that take-off might be cancelled—technical difficulties, or the pilot indisposed at the last minute. He looked up and saw a handful of clouds in the vast blue sky—no danger there. Then all at once it went quiet. Voices dropped, people stopped laughing; there were no more of those deadpan remarks so typical of the Berliners that Lahnstein found so hard to gauge. All was silent; only a soft whirr reached Lahnstein's ears. Wilma put a hand on his arm. He stood on tiptoe, straining to see the aeroplane; it seemed, he thought, to be trembling slightly, but that was as much as he saw, because other, taller men also stretched to look and children were hoisted onto shoulders. Then, suddenly, it appeared— the Wright brothers' flying machine. It climbed slowly into Lahnstein's field of vision, rising over the heads and hats of the people in front of him, over the children on their dads' shoulders, over the crowns of the trees and the roofs of the houses on the edge of the airfield until there was nothing but blue all around it and it was flying through the sky, in its element. Lahnstein was overwhelmed, moved by the delicate-looking machine and the small figure sitting between the spindly struts. A big, light-skeletoned bird. Orville Wright circled the cordoned-off part of Tempelhof Airfield a dozen times; he was in the air for nineteen minutes. Lahnstein timed it himself, hoping after every minute completed that Wright would defy gravity for another minute longer and another and another.

Lahnstein made the trip out to the airfield several times in the days that followed, but he preferred to go without his cousin; Wilma kept him earthbound in those precious minutes when Orville Wright soared through the sky— and Lahnstein wanted to soar with him. Perhaps, too, he was embarrassed by his zealous enthusiasm for the flying American, whom he cheered till he was hoarse and waved at till his arms trembled. Thirty-nine minutes—that was Orville Wright's Berlin record; after that, the Man of the

Skies left the city, and Lahnstein, feeling abandoned, sneaked into churches and climbed the narrow, winding stairs to the top of the towers. There, at least, he was high up and could see Berlin the way Orville Wright had seen it, but it was small comfort; he wanted to reel and soar through the air and instead he was standing in a belfry with both feet firmly on wooden boards.

'How do I become a pilot?' he asked his father when he was back in Bochum, but his father only laughed. Everyone laughed, even Lissy, whom he'd met in May 1914. Then the war broke out and Lahnstein's work in the force exempted him from serving at the front. This was a great relief to Lissy, and Lahnstein was glad, too, until he realised that part of the war was being fought in the air and that joining up would give him the chance of becoming a pilot. Lissy didn't understand; she refused to accept that he could be drawn to something so dangerous, that he was willing to risk their happiness just to satisfy some mad desire to be airborne. They argued—nasty scenes, unworthy of them both. Lissy ran away, came back, shouted at him, pounded his chest with her fists. But Lahnstein wouldn't be deterred from volunteering as a fighter pilot. They took him on. He started training in spring 1916.

And now he was back on the ground, no longer yearning to be in the sky—but Lissy was still up there with August, flying night after night. Lahnstein would have liked to promise himself that he'd fly after them and fetch them back to earth, but he knew he'd never set foot in a plane again. He didn't have the strength.

When he woke from his daydream he was sitting in the office, somewhat dazed. Slowly, groping his way back into the real world, he resumed the list in his head. He was in the habit of running through it from time to time, to make sure he didn't forget any of the names or dates.

Number Four: Hans Sonnenfeld, born on 1 June 1904, missing since late May 1923, factory worker, son of a trader.

Number Five: Ernst Ehrenberg, born on 30 September 1909, missing since 23 June 1923, schoolboy, son of a cobbler.

Number Six: Heinrich Struss, born on 23 July 1905, missing since 24 August 1923, office boy, son of a carpenter.

Number Seven: Richard Gräf, born on 13 February 1906, missing since late September 1923, unemployed, son of a casual labourer.

Number Eight: Wilhelm Erdner, born on 4 February 1907, missing since 12 October 1923, worker, son of a metalworker.

Number Nine: Hermann Wolf, born on 9 June 1908, missing since 24 or 25 October 1923, unemployed, son of a metalworker.

Number Ten: Heinz Brinkmann, born on 20 October 1910, missing since 27 October 1923, schoolboy, son of a widow.

Number Eleven: Adolf Hannappel, born on...

Lahnstein was stuck. He racked his brain, but the date wouldn't come to him, so he consulted his papers.

...28 April 1908, missing since Martinmas 1923, dairyman's apprentice, son of a carpenter.

—

Two days with no further missing boys. Lahnstein was relieved. His talk with the Hannappels had left him fearing a whole spate of cases—a boy a day, or maybe even more. It was all possible. He imagined a long queue stretching down the stairs and onto the street; parents thronging outside his office, pushing their way in—angry, despairing parents, shouting and crying and begging him to help. *Where's my boy? Bring back my boy to me.* He'd be to blame, unable to solve the case, or indeed, any of the cases; Müller would smirk and grin. Lahnstein saw it all: the twisted faces, the flailing arms, the hands snatching at him wherever he went—in his digs, in the cafe, in the office. He heard them shout and beg. Stop it, he told himself. Calm down. Since you came to work here, only one boy has gone missing and you have a lead; you can do something. For so long nothing had been done.

When Müller came in, Lahnstein asked if he'd ever thought of murder and robbery as a possibility.

'Ah, you've been talking to Number Three's mum. Have a nice chat?'

'*Nice* is not the word I'd use in the circumstances.'

'She thinks her boy's a cut above the others.'

'She's still getting over the loss.'

'So are all the other mothers we've seen. But they don't make such a song and dance about it.'

Lahnstein left the conversation there and went down to the archives to ask if there was a file on Franz Hörmann. There wasn't. Then he set off for Widow Sürmann's farm, sitting in the back of a Mercedes driven by a fat policeman. Neither of them spoke. The countryside was flat, the fields bare, broken only by hedgerows and the occasional tree. Sometimes Lahnstein caught the policeman looking at him in the rear-view mirror, doubtful, scornful. He knew that look from headquarters. *Who do you think you are?* it said. *You come here, a stranger, to show us how to do things, and you haven't got anywhere.* Boys were still going missing. The liver sausage had turned out to be pure pork. Hastily stifled laughter preceded Lahnstein down the corridors of headquarters.

It was more of an estate than a farm, though the house, a modest brick manor at the end of a winding gravel drive, was by no means palatial—large enough to suggest a certain pride and wealth, but free of pomp or flourish. Evidently it was a place of work, not leisure. A maid in peasant dress showed Lahnstein into a drawing room shrouded in gloom, the windows half covered by heavy curtains. Widow Sürmann sat in a winged armchair where Lahnstein guessed her husband had sat before her. She was about forty, an elegant woman— not a farmer's wife, but the wife of a gentleman-farmer and now a lady-farmer in her own right. She was wearing a long, black skirt, a high-buttoned black blouse, and a black lace ribbon in her hair. She rose but didn't come towards Lahnstein. He walked over to her and held out his hand.

'Inspector Lahnstein,' he said. 'I'm sorry about your husband.' It sounded clumsy. They sat down; the maid brought tea.

Her husband had been a reserve major. He'd signed up in August and fallen in Belgium a few days later.

'I'm sorry,' Lahnstein said again.

'What about you?'

'Pilot, stationed at Verdun.'

Verdun was a word that resonated. Lahnstein hoped it would put an end to the questions. It didn't.

'Shoot any down?'

'Nine.'

Two was not a respectable number in the circumstances. Richthofen had shot down eighty planes, Udet sixty-two, Göring twenty-two and Immelmann fifteen—despite being shot down himself by the Brits in June 1916. The figures were common knowledge; Lahnstein just had to hope that the widow didn't have a complete list in her head. Some people did, though most, luckily, were only interested in the real aces—those who had shot down at least ten or twenty. That made nine the perfect number for him—the highest he could safely name, though still pitifully low.

The widow looked disdainful, but made no comment.

He turned the conversation to Adolf Hannappel, who had indeed, it seemed, been caught with a gun. The head-dairyman had seen him doing target practice in a field and reported him to the widow. When questioned, Hannappel refused to say how he had come by the gun or what he was intending to do with it. Lahnstein asked the widow why she assumed that Adolf Hannappel was a Communist.

'Communists want to wreak havoc,' she said. 'That's why they have guns.'

'Was Adolf Hannappel a member of the Communist Party?'

'I don't know, I never spoke to him.'

'So what makes you think he was a Communist?'

'The gun.'

She was sure it was only a matter of time before the Revolution reached Germany, and German farmers were bled white or expropriated. She believed that the Communists were being supplied with guns by the Russians and hoarding them until the order to strike came from Moscow. The gentleman-farmers would be hit first, not a doubt of it. Like in Russia.

'I don't understand why you do nothing to stop the Communists,' she said.

The maid came and poured more tea—a Mcissen tea service. The walls were hung with the heads of stags and wild boar. Antlers, a well-stocked rifle cupboard, heavy leather chairs, cigar smoke. Who was the smoker?

'As long as they're not breaking any laws,' Lahnstein said.

'The insanity of our times,' she said, 'is that we punish those who break our laws, but do nothing to stop those who want to abolish them.'

'If the Communists were elected,' he said, 'they'd be in their legal right to abolish the laws and replace them with new ones.'

'Are you a Communist too?'

Her eyes were blue, her hair reddish blond. She looked at him teasingly, as if she'd made an amusing remark. Perhaps she couldn't imagine that a policeman could be a Communist.

'No,' Lahnstein said, 'I'm not.'

'No,' she said, 'I didn't think you were.'

'Are there Nazis here?' he asked.

'On the farm? I don't think so. But then, what exactly is a Nazi?'

'One of Hitler's people.'

'Oh, we heard about the Munich Putsch, even here in the country. But what do those men want?'

'A new order.'

'Don't we all?'

Lahnstein set down his teacup and stood up. 'May I speak to the head-dairyman?' he asked.

'By all means. You'll find him in the cowshed.'

She accompanied Lahnstein to the door.

'Keep an eye on the Communists,' she said in parting. 'They're not as harmless as you might think. It's my belief that Hannappel has gone underground with that pistol of his. One of these days he'll be back, and depend upon it, he will shoot.'

The head-dairyman told Lahnstein that one of the assistant dairymen, twenty-year-old Jens Sieversen, had gone missing two days before the attempted coup in Munich. He said he thought he was a Nazi. Sieversen, it seemed, couldn't stand Hannappel's guts, but the head-dairyman didn't know why.

'Do you think Sieversen might be behind Hannappel's disappearance?' Lahnstein asked.

'I'd say it's more likely that Sieversen went to Munich and had to go into hiding after the putsch.'

'It's possible, but he could have killed Hannappel all the same—in rage or revenge.'

The head-dairyman shrugged. 'Suppose so,' he said.

Lahnstein returned to Hanover satisfied. He hadn't been refuted in his hypothesis; you might even say he had been a little confirmed in it. That was one way of looking at things, anyway, and he decided it was a good one.

Sitting in the back of the motor car, he closed his eyes so that the chauffeur wouldn't attempt conversation. He thought of the green hills of Yorkshire, the pastures and fields. More than a year he had spent there, writing to Lissy, waiting for her letters. They had lived in barracks and been left largely to their own devices; occasionally, people from the International Red Cross had dropped in to make sure they were being well-treated, which they were—always being called *sir*, always being told *please* and *thank you*. That wasn't the trouble. The trouble was the yearning—and some of the Germans. The Brits were no trouble at all.

The barracks were in passable condition; the latrines were all right too. The food was revolting, but there was enough. Sometimes British newspapers were handed out, and those officers who had a good command of English would read aloud to the others, translating as they went along. That way, they knew broadly how the war was going—though it was generally assumed that British journalists were conduits of government propaganda, and the prisoners remained, to the end, more optimistic than the reports warranted.

Life in the camp wasn't even particularly boring—no more so, at least, than a quiet weekend, except that it went on day after day. There was plenty of erudition in their circles;

almost all the men could lecture on some topic or other—
the medics on the state of modern medicine, the engineers
on the state of technology. Groups were formed and met
regularly to discuss history, philosophy, literature and music.
There was a drama club and a choir. Lahnstein attended the
philosophy and literature groups and played Karl Moor in
Schiller's *Robbers*.

Sometimes a plane crossed the sky. Lahnstein would hear
the hum of the engine and glance up, but it always made him
feel dizzy and he had to stop looking and go inside.

Lissy wrote twice a week, but the post wasn't regular;
sometimes he waited a whole month, only for three letters to
arrive at once. At other times they came in the wrong order
and he had to fill in the gaps. Or they were late and full of
out-of-date news. He didn't mind. What mattered was that
he heard from Lissy. Chronology was neither here nor there
in the camp, where all days were the same.

But the letters left him unsatisfied. Lissy wrote lovely
chatty letters about her day-to-day life with August, but she
wasn't good at telling Lahnstein what she felt for him. She
never had been one to express her feelings. Though she had
always showered Lahnstein with hugs and kisses, it was rare
for her to put her emotions into words. That hadn't mattered
as long as they were together in Bochum. Lissy threw her
arms around him whenever he was within hugging distance,
and since the flat was so tiny there was plenty of opportunity
for such shows of affection. She would even kiss him on the
street if she thought no one was looking—Lahnstein lived in
fear that someone would round the corner and catch them at

it, but he couldn't pretend he didn't like the attention.

In the camp, it was different. He needed words to reassure him of her love, but no such words came. Lissy wrote sweet, witty letters about her day-to-day ordeals. Things were in short supply in 1918, especially food, and she made Lahnstein laugh with her tales of onerous quests for groceries. But each time he reached the end of one of her letters, he felt sad. Lissy never used the word 'love'; she never spoke of longing or desire. She might at least, he thought, have put her everyday affection, her hugs and kisses, into words. Though no substitute for the real thing, it would have been nice. But it never happened.

He brooded over this, trying to puzzle it out; there was plenty of time for brooding in the camp. But he didn't dare raise the matter with Lissy, let alone ask her to write more lovingly. Was there another man? Had she stopped caring for him? The frequency of her letters suggested otherwise; she seemed to write more than most wives. Lahnstein couldn't explain it and, as the months went on, he became more and more despondent. He longed for Lissy's letters, but as soon as he held one in his hands he was terrified of disappointment. At the same time, his desire to see her—to be hugged and kissed by her—was stronger than ever.

Most of the officers remained loyal to the Kaiser, some of them fanatically so. Lahnstein steered clear of them; they believed the Germans would emerge victorious and vied with each other in thinking up punishments for all those they saw as getting in the way of victory and prolonging the war: Communists, Social Democrats, Jews, pacifists, sissies. Some officers wanted little less than mass murder; the milder among them favoured re-education camps or forced exile.

There were no Communists in the camp, but there was a small group of Majority Social Democrats, which Lahnstein joined. Before the war he had taken no interest in politics, more or less satisfied with the order he had been born into. He thought the Kaiser an embarrassment, but didn't question his birthright to rule over Germany. In the military hospital he had begun to change his views, becoming a democrat because he didn't think the Kaiser had the right to send so many of his people to die in such pointless battles. In the camp in Yorkshire he became a Social Democrat because somebody had to take care of the people, and if the Kaiser couldn't or wouldn't, the Social Democrats were their only hope.

There was a man in their group called Franz Hartwig, a twenty-four-year-old lieutenant from Würzburg who'd fought on the Eisack in a machine-gun company and was missing two toes on his left foot after catching frostbite in the Tyrol. He and Lahnstein went for walks along the fence together, ten or twelve rounds at a time, telling each other about their lives, never tiring of listening to one another. After six months, Lahnstein knew so much about Franz's life that it began to feel as if he'd always known him. They put their camp beds side by side so that they could carry on talking at night, sometimes into the small hours. Lahnstein confided his worries about Lissy to Franz, and Franz reassured him. There was no other man, he said. Her letters would be colder if there were. Lahnstein read passages aloud to Franz and showed him the photographs Lissy had had taken of herself and August. She wrote fondly and tenderly of the little boy—also without using the word 'love'.

'That's just the way she is,' Franz said. It was clear from her letters what hard work it was, alone with a baby in Bochum, while her family was far away on Lake Irr. She had few kind words for Lahnstein's parents.

Franz had no wife or children. All his letters were from parents and siblings and friends.

One summer's night, as they lay under the stars talking, they suddenly fell silent. Neither spoke for a while, until Franz moved very close to Lahnstein and said simply, 'If you'll help me, I'll help you.'

Lahnstein understood at once. The atmosphere between them had been strange the last few nights—oddly mawkish. Thoughts had surfaced in Lahnstein's mind as he lay there next to Franz and he had fought them back—but now Franz's words burst into the night, demanding a response.

'It's easier if you close your eyes,' Franz said.

Lahnstein closed his eyes and thought of Lissy. The next thing he knew, Franz was holding his mouth shut, his firm hand an almost brutal muzzle.

When it was over, Lahnstein wished he could jump up and run away, but he was Prussian enough to keep his side of the bargain. He kept his eyes shut as he 'helped' Franz, and was soon through it. They sat up, as if in sync, doing up their flies together.

'You go first,' said Franz. 'I'll wait a bit.'

Lahnstein stood there, wondering whether to say anything, and then walked off in silence, without looking back. A moment later he was lying on his camp bed, doing his best to think of Lissy and August. When Franz came to bed, he pretended to be asleep. Some of the officers were snoring. Franz was soon breathing steadily, but Lahnstein lay awake for a long time.

For a few days they kept out of each other's way, but it wasn't long before they resumed their walks and conversations. It had happened; there was no undoing it. And you couldn't fight an urge like that—could you? Still, Lahnstein felt ashamed; he would have liked to write to Lissy and tell her about it, ask for her blessing—and make clear, too, that it was nothing like the lovely times with her. But he couldn't. Franz played an important part in his letters to Lissy, but not that particular part, for which Lahnstein knew no name.

'Headquarters or home?' the chauffeur asked.

Lahnstein started from his thoughts and saw the streets of the city, still strange to him after the mines and furnaces of the Ruhr District. The French were in power there now, of course, but he missed it all the same.

'Headquarters,' he said. Back at his desk, he ordered a search for Jens Sieversen. Then he walked home.

The next day they drove to the station in two motor cars—six men, armed, but relaxed. They had no plans to intervene—only to look. It was ten in the morning, a crisp, cold day. The cars stopped on the station forecourt where there was the usual bustle of people coming and going, hawking and trading. Lahnstein was disappointed; everything looked the same as any other day—men in hats and coats, women in peasant dresses and headscarves, coaches, a few cars. He leant over into the footwell and rubbed his shoes with his handkerchief.

When he sat up again, the pattern had changed. The throng of people was denser, their movements more structured; there was a marked thrust towards the right of the forecourt.

'Everybody out,' Lahnstein said.

The chauffeurs remained in the cars; the other men scattered, approaching the crowd from all sides. Four broad-gaited policemen. It didn't matter, Lahnstein had explained, if they were recognised as police; on the contrary, their presence was to have an effect, provoke a response. Lahnstein was hoping to pick up fragments of evidence—looks, gestures, words. He wanted to rattle people; he was searching for clues, not for the key to the case. That, he knew, was still a long way off.

He was surprised at the men in the crowd. Until then he hadn't given much thought to what Nazis might look like. He had seen Hitler's face in the papers, of course, and remembered Göring from that time on the airfield, but that was all. The photos of the attempted coup hadn't revealed much. Göring still hadn't been found. The state wasn't doing its work properly; that was a worry. But wasn't the same—or worse—also true of Hanover? Wasn't it true of him?

These were men such as he saw every day, on the street, in shops, at the police station. They were part of the crowd on the station forecourt; there was nothing to distinguish them. Lahnstein had expected something different of members of a putsch party—a party that had tried to overthrow a democratically elected state. These men didn't look like outlaws; they gave every appearance of belonging. Only a small group in light-brown uniforms stood out from the rest, but they looked even more ill at ease, hovering uncertainly, as if they weren't sure how to go about things, holding up passers-by as they made their way to or from the station, causing diversions and collisions and resentment, and then backing off, apologising, clueless to respond. Lahnstein was afraid that their embarrassment and indecision would get the better of them—that they would disperse before they'd even begun. He wanted them to muster all their courage and set off at last, shouting their anger. He'd never find a serial killer in this pathetic little group.

Then suddenly an order was barked in that clipped military tone that evoked hatred in some and nostalgia in others. The men threw back their shoulders, fell into formation and marched off, with such speed and power that the policemen were caught off guard and took a while to catch up.

'Freedom for Adolf Hitler.'

'Death to the Jews, death to the Jews.'

'Ludendorff, Ludendorff.'

'Shame on Versailles, shame on Versailles.'

They moved swiftly, ploughing through the streets like a phalanx, two hundred men forging a path through the centre of Hanover. Set off as ordinary citizens, Lahnstein thought, and now they're a mass of hatred. Passers-by dodged them and looked on from the pavements, bemused or startled; some laughed or smiled to themselves, but none of them joined the march.

Only two hundred—Lahnstein had expected more. He spotted some boys about the age of the victims and felt alarm until it occurred to him that if his theory was right, those boys were in no danger. Was it even a theory? Not really, he thought, correcting himself; it was more of a hypothesis, a hunch. Mere idle speculation? No—he might tend to modesty, but it was more than that. Lahnstein turned his mind to the party leader in Hanover—he had asked to see the file. It dated back to the coup in Berlin, the Kapp-Lüttwitz Putsch.

Hinrich Schreyer, forty-one, married with three children, ran a stationery shop that he'd taken over from his father. During the war, he'd served first as a pioneer on the Eastern Front (Iron Cross Second Class) and later in France; afterwards, he'd taken part in the 1919 uprisings in Berlin, fighting with the Freikorps—which meant, Lahnstein realised with a start, on the side of the Social Democrats. The file was hazy about what he'd got up to in Berlin. Had he, perhaps, shot demonstrators? Played some part in the murders of Rosa Luxemburg and Karl Liebknecht? Lahnstein's imagination began to run riot: he heard shots in the woods, bullets fired from behind, in the back, in the head, though there was no hint of any of that in the file. The only facts recorded were that Schreyer had been in Berlin at the time, in a Freikorps, and that after the putsch he'd been arrested, registered and released. There the file ended.

Schreyer was marching in the front line, bawling slogans. Lahnstein walked level with him, alongside the demonstrators; at one point their eyes met.

Was this a man who butchered boys? Schreyer wore a tweed coat, brown brogues and a small hat with a narrow brim. He was sleek but not fat; his oval face was unremarkable,

55

well-proportioned, not unappealing. The war had left no trace on him. He must have been good-looking as a young man, and perhaps he still was.

'Freedom for Hitler, freedom for Hitler.'

It made no sense to Lahnstein. Why was this man, who seemed to have everything in life, following a cove like Hitler, a war messenger, a street painter? It wasn't as if he was the only one cursing Versailles; there were plenty doing that—many of them more formidable politicians. And was Hitler even a politician? Was attempting a coup sufficient qualification? Hating Jews was nothing out of the ordinary either.

The approach of a second demonstration interrupted Lahnstein's train of thought. Men carrying red flags shot out of a side street onto the main road with such force that the Nazis were pushed to the edge.

For a while, they marched side by side. Lahnstein estimated that the new group was about a hundred and fifty men strong. He looked around for his own men, but could see only Müller; the others must be lost in the crowd or at the tail end. Together, the demonstrations took up the entire breadth of the street. Passers-by sought refuge in shops and doorways; a woman fell to the ground. Lahnstein shouted at Müller that they must get between the two groups, but it didn't look as if he'd understood. Lahnstein's heart was pounding; he needed twenty men, at least. He saw fierce jostling at the seam between the two marches, flying fists, furious pushing and shoving.

He tried to make his way to the middle. The seam was no longer a straight line, but a zigzag, depending on who had the upper hand where. Red flags crashed down on heads.

Lahnstein elbowed a path between the rows, taking blows, getting trapped, burrowing his way through the crowd. He didn't reach the middle. But what could he have done if he had? The marches slowed and came to a halt. The two sides went for each other and were soon rolling around in horse shit. He saw a knife flash; he must get in there and prevent the worst—and mustering all his strength, he fought his way through. But it was too late—still a few yards to go and already he could see blood. Please, let it not be a boy, he thought, not another boy to add to the list. Number Twelve, the full dozen.

Then again, it might be his chance to catch the culprit— the man with the knife who had vanished into the brawling crowd. Lahnstein flailed around more wildly than ever.

Suddenly the path was clear. The crowd thinned and dispersed. The men ran away. Lahnstein was knocked to the ground and for a while he lay on the cobbles in a daze. When he came to, everything was back to normal; people were emerging from the shops and doorways where they'd been sheltering—hurrying now, to make up for lost time. Müller helped Lahnstein up.

'Where's the victim?' Lahnstein asked.

'What victim?' Müller said.

'The man who was stabbed.'

Müller shrugged. 'No one was stabbed,' he said.

'I saw it.'

'Was it fatal?'

'There was certainly blood.'

'No sign of a corpse,' Müller said.

Lahnstein looked about him. It was true; there was no one lying on the ground, no one dragging his injured body to the side of the road.

'Was anyone carried off?'

'Not that I saw.'

Lahnstein felt a sudden fear that in his dazed state he might have dreamt it all. He scanned the ground for a pool of blood.

He hadn't seen much blood in the war—less than most men: his own blood-soaked bandages in the military hospital and a heap of gory arms and legs behind the operating tent—a memory he'd been fighting for years, more or less successfully. Now it was back. Looking down at the cobbles, he saw severed limbs swimming in shit and piss.

Pull yourself together.

The arms and legs vanished. He saw a few dark stains that might have been blood. He dipped his fingers in the stuff, peered at it, sniffed it. It *was* blood.

'It's blood,' he said.

'Only a few drops,' said Müller. 'Can't have been more than a scratch.'

But there had been a knife. Blood had been shed. Lahnstein was relieved to know that he hadn't been imagining things.

They got back in the cars, which had brought up the rear of the demonstration. One drove to hospital, because an officer had broken an arm in the crush. The car Lahnstein was in returned to headquarters. The drive passed in silence.

There was, thank God, no one waiting for him in the office. A missing boy on the day of the demonstration would have been a disaster. He could just imagine what the papers would say: *Inspector Lahnstein of Bochum today led Hanover's police into a trap while failing to prevent a murder on the other side of town.* He went to the lavatory and tried, without much success, to wipe his coat and trousers clean. Then he tackled his shoes, rubbing and rubbing until they shone. Back in the office he wrote a report for the chief of police.

That evening Lahnstein stopped off at Burschel's tobacconist. A bell at the door announced his arrival and a man glanced round from in front of the counter. The woman who ran the shop was standing on a stool, reaching for a small box on one of the upper shelves. Lahnstein saw her calves, the backs of her knees. The man at the counter was staring openly. She put the box on the counter, smoothed her skirt, opened the box and held it out to him. He took a cigar, sniffed it, shook his head, replaced the cigar and pointed up at the same shelf, a little further to the right.

The woman kicked the stool a short distance along the floor, climbed onto it and stretched up to the shelf. Again, Lahnstein saw her calves, the backs of her knees. He looked away and watched the other man watching her legs.

She came down, smoothing her skirt. Once more, the man sniffed a cigar, shook his head and put the cigar back in the box. This time he pointed a little further to the left.

'Get out, please,' the woman said.

'Excuse me?'

'I'm asking you to get out.'

'How dare you. I want you to sell me those cigars and you'll bloody well do as I say.'

The woman didn't budge from behind the counter. The man made a grab for her left arm, but soon let go because Lahnstein had taken hold of his other arm and twisted it behind his back. The man went down on his knees and tried to wriggle free, but he didn't have a chance. He gave a cry of pain and slumped to the floor.

'You'd better go now,' Lahnstein said. He loosened his grip to let the man up, piloted him to the door and pushed him out.

'Thank you,' the woman said.

'Impudent fellow,' Lahnstein said.

She smoothed her skirt again, this time from embarrassment, and closed the box of cigars that was lying on the counter. 'What would you like?' she asked.

She was small and delicate and tired-looking—even more so, he thought, than the last time he'd seen her—and she had a round face and narrow eyes that seemed to extend almost to her ears. This looked strange at first glance, but it had a charm of its own that disarmed Lahnstein.

'What would you like?' she asked again.

'Cigarillos,' he said.

'Cuban?'

He nodded.

She turned, took a packet from the shelf behind her and placed it on the counter.

He dug in his pockets for money. A little boy came

through the door at the back of the shop, wrapped his arms around the woman's leg, and stood looking at Lahnstein, his cheek snuggled up to her hip. He was about the age August would have been, or perhaps a little older. Lahnstein thought of asking him his name, but decided against it. He paid for the cigarillos and went to the door.

'Thank you again,' the woman said.

He glanced back, but she was already up on the stool, turned away from him, box of cigars in hand. A few yards from the shop he paused to light a cigarillo, then continued to the Leine, stopping in the middle of the bridge to look down at the sluggish water, his arms resting on the parapet. Luckily the boy in the tobacconist's shop was too young to be a victim. Unless, that was, Lahnstein still hadn't solved the case ten years from now. It wasn't impossible.

When he approached his office the following morning and saw a woman sitting in the corridor, he hoped she was waiting outside the office next door, waiting for some other inspector who was working on some other murder case. Perspective could be deceptive, he told himself, but he knew full well that the woman was outside his office—and the nearer he got, the clearer it became that she was exactly the right age to be a victim's mother, the mother of a fifteen- to twenty-year-old boy. He felt like turning and leaving, going to the station and buying himself a ticket to some faraway place—Salzburg, perhaps; he could hide out at Lake Irr.

But there were other cases beside the missing boys— shorter murder series, isolated murders. This woman might be missing her daughter, husband, father, sister. Or she might be a witness to some long-past crime. There were all kinds of possibilities.

When he was five yards from her, she stood up.

'Are you Inspector Lahnstein?' she asked.

'I believe I might be,' he said.

She looked at him uncertainly.

'I was told to wait here for Inspector Lahnstein. They said he could help me.'

'Did they indeed?'

He must stop this; it wasn't her fault. She looked about fifty, so was probably, he guessed, in her early forties. Minus ten for working people—that was the rule of thumb. He'd already done the sums. Her face was grey; her dull, worn skin deeply furrowed; her blue eyes clouded. She wore two skirts on top of each other—maybe she had no stockings and was trying to stave off the cold of autumn—and her dark, baggy coat was buttoned up, but he could see even so that she was a heavy woman. Her hat had lost whatever colour it once had. She was the wife of a tradesman or a worker and evidently worked hard herself.

'It's about my boy, Adolf,' she said.

He felt a glimmer of hope. Adolf was Number Eleven. It was an old case.

'Hannappel?'

She started to cry. He looked at her, less sure of himself.

'Is he your nephew?'

He put a hand on her arm.

'I'm so frightened about my boy and you say such strange

things,' she said.

His hope vanished.

'What's your name?'

'Hennies.'

'And Adolf is your son? Adolf Hennies?'

'My son, yes.'

Number Twelve. The full dozen.

'Come in,' he said.

She followed him into the office and he motioned to a chair in front of his desk. When she sat down, he saw feet and calves swaddled in cloths, flat shoes with worn rubber soles.

'So your son's called Adolf too? Is that right?'

'Yes, that's right. Why *too*? Is there another Adolf missing?'

'Reported missing last month. How long has your Adolf been gone?'

'Two nights. He's never stayed away at night, and now it's been two in a row. And he'd have got in touch, I know he would. Mr Eisenschmiedt says the same.'

'Who is this Mr Eisenschmiedt?'

'Schmiedt, with an *ie*.'

'Mr Eisenschmiedt—who is this man? And what does he say?'

'He's my lodger. He shares Adolf's room. It's the only way I can make ends meet.'

She was a widow, like so many others, but her husband hadn't fallen in the war; he'd died of cancer. You wondered what they needed cancer for, when war and influenza alone filled the cemeteries, but ordinary peacetime diseases did sometimes carry people off during the war. *Remember us?*

they seemed to say. *What the trenches do, we've been doing for centuries. What the flu can do, we can do too.* Mrs Hennies spoke with a certain wistfulness, as if the war had done her out of her share of pity, her status as a young widow. So many young women were widowed these days that it no longer set them apart; it had become ordinary. Death by cancer was never more senseless than in a war, when only death at the front—a sacrifice for the fatherland—was considered meaningful. Mrs Hennies seemed a little resentful towards her husband for leaving her with such a banal story—a story that nobody wanted to hear and that she didn't stand to profit from. People were calling for better pensions for war widows, as if they were the only ones who needed it.

She told Lahnstein that she'd worked at the Continental rubber works during the war. They'd put her at the machines because all the men were away, but when the war was over and the men came back—or some of them, anyway—there was no more work for women at the machines; part of it went to former Continental workers, and the rest to men from other companies that had gone bankrupt. These days, she earned a living working nights as a factory cleaner, but it paid less and she'd had to take in a lodger—which was why her son now shared his room with Mr Eisenschmiedt. She slept in the only other room.

'Doesn't Adolf earn anything?' Lahnstein asked.

'He's out of work at the moment,' she said. 'But he applied for a job three days ago.'

'The day he went missing?'

'Yes. He was an errand boy at Ahrberg's, the wholesale slaughterhouse, but business wasn't good and he lost the job.'

'Where's he hoping to work next?'

'At Grusen's on Alte Celler Heerstrasse. He's applied for a job as a travelling soap salesman. But I don't want him working there.'

He looked at her in surprise.

'Why not?'

'Grusen's not a good man.'

'What does he do?'

She looked embarrassed.

'Does he beat the boys? Doesn't he pay their wages on time?'

'He's not got a good reputation.'

'What do you mean?'

'I can't say it.'

'But you want us to find Adolf, don't you? You want it as much as I do. If we're going to find him, we need to know everything.'

'He's sweet on a girl, I know he is, he told me.'

'What of it?'

'He met her when he was an errand boy at the slaughterhouse. She worked in a pub. He mentioned her to Mr Eisenschmiedt too.'

'Why are you telling me this?'

She stared at the floor.

He felt bad. He knew he'd made a mistake, a big mistake, and that this woman's son might be alive if he hadn't. He looked at her; she was still staring at the floor. He felt like taking her in his arms and begging her forgiveness—but how could he? You didn't own up to a possibly fatal mistake.

He couldn't, at any rate. Instead, he swore to himself that he would do everything in his power to distract from the mistake and, if possible, to make it good.

'Mr Grusen has a nasty reputation, doesn't he?' he asked rather sharply.

She didn't reply.

'You needn't say anything, but you could nod or shake your head.'

She hesitated, then nodded, without raising her eyes.

'It's to do with boys.'

She started, as if she might leap to her feet and run away, but again she nodded.

'He likes boys.'

This time she shook her head, though not, he realised, in disagreement, but in incomprehension, disapproval, embarrassment.

'You don't want Adolf working there, because you're afraid Grusen might mistreat him.'

'Adolf isn't like that, I know he isn't, but he needs the work.'

Lahnstein nodded. 'He needs the work.'

'He likes girls.'

'I'm sure he does.'

'My son's respectable. He always comes home at night.'

'So you said.'

'He sometimes went dancing with his friend Wedemeyer, but he always told me where he was going and he never stayed out past midnight. I can't sleep till he's home.'

She cried—not for fear this time, but for shame. Lahnstein looked at her, wondering why he was being so harsh on her, so ruthless. But he knew really. It was because her son was missing; because she'd come in here with a case for him to solve—a case that probably proved him guilty of a grave mistake. Why did she have to have a queer son? Oh, stop it, he told himself. It's not her fault that you're an idiot.

'What will you do?'

Her voice tore him out of his thoughts.

'We'll look into this Mr Grusen and ask him about his interview with your son...'

'I've already been to speak to him.'

'Well?'

'His hair's quite blond, but unnaturally so. Like a woman's.'

'What did he say?'

'He said he'd given him the job—said a bright boy like Adolf was just what he needed— but then Adolf didn't show up, not on the first day and not on the second either. Grusen said he'd let him down—that he was a good-for-nothing and how could he trust a boy like that to sell his soap. But he couldn't say where Adolf might be.'

'We'll question him in a bit more detail,' Lahnstein said, 'and I'll send a man round to look at your son's room and speak to your lodger. Is he a young chap too?'

'He's an elderly gentleman.'

Now her voice was sharp.

'An upright man, and if you think I'd stand for...'

He raised his hands defensively.

'I assure you,' he said, 'I think no such thing.'

He got up and held out his hand.

'We'll do all we can to find your boy,' he said. 'I promise.'

The same old words. He couldn't help himself.

—

He washed at the bowl on the dresser, splashing two scoops of water onto his face and rubbing a handful of water into each armpit. Then he dried himself, put on a singlet, a white shirt, his good suit and his pointed shoes. The fake moustache he slipped into his jacket pocket along with the warrant card. He had a last look around the room to make sure it was clean and welcoming, wiped a dark stain from the table, and went out, locking the door behind him.

It was dark, ten at night, the streets were empty. He heard the babbling river, crossed the bridge and turned off towards Cafe Köpcke. Along the last stretch, he was accosted by boys, some familiar to him, others not. There were always new ones. But he wasn't interested today. He knew their kind. They were diseased and took drugs that made their eyes shine. First they were lively, then silent and listless. They were cautious, too, always on their guard, knew every trick in the book.

He'd hoped to find Hans in the cafe, but he couldn't see him. The place was heaving with people—men to look like men; men to look like women, and a handful of women who would remain women whatever their state of undress. Shrill laughter, heat, sweat-smeared make-up. A bad pianist, though they sometimes had good ones. People dancing. He ordered a beer at the bar, avoiding the looks and winks. Someone shouted in his ear, but he couldn't make out the words and went to lean against a pillar with his beer. Not for long. He felt a hand on his backside, wheeled round, grabbed a man by his collar, raised a fist. Eyes met his—humble, beseeching.

It was an old man; he thrust him away.

Hans came in, talking to Hugo. Hans saw him and waved, but made straight for the bar, deep in conversation. He left the pillar and greeted Hans with a kiss on the mouth. Hans turned his head away. How are you? Fine. Yourself? Not bad, good to see you again, you must drop in some time. The conversation petered out. Hans spoke insistently to Hugo. Then a couple of girls showed up who worked for Hans; they handed over their earnings and danced with the two men. How lovely Hans was with that beautiful blond hair. Good to touch, too.

He went out, back past the boys. This time he laughed them off and went behind a tree to stick his moustache on. It was cold, but he had a good coat—and, with a grateful thought to the previous owner, God bless him, he set off for the station, walking at a leisurely pace. He was in no hurry; it wasn't yet midnight and he was in a good mood; his hopes were high. The station loomed before him—vast, imposing, his territory.

3

After half an hour, the doors were opened and they were allowed to get out and stretch their legs. The boy was one of the first off. The train had stopped on a bend in the line at the edge of a wood and there were men busy with something up by the engine, but he couldn't work out what. They stooped down, stood up again, gesticulated. The boy's carriage was the last of four and he made his way to the front to investigate. Maybe there was a body on the lines. He'd never seen a corpse, but he knew all about them from his older brother who'd seen dead men every day in the war, many of them mangled and dismembered. The boy had pretended to be unimpressed by the stories, but for a long time his waking dreams had been full of stumps and guts, chinless, noseless faces, empty eye sockets. Now he was older and felt strong enough to confront a corpse—longed for it, in fact. It was as if he needed a real dead man to crowd out the images in his head.

But it wasn't a man; it was a cow, and didn't look as bad as it might have done—it must have been knocked down, rather than run over, then caught under the engine and shunted along. The men were having trouble pulling it out. They tugged and heaved, but the dead animal wouldn't budge. The boy offered to help, but the engine driver and the stoker wouldn't let him. They decided to cut the cow up and sent him away. He went reluctantly; it would have made a good story for his brother. Then he remembered that he wouldn't be seeing his brother for a long time, maybe never.

At first he'd thought it was the journeyman the vicar's daughter came to see, but most of the time, as she stood at the door, watching them work, her eyes were on him. She came in the early afternoon; he supposed she had school in the mornings. On the third day he mustered all his courage and left his cap in church, and when they reached the bottom of the hill he told the journeyman and the apprentice master that he had to go back for it. But when he got there, it wasn't where he'd left it. He looked all over until a sound overhead made him look up at the gallery, and there was Monika with the cap on her head, his green cap. He climbed the stairs and that was how it began.

He glanced at his watch. It was ten o'clock; they'd been standing for about an hour and he had three hours in Hanover before the last train left for Bremerhaven. Should be possible. He looked down the line towards the engine and saw the stoker swing an axe above his head and bring it sweeping down. He heard a sound that he thought might be splintering bones. The green cap was perched on his head.

—

'More boys missing, eh?' Lahnstein's landlady said when he came out of the bathroom that morning, outdoor shoes on his bare feet beneath his pyjamas. The other rooms were occupied now and the shoes were a necessary precaution.

'Is that so?' he asked.

'It's what the papers say.'

She was wearing the same grey housecoat and slippers.

'It's got to stop.'

'It will.'

'Lock Haarmann up. That'll put a stop to it.'

'Who's Haarmann?'

'He was born on the seventeenth of the fifth.'

'What's that supposed to mean?'

'Haarmann's a boy-fancier and the boys he takes home vanish. Klobes'll tell you.'

'Who's Klobes?'

'Fellow who runs the tobacconist's across the road from Haarmann's old digs. He noticed that there were boys went in there that didn't come out again. Haarmann had to move in the end, because Klobes was on his trail.'

Lahnstein was less than electrified. The woman wasn't right in the head.

'Haarmann sells meat, too,' she said.

'But who is this Haarmann? A butcher?'

'No, he sells clothes and meat.'

'And who's Klobes?'

'Christian Klobes, the tobacconist, I just told you.'

'Not Burschel?'

'No, Klobes.'

'And he said the boys went in but didn't come out?'

'He watched all day and all night, and none of them came out.'

'Why didn't he go to the police?'

'He did. They didn't believe him.'

'What's Klobes' address?'

'Neue Strasse, in Little Venice.'

'On Leine Island?'

'Yes, Klobes the Tobacconist.'

'Klobes, Neue Strasse, I'll remember.'

He went back to his room, hearing her slippers shuffle over the linoleum behind him.

They had made a raid on Cafe Köpcke, questioned the renters and drawn up a list of thirty men from Hanover and its environs who had repeatedly offended against Section 175. Most of the cases involved boys. Six of the men were violent enough to be considered potential culprits. The police had watched them intermittently, but that was as much as they could manage. 'Versailles,' they said, with a shrug of their shoulders.

The questionings yielded nothing. No one had heard or seen anything—certainly nobody said anything. The men from Cafe Köpcke and the Queer Kettle were cagey with the police, diffident. They'd learnt to play a role, to hide their true selves; they were on their guard. And they stuck together. They wouldn't peach on one of their kind.

Most of all, they were scared of Müller. Lahnstein noticed this when the two of them interrogated a suspect together.

Müller was calm and friendly, but there was a disdainful curl to his lip. Lahnstein had the impression that there was a hidden substructure to the interrogations, an unspoken arrangement permitting certain words and prohibiting others. Müller heard only what he already knew—what he wanted to hear.

Lahnstein broached the matter to him.

'You seem to know them all,' he said.

'Are you implying…'

'No, you misunderstand me. I mean professionally.'

'I am glad to hear it.'

'What I'm getting at is, these men seem to have a clear notion of what you expect of them, what you want them to say.'

'We've had occasional dealings with them. On the whole, we leave them in peace. We could nick them all under Section 175, of course, but we don't. Can't lock them all up—they only pollute the prisons, and really they're quite harmless. Poor sods, eh? Can't help it.'

Lahnstein felt uneasy, but refrained from commenting.

'So what are these *dealings* you have with them?'

'We try to contain them. We don't want them visible in town, especially in the daytime. People don't want to see them; they disgust the public.'

He felt unease again. Or was it shame?

'Let me tell you something. If the one-seven-fivers spread, everyone will say the police has failed them, the state's failed them.'

'Wouldn't it make more sense to say that the best state

is the one that treats them well? They're citizens, and in a democracy, if I understand correctly, all citizens are equal. Everyone has a vote and each vote counts the same.'

Had he gone too far? Would Müller make inferences?

Müller laughed scornfully and said, 'Even women have the vote these days, in this fine democracy of yours. But then again, if sodomites have the vote, why shouldn't women?'

Lahnstein said nothing.

'Listen,' Müller said, 'we aren't judged solely in terms of our efforts to suppress sodomy, but it's one criterion, and it's an important one. Sods are depravity and depravity is something we guard against. But nobody thanks us anymore. Times have changed.'

Lahnstein had a sudden thought.

'If someone's born on the seventeenth of the fifth does that make him a one-seven-fiver?'

'That's right.'

Returning to the office after lunch a few days later, Lahnstein was surprised to hear Müller's voice from some way down the corridor; he'd never known him to shout. He and a colleague called Gerst were questioning a man of perhaps forty who wore a dark-red velvet suit, a white shirt, pointy brown shoes, and chains of gold—or what looked like gold—at his wrist and neck. He had a moustache and his jet-black hair gleamed with oil. A brass-knobbed stick was propped against Müller's desk and Gerst was propped beside it, looming over the man, who sat on a chair in front of the desk. Müller was sitting in Lahnstein's seat, shouting questions.

'You like fucking little boys, don't you?'

'How dare you. I have a steady lover and he's forty-seven.'

'You expect us to believe he's the only one you fuck?'

'We've been together for ten years.'

'Oh, come off it,' Gerst said.

'Together and faithful. But what concern is it of yours, gentlemen?'

Müller kicked the leg of the desk, sending the stick clattering to the floor. The man retrieved it and propped it up again.

'What brings you to Hanover?' Gerst asked.

'I told you. I'm here on business.'

Again, Müller kicked the desk, knocking down the stick. This time the man laid it across his lap.

'May I ask why you're questioning this gentleman?' Lahnstein asked.

'We picked him up at the station,' Gerst said. 'Looked to us like a one-seven-fiver and so he has proved. Confessed at once. Now we're trying to find out if he's here to nab another boy.'

'I import cloth from Italy,' the man said. 'I have customers in Hanover.'

A policeman came in and said there was a woman downstairs to see Lahnstein.

He got up and walked unhurriedly to the door, as though to put off meeting this person for as long as possible. Unlucky Number Thirteen.

On his way out, he heard Müller say to the man, 'You see, no sooner are you in town than it all starts up again.'

—

Lahnstein leapt down the stairs in a panic. Another boy, another boy, another boy. He'd let it happen again. Then he saw her: sitting on one of the visitors' benches, in a hat with a feather, was the woman from the tobacconist's. *Her* son, he thought, appalled—but her boys are too little, far younger than the others. She stood up and came towards him.

'I'm so sorry to bother you, but I'm awfully...'

'No need to be sorry,' he said quickly. 'It is, I am afraid, my duty to deal with these sad affairs.'

'That's just it. This isn't your duty. You told me you dealt with murders.'

He was getting to be a regular in her shop, often stopping by for a chat—settling down in one of the worn leather armchairs and telling her a bit about his work. He'd even mentioned the missing boys, but she'd listened without curiosity, apparently unimpressed by the story, though she had two sons of her own—younger than the victims, it was true, but surely she must feel something at the thought of all those boys losing their lives. Lahnstein was used to being admired for his work on the case, and he was used to being spurned, despised, attacked. He had never encountered indifference. But this woman—Emma Burschel, as he now knew her to be called—hadn't asked a single question. She was altogether reserved, asking nothing, volunteering nothing—though she seemed to find it agreeable enough when he sat and talked to her after buying his cigarillos.

'I'm not here about a murder,' she said, 'thank goodness. I'm here about a burglary. Someone broke into my shop last night and took some boxes of cigars, the expensive Cuban kind.'

'I'm sorry to hear that,' Lahnstein said.

'I've been waiting for the police all morning,' she said. 'The constable looked in and said he'd send someone round who knows about burglary, to check for fingerprints and take a report from me. But no one's showed up. And I need the report for the insurance. So I was thinking that maybe— forgive me, but I was thinking maybe you could help.'

Why not? Of course he could. No trouble at all. It wasn't his department, but it was a way of winning this woman's sympathy, of being with her without betraying Lissy, whom he was loath to deceive as long as she was up in that aeroplane— though mind you, maybe thinking of another woman would get that out of his head. He did think of Emma Burschel from time to time, but perhaps not enough—the plane still flew almost every night. It was a dilemma he knew no way out of. What he did know was that he needed a woman. Maybe they could just talk, to begin with. Might be better than nothing.

'I'll fetch my hat and coat,' he said.

He went upstairs. The office was empty now; even the stick was gone. It occurred to him that he hadn't seen the man in the velvet suit leave headquarters. There were other doors, at the back of the building, but it wasn't usual to send witnesses or suspects out that way. He asked in various offices, but nobody knew where Müller and Gerst had got to.

Lahnstein took the back stairs to the basement where the cells were and some interrogation rooms with no windows and thick doors. He listened at these doors and hearing a scream behind one of them, he pushed it open. The man was lying on the floor; Gerst was beating him with the stick. The man was writhing, screaming, trying to protect himself with his hands, but the stick came down fast; every other blow struck home, hitting his shoulders, his chest, his groin. Müller stood at the wall and watched, arms folded.

Lahnstein threw himself at Gerst, wrested the stick off him and pushed him away, sending him staggering against the wall.

'Those days are over,' he said.

Müller didn't move. He was still standing at the wall, arms folded.

Lahnstein helped the man up and returned his stick to him. The man groaned, doubled up with pain.

'Wait for me in my office,' Lahnstein said.

The man hobbled out.

'What is this?' Lahnstein yelled at Müller.

'You want progress too, don't you?'

'Not like that. We don't torture anymore. We stopped all that long ago.'

'A bit of a beating isn't torture. We have twelve missing boys and we're getting nowhere. We know nothing. You were supposed to change things, but a fat lot of good you've done. Boys are still going missing. Do you want us to look on and do nothing?'

'Beating *is* torture; it violates fundamental rights in our constitution. You know that.'

'Of course I do,' Müller said scornfully, 'but that constitution makes it hideously difficult for the police to do their job. It makes it impossible for people to live in safety. Twelve dead boys in one year. That didn't happen in the Empire.'

'Torture was forbidden in the Empire too.'

Müller gave a loud laugh. 'That's true,' he said, 'but nobody gave a damn if we dealt the odd blow. It was the results that mattered, public safety—and that was better served under the Kaiser.'

'Do you think so? Didn't he send two million men to their deaths? And how many women and children did he let starve? Is that what you call public safety? Our serial killer has a long way to go before he has as many lives on his conscience as the Kaiser.'

Müller detached himself from the wall and took two steps towards Lahnstein.

'You will not insult the Kaiser,' he hissed.

Gerst moved in on him from the side.

Lahnstein pulled his gun and rapidly pointed it at Gerst and then Müller.

'Stay where you are,' he said.

Müller laughed again. 'You idiot. Your democracy won't last long if you carry on like that.'

'The Empire only lasted forty-seven years,' Lahnstein said. 'We can manage that, no trouble.'

'Forty-two to go,' Müller said. 'Good luck to you. May I leave now?'

Lahnstein lowered his gun. Müller passed him with a smirk. Gerst followed.

Lahnstein put his gun away, left the interrogation room and hurried up the back stairs. He had sounded surer of himself than he was. Sometimes, it was true, he imagined detaining the culprit and manoeuvring him delicately into confession; he had visions of a brilliant piece of interrogation that would be cited at police academies for decades to come. On other days, however, his imagination took a rather different course and he set to and thrashed the monster, beating out of him the words he needed to save himself and Hanover and the German Reich. He laid into him with a certain gratification at the thought that he was, at last, getting somewhere, after weeks of failure. And he laid into him all the harder when he remembered that he was beating a man to get a confession out of him.

The office was empty. He looked in the lavatory to see if the man in the velvet suit had gone to wash the blood from his face, but he wasn't there. Lahnstein fetched his hat and coat and went down the front stairs to accompany Emma Burschel to the tobacconist's.

The back door had been broken down with a crowbar—clean, professional work, as far as Lahnstein could judge. He'd investigated quite a few burglaries in his early years with the police and wasn't entirely clueless.

'Any idea who might have done it?' he asked Emma Burschel. 'Customer? Neighbour?'

'What makes you think he knew the place?'

'The back door doesn't lead straight to the shop; there's a passage that takes two turns. You wouldn't risk breaking down a big door like that just on the off-chance. Could have been one of your suppliers.'

'Could have been my brother.'

He looked at her in surprise. Her face showed no emotion.

'Your brother?'

'Yes, he's here a lot. Comes for his cigars. Minds the boys for me sometimes. He knows the passage. He broke in once before, but that time he smashed the shop window.'

'Do you want me to deal with your brother?'

She shook her head.

'I'll settle it with him,' she said. 'I just need a stamped report. Can you get me one?'

'Of course. But I'd be happy to speak to him.'

'He was trying to help,' she said. 'Last time, the insurance said they wouldn't pay for the window. It was the third in a row. But my brother only smashed the last. Someone else did the first two. Will you have a cup of coffee?'

She told him she hadn't stuck it out long with the boys' father, who was a drunk and a gambler. He'd spent the war on a submarine and survived. The last she'd seen of him was in November 1918, when he came down from Wilhelmshaven to help the local soldiers set up councils. He'd called in to see the boys, and then gone on to Berlin to join the revolution. She hadn't heard from him since.

'Is he still alive?'

'I don't know,' she said. 'A lot of people died in Berlin in the revolution. Where were you in November '18?'

'Yorkshire,' he said, 'in a POW camp.'

They heard the news from the guards, with a few days' time lag.

9 November: abdication of the Kaiser, proclamation of the Republic.

11 November: ceasefire.

The guards were happy, but gloating. *You've had it.* The monarchist prisoners grieved; two of them committed suicide one night after hearing of the Kaiser's escape to Holland. The Social Democrats celebrated, earning themselves monarchist hostility, hatred, blows. As the Kaiser's adherents were in a clear majority, the situation grew dangerous. The Social Democrats, who had previously slept scattered about the barracks, closed ranks, setting up night watches and going in groups to wash and eat. They were looked on as traitors, blamed for the defeat.

Franz no longer slept next to Lahnstein. They had met outside at night another two or three times, but otherwise kept out of each other's way, hardly speaking, avoiding eye contact. When they moved their camp beds into a new barracks, neither approached the other, so they ended up at opposite ends of the room. Once, they were on watch together, but they didn't talk. There was a half moon; they sat five paces apart, smoking solitarily, glancing at the moon from time to time, listening out into the night. Spears whittled from branches lay ready. Somewhere, far away, people were celebrating. Lahnstein felt no anger or contempt towards Franz; he bore him no grudge. It had to happen, he told himself, for reasons that had nothing at all to do with either of them. But now that it had happened, they could no longer bear each other's presence. That was the price they had to pay.

A few days later a Social Democrat was found dead with signs of strangulation at his throat. The English mounted an inquiry, but it yielded nothing. Nobody told them what was going on in the camp. They were English.

Such incidents meant nothing to Lahnstein. It was like watching a play from the front of the stalls—so close, and yet so far removed from his thoughts. It was three months since he'd last heard from Lissy. The Republic, peace—all that was very well, but Lahnstein had only one thing on his mind: what had happened to Lissy and August? Where were they, if they were still alive? Not in Bochum, that much he knew from his parents. They hadn't come back from Lake Irr.

Were they dead? Impossible. The war hadn't penetrated to Germany. An accident? Lahnstein couldn't believe it, though part of him would have liked to. Because the alternative, surely, was worse—the possibility that Lissy had left him, taken August and gone off to live with another man, hoping that he'd give them up for lost and wouldn't go looking for them. She was wrong there, he thought angrily. 'I'm going to look for you. And I'm going to find you. Both of you.' He said the words softly, barely opening his lips, and decided that perhaps, after all, it was better if they weren't dead. Then at least there was a chance that he could fetch them back—if not both of them, then August. The thought kept him alive. In the summer of 1919, the Germans accepted the Treaty of Versailles and Lahnstein was released.

'Are you married, Mr Lahnstein?' Emma Burschel asked— they weren't on first-name terms. They were sitting in her flat, drinking cognac; Lahnstein was smoking a cigarillo. She hadn't bothered opening the shop after the break-in. The boys had said a brief how-do-you-do and vanished into their room.

'No,' he said. But it's not true, he thought, you're married to the woman in the plane.

'You look sad,' she said.

'I like being on my own,' he said.

'I don't. I hate it.'

Silence.

'What if he strikes now?' Lahnstein asked.

'Who?'

'The boy killer.'

'What makes you say that?'

'It's dark. Not that it need be; he could strike at any moment. We know nothing. He could be killing as I speak.'

Lahnstein got up. 'I must be going,' he said.

He saw her disappointment, like a rip in her face.

'I'll write the report,' he said, 'and bring it round tomorrow. I'll say there are no suspects, all right?'

She nodded, somewhere else with her thoughts. He stood there but didn't move.

'I'll be going, then.'

She saw him to the door. He gave her his hand and went out. After a few yards, he turned around, but she had gone in and closed the door; he couldn't see her.

It was cold. He pulled up his collar, plunged his hands into his coat pockets and set off towards Little Venice. If it was true that the killer could strike at any time—and it was—then he could also strike in any place; he could strike right here where Lahnstein was walking. He walked briskly, keeping his eyes on the edges of the streets. The middle of the road wasn't a place for crime; criminals stuck to shadows and corners and passageways. It was seven in the evening and the streets were full of people, most of them on their way home, tired, but hurrying. Lahnstein paid particular attention to couples—older men with younger men—but all those he saw turned out to be fathers and sons. This was reassuring, though it was a pity not to be able to take action. He came to the bridge over the Leine with Little Venice beyond and slowed his pace. Whores and renters, lively in anticipation of the evening's business, not yet ravaged by drugs—and in among them, children who hadn't been called home, workers coming from their shifts, decent people who couldn't afford to live elsewhere. Rubbish outside the houses and in the gutters. A woman stood in Lahnstein's way, heavily made up, a shiny red mouth, big eyes—*yellowish* eyes, as far as he could make out in the light of the gas lamps. 'Come with me, sweetheart.' Bad teeth, her tongue circled, she clutched his arm, he tore free, went on his way. 'Bloody fairy,' she called after him. He drove his hands deeper into his pockets. I'm not, he thought. I am not.

Suddenly he saw the man in the velvet suit—heard him first, tapping his way along the cobbles with his walking stick, *tock, tock, tock*. He came out of a side street in front of Lahnstein. His coat was long, but the dark-red trousers were visible underneath—and with that stick of his, there was no mistaking him. Lahnstein dropped his pace again and followed at a distance, hoping the man would meet a boy so that the case could at last be brought to an end, solved thanks to Inspector Lahnstein and his respectable constitutional methods.

The man made for a porte cochère where a boy of about fifteen stood, apparently waiting, but without the nonchalant, leering air of a renter; he looked troubled, barely managing a smile as he held out his hand to the man. They held each other clasped for a strangely long time, and then the pair of them went in at the porte cochère, the man with a hand on the boy's back, tender rather than controlling.

Lahnstein couldn't fathom the situation and followed them into the yard, where there was a saddler's workshop, closed at this hour. All was deserted, silent. The man and boy disappeared through a door on the left. There were lights in all the flats. Lahnstein pulled his gun, pushed open the door and found himself at the bottom of a narrow staircase. He heard another door shut upstairs, on the third or fourth floor. In a less distant flat, someone shouted. Somewhere else, opera was playing on a gramophone. Lahnstein hurried up the stairs, two or three at a time. On the third floor he listened at the doors on either side—silence on the left; the gramophone on the right. He sprinted up another flight of stairs to the top floor. Sloping walls, only one door. His heart was racing. Should he go in? Somebody laughed—a bright voice, a woman's rather than a man's—and Lahnstein was thrown into such confusion that he forgot to put away his gun before he knocked, and found himself face to face with a frightened boy who flung up his hands when he saw him.

'Police,' said Lahnstein, lowering the gun awkwardly and putting it away.

'What do you want?' the boy stammered.

'You have a gentleman visiting?'

'My dad.'

'Your dad? But...you can put your hands down.'

The boy lowered his hands.

'May I come in?'

'Please do.'

The boy stepped aside and Lahnstein followed him into a sitting room. He saw the man, still in his coat, and a woman. As he entered, they moved apart, as if from an embrace. The woman was plump, of medium height, and wore thick-lensed glasses.

'What are you doing here?' the man asked. He had bruises on his face.

'I'm not so sure myself.'

The man laughed. 'This policeman came to my rescue today,' he said.

The woman offered him a seat and he collapsed into an armchair. The sitting room was crowded, though by no means small—too much furniture, too many lamps, too many pictures, chests-of-drawers, vases. Very little light. Soon they were drinking liqueur and the man, who introduced himself as Karl Sass, told the woman the story of his arrest—vividly, but without reproach or complaint, as if pain were the price you paid for a good story. 'Wasn't that so?' he kept saying to Lahnstein, and Lahnstein nodded.

It turned out that Sass and the woman had been married for ten years before Sass realised, as he put it, that he liked a squiz at the other side. He laughed. 'Seriously,' he said, 'whenever Hilda talked about fancying a man—and she was always very frank on the matter—I'd think to myself, well, yes, I quite fancy him myself—and if I didn't, it wasn't a fundamental thing, if you get my meaning, it was just that there was something about his face or build that didn't appeal. Eventually it began to dawn on me that I saw men with the eyes of a woman. That was my second birth, on the seventeenth of the fifth.'

He laughed again, but he was the only one. His wife looked at him intently.

'Stop it, Dad,' the boy said.

'I come here once a month to visit my loved ones and leave them a bit of money. Then I go back to my beloved in Berlin.'

Silence.

'You can be sure, Inspector Lahnstein, that I don't lay a finger on my son.'

'Dad!'

'But that's why this policeman's here. He thought I was going to slaughter you—isn't that so, Inspector?'

'It was pretty much chance that I found you,' Lahnstein said.

'Quite some chance.'

'I should be going.'

The boy showed him to the door. 'Take care of yourself,' Lahnstein said. On his way downstairs, he realised with annoyance that his words could be misconstrued.

He felt the way he always did after interviewing someone in connection with the case. No lead, no clue, nothing. Almost eight weeks had passed and he was no further. They'd had the soap merchant watched and found out all they could about the two Adolfs, but it had got them nowhere. Nothing but mysteries. The only good news was that no boy had gone missing for two weeks. In four days it would be Christmas and he would go and see his father in Bochum.

The next morning, for want of anything better to do, he sought out the tobacconist on Neue Strasse. Klobes was a tiny mannikin, short and thin, a mere brushstroke in a shop that was a good deal less orderly than Emma Burschel's. Boxes stood in rough piles or carelessly stacked towers, close to collapse; dust and cobwebs hung in air that was thick with stale and fresh smoke. Klobes was sucking on an almost black cigar. Lahnstein showed him his warrant card and received a look of contempt.

'Do you know Fritz Haarmann?'

'Used to be a customer.'

More contempt.

'I've heard that you harbour certain suspicions about him.'

Klobes took a long drag on his cigar. For a while he said nothing, and then: 'Since when have the police been interested in that?'

'Was there a time when they weren't?'

'They never gave a toss.'

'You mean to say, you went to the police and told them of your suspicions?'

'You know I did.'

'I know nothing. I'm new.'

'I went to the police several times.'

'And then?'

'Nothing happened.'

'What were your suspicions?'

'Last time they laughed in my face.'

'I'm here because I take you seriously.'

'Haarmann lived across the road in Number Eight in a room let by Miss Rehbock. He turned the place into a slaughterhouse.'

Two men came in, both workers, and bought cheap cigarettes.

Lahnstein stayed half an hour at the tobacconist's. Klobes told him that Haarmann had moved into Miss Rehbock's in the summer of 1921. Had a lot of visitors, he did, and all boys, so it was soon clear what sort he was, though it was nobody's business what people got up to—you could do what you liked these days; it was all allowed—but it did strike him as odd that some of the boys who went in never came out again, and he had a very good view of Number Eight from the shop—the Inspector could see for himself, if he liked.

Klobes came out from behind the counter and led Lahnstein to the shop window.

'Over there,' he said, pointing to the left, 'the very old house with the wide gateway. It backs onto the river. Haarmann's room was just to the right of the gateway. There's a spinster living there now.'

'The boys might have left at night,' Lahnstein said.

'I watched at night too, once my suspicions had been aroused. But they didn't come out—or only a few of them. "There's some funny business going on in there," I said to Lammers next door, "all those boys." "What I think," he

91

said to me, "is that he sells the lads to Africa, to the Foreign Legion." And that reassured me for a while. But the boys kept going in and not coming out and I stopped believing in the Foreign Legion story.

'I asked Haarmann about it, but he dodged my questions. And the strange goings-on continued, especially at night. When I went down the passageway, past his window, I'd see shadows moving up and down behind the curtains and sometimes it looked as if the people in there were in the nude.'

'How could you tell?' Lahnstein asked.

'I could see.'

Klobes puffed at his cigar. He spoke in an affected manner, in a high, pompous voice that cracked when his own importance was almost more than he could bear.

He told Lahnstein that he'd heard a banging and a hammering at Number Eight into the early hours of the morning—gave him the creeps, it did. Haarmann had come out carrying parcels of meat.

Meat?

Parcels of meat—though, mind you, the boys did take Haarmann the odd rabbit or pheasant—sometimes even a dog. There was a mincer in Haarmann's room—Miss Rehbock had seen it—but Haarmann was very careful not to be caught in his room and always locked up when he left the house. Another thing Klobes had noticed was that Haarmann sometimes went out in the dark with a heavy sack. One night, after reading about all those missing boys, he'd followed him and watched him from behind a bush and he'd seen him throw the sack into the Leine. Probably—for sure—the sack was full of bones and innards.'

'Probably or for sure?'

'Beg pardon?'

'You said there were probably bones in the sack. Then you said for sure there were.'

'How could I be anything but sure?' Klobes asked. 'What else could have been in that sack?'

He came close to Lahnstein and lowered his voice. 'Those weren't rabbits in there,' he said, 'and they weren't pheasants and they weren't dogs. They were human bones.' The last words were a shriek.

'How do you know?'

'Couldn't have been anything else. The boys went in and what was left of them was carried out of Haarmann's room in a sack. He sold the meat—everyone knew he traded privately in horse and other meat that supposedly came from a certain Karl the Butcher. Good-value fillets and mince.'

'And you told the police all this?'

'Every word.'

'Was your statement taken down?'

'Oh, yes, I signed it. But nothing came of it. Haarmann was left to carry on his monstrous deeds.'

'And then he moved?'

'A few weeks later. Things were getting too hot for him here. He realised we were on his trail and weren't going to put up with things any longer.'

Lahnstein bought the cigarettes he had wanted to buy from Emma, thanked Klobes and said goodbye.

'What happens next?' Klobes asked.

'Something will happen, I assure you. One last question: where's Haarmann living now?'

'That I don't know.'

Lahnstein left the shop and crossed the road to Number Eight—a crooked half-timbered building. He passed the gateway and saw children playing in a big courtyard. 'You can feel a crime scene,' his father had once said, but perhaps it was tongue-in-cheek; Lahnstein never knew how seriously to take those sayings of his. He stopped for a moment, but felt nothing. The children gawped at him.

The following morning, Lahnstein received a call saying that Kogel, the chief of police, wished to see him. He supposed he would be dismissed, or at least reprimanded, and prepared his defence on the stairs: Versailles, an understaffed force, the one-seven-fivers' reticence towards the authorities—he might even mention Müller's unreliability. But he knew it wouldn't save him. After more than two months in Hanover, he'd made no progress at all. That was the truth and it was enough to get him sacked. Then again, as employers went, Kogel had always seemed lenient—a man of few words, who listened and nodded and seemed glad when a meeting was over.

Today he was not alone; with him was a man whose photograph Lahnstein had often seen in the papers. He immediately thought of the picture of this man with the president of the Reich, the pair of them—president Friedrich Ebert and defence minister Gustav Noske—up to their knees in the Baltic Sea, dressed in bathing trunks. That photograph, taken in the summer of 1918, had been a long-running scandal.

The war and the revolution weren't long over; the Treaty of Versailles was only just signed, and here were two eminent representatives of the Republic paddling in the sea. They hadn't even had the decency to wear proper bathing costumes. Ebert was grinning, Lahnstein recalled; Noske, at least, looked serious. People were suffering and the president was grinning at them in his bathers. The photo had even made it into the English papers, accompanied by a sardonic caption; Lahnstein had seen it in the camp.

'What did we tell you?' the monarchists had cried. 'That's the Republic for you! Just look at it! A disgrace.'

More recently, the photograph had been set side by side with one of the Kaiser in his uniform, all spruced up. As if people had forgotten how ridiculous Kaiser Bill had been, with that affected military air of his.

Noske looked just the same as in the photo—the same broad, bushy triangle of a moustache, the round glasses, the earnest eyes.

He and Kogel were sitting in heavy armchairs at the window and rose when Lahnstein entered. Kogel towered over Noske as Noske had towered over Ebert. He was a gaunt man with sallow skin and a beard too big for his narrow face.

'Good morning, Inspector Lahnstein. You know Mr Noske, the Governor of the Province of Hanover?'

'But of course.'

Lahnstein held out his hand to Noske.

'Who doesn't, eh?' Kogel said.

Noske seemed to flinch at this remark.

'Please, take a seat.' Kogel waved Lahnstein into an

armchair opposite Noske. 'You can imagine,' he said, 'why we want to speak to you?'

Lahnstein nodded.

'The governor and I are greatly concerned. You will have read the papers, heard the rumours. People are afraid; they complain that their maids are frightened to go into town on market days.'

'No woman has yet come to any harm,' Lahnstein said.

'I know, I know. But when people panic, such distinctions go by the board. All that registers is that it isn't safe in town. What do you have to say to that?'

Lahnstein said all that he had planned to say, but without mentioning Müller.

'It may be over now,' he added, 'though of course there are still the cases to be solved. We're doing our utmost.'

Throughout Lahnstein's speech, Noske had sat motionless in his armchair, legs crossed, elbows on armrests, hands clasped, eyes fixed on Lahnstein. Kogel was fidgety and kept shooting glances at Noske.

For a moment there was silence. Then Noske said, 'Thank you for your lecture, Inspector Lahnstein. You have not convinced me. Do you mind my being so frank with you?'

Lahnstein was taken aback, both by the bluntness with which Noske spoke and by the question.

'Not at all.'

Kogel's face was twisted with fear and only slowly recovered its composure.

'Do you know what's at stake here?' Noske asked, but he didn't wait for an answer.

'It is your job to defend the achievements of 1918. The revolution, you know, democracy, the Republic. I was there in Kiel. I was part of it from the beginning. Did you know that?'

Lahnstein nodded. After the mutiny in Wilhelmshaven, the uprising had soon spread to Kiel, and the soldiers and workers had set up councils. Noske was sent along by the Social Democrats to calm the situation.

'We Majority Social Democrats were part of the revolution, but we also contained it. You know that. Bolshevism was a threat. Do you think we hadn't seen what had happened in Russia? Civil war, persecution—atrocious, quite atrocious. Our brothers, the Independent Social Democrats, wanted to go that way; they wanted a soviet republic. Not us. Do you know what we stood for in people's minds?'

Lahnstein hesitated. He couldn't tell when Noske expected an answer and when his questions were rhetorical.

'Well?' Noske said. 'You ought to know that.'

'I suppose…'

'Security. People wanted security, law and order. They could live without the Kaiser, but they couldn't live without security. It was something they clung to, during the revolution, after the revolution. Ebert and I understood that and he charged me with providing for security, for law and order. You know that.'

He looked at Lahnstein, challenging him to respond.

'You were the People's Representative for Army and Navy, and then Defence Minister.'

He spoke like a schoolboy, reciting a lesson.

'That's right. You know your stuff. I was conscientious in my execution of Ebert's orders—the orders of the people.

Security, no chaos, no anarchy, no Bolshevism. The public has us to thank for that, the Social Democrats.'

'I am a member.'

'Oh, are you?' Noske said. 'Then we're comrades; you must call me Gustav.'

'We'll find the culprit, Gustav,' Lahnstein said. 'You can depend...'

Noske waved him aside.

'The Communists wanted chaos, constant uprisings, the People's Naval Division, the Spartacus League—we had to take drastic action; there was no other way. Fighting in the Ruhr District, fighting in Bavaria, that ludicrous writers' and journalists' republic in Munich—a pack of idiots, we soon put paid to them. Just think, if it hadn't been for us, Bavaria would now be part of the Soviet Union.'

He laughed.

Lahnstein saw Noske and Ebert in their bathing trunks, but this time they were standing in a sea of blood. There had been a trick photograph in one of the papers.

'Democracy was strong, able to defend itself,' Noske said smugly. 'We called elections almost immediately, in January '19—the national assembly, the constitution and so on. You know all that. These days people reproach us for getting involved with the wrong types—the generals of the Reichswehr, the Freikorps. But who else could we have joined forces with? The Communists? And let them open the gates to the Russians? I ask you.'

'Of course not,' Lahnstein said.

'Who had rifles and experience? Who could provide

for security? The soldiers who had been in the war. Quite straightforward.'

But they also killed Liebknecht and Luxemburg, Lahnstein thought.

'Rosa Luxemburg and Karl Liebknecht,' Noske said. 'Frightfully sad business. Communists, of course, but they didn't deserve to be shot dead like that, the woman's body in the canal. Not nice. People blamed me for those murders, but it wasn't me. It was Pabst, Captain Pabst, who was to blame. I knew nothing, would never have sanctioned it. You know that, don't you?'

Lahnstein wasn't sure what to say. 'But you never distanced yourself from those murders,' he said at length.

A look of panic from Kogel. One of Noske's eyebrows shot up.

'I couldn't. As I said, we needed the Freikorps. We wanted security, law and order—and most Germans wanted the same. You know that as well as I.'

Silence. Lahnstein could smell Kogel's sweat.

'The coup in 1920. Kapp, Lüttwitz, the Ehrhardt Naval Brigade—and Captain Pabst, whom I trusted. Mistakenly, as it turned out. Mistakenly. Isn't that so?'

Lahnstein nodded.

'Now, to come to you, my dear...'

'Robert.'

'...Robert. We have achieved democracy, we have defended it. It hasn't always been easy—we've had to make compromises, some of which have been painful, but the Republic has survived; it even survived 1923—hyperinflation, the occupation of the Ruhr, Hitler's putsch. Appalling year. But look, we're still here, we're living in the Republic, aren't we?'

'Absolutely,' Lahnstein said.

'Even if the SPD is not, alas, in government. But that's another matter. How many dead?'

'Twelve, so far,' Lahnstein said, immediately regretting the *so far.*

'The public are nervous,' Noske said. 'They're afraid. And do you know what people are asking?'

Lahnstein said nothing.

'Is democracy to blame?' Kogel said.

'That's right,' said Noske, but he wasn't looking at Kogel; his eyes were on Lahnstein. 'They're asking: is this what it means to have a democracy, a republic—twelve deaths in one year and no culprit, no clues? That wouldn't have happened under the Kaiser, they say. Is there no security in a democracy? I hear what they're saying, I talk to them.'

'We have too few policemen,' Lahnstein said.

'We mustn't appear weak,' Noske said. 'We, least of all— we democrats, I mean. We didn't then and we mustn't begin now.'

You never got rid of the old crew, Lahnstein thought. You kept them on, all those monarchists and militarists, weakening democracy right from the start, hindering me in my work. They're all still here. He said nothing.

'I think you know what I mean,' Noske said.

He rose from his chair, followed by Kogel.

'I have another appointment now. We'll keep in touch.'

A firm handshake.

—

Lahnstein headed for the archives and asked for Fritz Haarmann's file. The man who worked there showed no reaction to the name. He shuffled off to a distant row of shelves and shuffled back again. 'No such file,' he said.

'Sure?'

'Sure.'

'May I have a look?'

The man raised the barrier to let Lahnstein through and followed him to the shelves. *Gunther, Gutter, Guzel, Haan, Haar, Haas.* There were no gaps; the files were closely ranged. 'Has anyone taken out Haarmann's file?' Lahnstein asked.

'Not that I know of.'

'Would you check, please?'

They returned to the counter. The man put on a pair of glasses and turned the pages of a ledger, peering and mumbling.

'No record of it,' he said at length.

'May I see the list of files, please?'

'Certainly.'

He pulled out a handwritten list and handed it to Lahnstein. No Haarmann there either.

'Is there another list, a classified one?'

The man shook his head diffidently and Lahnstein saw sweat on his brow.

'Not that I know of.'

'This will have to be looked into,' Lahnstein said.

Müller was reading the paper with his feet on the desk

when Lahnstein came in. He greeted him curtly, removed his feet and went on reading. They had hardly spoken since the incident in the basement, but each had refrained from reporting the other. They were waiting for the next missing boy.

Lahnstein hung up his hat and coat, sat down with his hands on the desk and looked at Müller. Feeling his gaze, Müller looked up.

'Anything wrong?'

'Where's Fritz Haarmann's file?'

'Name rings a bell. Help me.'

'Man Klobes said had boys round who disappeared.'

'Who said that?'

'Christian Klobes the tobacconist.'

'Don't know what you're talking about.'

'There must be a file somewhere. Klobes' statement was recorded here. Where is it?'

'Klobes, Klobes. Where have I heard that name?'

'Neue Strasse.'

'Oh, that lunatic. Have you been talking to him?'

'Yes.'

'He made utter fools of us. Did he tell you that?'

'He told me about his observations.'

'Ah, yes, his famous observations. We fell for them, too.'

Müller said that Klobes had claimed to know the faces of all the boys Haarmann had taken into his room. When he read in the papers that the son of a high-up official from Darmstadt had gone missing in Hanover, he went to the police and asked to see the photo. He swore that the boy had gone into Haarmann's room with him, never to re-emerge.

'We had the house searched, of course,' Müller said.

'And?'

'We found clothes belonging to the boy.'

He paused, looking defiantly at Lahnstein.

'And?'

'We questioned Haarmann sharply and he admitted that he'd had unnatural intercourse with the boy.'

Another pause.

'Go on.'

'We thought we'd solved the case, but then the boys' parents rang from Darmstadt to say that he'd turned up safe and sound, and as impudent as ever. So much for Klobes.'

'But where's the file?'

Müller shrugged.

'An accusation,' Lahnstein said, 'a house search, a confession to a violation of Section 175—there must be a file.'

'Ask in the archives.'

'There's no file there and you know it.'

'Files go missing.'

'I know they do, but they don't go missing for no reason; they go missing because it's in somebody's interests that they should.'

'Why would it be in anyone's interests that Haarmann's file go missing?'

Lahnstein rose abruptly. He went across to Müller and stood over him, leaning on the desk.

'I don't know,' he said firmly. 'But I know there's a file and I know that if you don't find that file, I will see to it that the man you beat up brings charges against you. I will also see to it that the press hears of it—that the case is held up as an example of what happens in the Republic when police violate basic rights. After that, you can kiss goodbye to your career. And your income. And your pension.'

He pulled himself straight again. 'I'm spending Christmas at my father's in Bochum. When I get back on 5 January, Haarmann's file will be lying on my desk.'

He left the office. *Unnatural intercourse.* The words hurt, every time.

—

He went to the buffet at the main station entrance, bought himself a cup of coffee and stood at one of the tables on the concourse, watching people come and go. There weren't many left to watch. Only two trains due to depart and two to arrive—he knew all the times. But it was still too early to see who was in the waiting room; it was so easy to be disappointed at this hour. You invested time in a conversation and then the boy turned out to be catching the last train. Still, he wouldn't mind a quick squiz; it was so exciting to spot someone likely looking, to feel his hopes rise, even if they did come to nothing.

For the present he stayed put, blowing on his coffee, studying the passers-by. It was a Tuesday; there wasn't much going on. On the weekend, people came from all over, even from Berlin, because there was so much more fun to be had here in Hanover—more of those nice drugs, more cheap girls. More boys, too, a lot more boys. But his kind didn't come at the weekend; the weekdays yielded more. The station was emptier then; the city too. The thought of lingering here was creepier; the prospect of a long night, alone and vulnerable, helped decide them to go with him. Maybe he'd be lucky today.

He sipped his coffee. Hans had been different in the past— nicer, more loving; he'd even spent the occasional night with him. Hans liked women, but he wasn't averse to a bit of a cuddle and they'd had some lovely nights, the two of them. All that was over now, though, thanks to Hugo. Something Hugo had said had stopped Hans from staying the night with him, and now he couldn't kiss and cuddle Hans anymore—couldn't get anywhere near him. Of course, Hans had never let him kiss him on the neck—he'd been careful. He chuckled to himself. Not that he'd ever harm Hans; that could never happen and Hans knew it. But he'd stopped staying the night with him all the same.

A last gulp of coffee and he sauntered off, hands in pockets, a man with time to spare. He never acted as if he had a train to catch; people would have noticed that he didn't ever board a train. At the barrier, he showed his warrant card and was waved through without a platform ticket. The warrant card confirmed that he was a detective—what a joke. He approached the waiting room, his heart pounding, but there was only an elderly woman with a younger woman, presumably mother and daughter. He tipped the brim of his hat, smiled and went on his way, disappointed. He hadn't reckoned with that. No one, not a glimmer of hope.

He was almost out of the station when he saw a boy negotiating with the man at the barrier, showing him a ticket. If only the man would let him through. If only. He stopped to watch and the boy passed through the barrier and made his way to the waiting room.

4

After two and a half hours, the journey was resumed. The boy felt reassured; he'd have no trouble catching the next train. Back in his seat, he closed his eyes and thought of Monika—not about the time they had spent together, but about the future with her, when he returned from Dunedin. For that was what he meant to do, in ten or fifteen years, say, when he'd made his fortune as the owner of a big carpentry shop full of machines—a vast furniture factory supplying the whole of New Zealand and Australia. He would book a passage to Hamburg and go back to the village. First, he would go and see his parents, riding in a motor car and dressed in a fine suit. His eyes filled with tears at the thought of the reunion, and furtively he wiped them away. His poor parents—how pleased they would be. Afterwards, he would get his chauffeur to drive him up the hill to the vicarage to see Monika. He decided it was there that he wanted to find her, and having decided that, he had to work out what had kept her there. Had she remained unmarried and stayed on to look after her old father? Or had she married her father's successor and become the vicar's wife? He preferred the first version: Monika and her son—their son—would be living with her father. She'd be angry with him to begin with, but not for long. The only question then was whether he had a family in New Zealand, and he was inclined to think he did; he couldn't see himself living a lonely bachelor's life out there. In fifteen years, he determined, he would be a widower, his wife having died in an earthquake a few months before his departure—a swift, painless death. He knew there were earthquakes in that part of the world; Craig had mentioned them when he came to their school. The boy—a man by then—would fetch his children over and set up a furniture factory in the village, like the one in New Zealand. He and Monika would marry—he wiped his eyes again. But what about Heiner? Would he come to the wedding?

The train stopped in a small town; it wasn't due to leave for ten minutes. The boy got out and bought a bottle of lemonade from the station buffet. He'd look for a job in Bremerhaven the very next day to earn money for the ticket to Wellington. From there, he supposed, he would travel overland to Dunedin. He had no idea how long he'd have to work to pay for his passage. The longer it took, of course, the higher his chances of being discovered and fetched back to the village. It was a good thing he hadn't told his parents or his brother about his dream of going to Dunedin; he didn't want them fretting at the thought of their younger son in the antipodes. The conductor called to the passengers to board the train. The boy finished his lemonade and returned the bottle. When he got back to the platform, the train was already moving. He ran. His suitcase, containing all he had left in the world, was on the train. He ran, afraid he wouldn't make it, but at the end of the platform he caught up with the last carriage and leapt aboard. As he got his breath back, he remembered that he had told Monika about Dunedin—about the penguins there and how, with a pair of binoculars, you could see polar bears. There aren't any polar bears at the South Pole, Monika had said.

—

When Lahnstein returned to work a few days into the new year, there was a file waiting on his desk. He saw it the second he walked in the door and rushed to snatch it up. *Friedrich Heinrich Karl Haarmann*, it said on the front. Lahnstein hung up his coat and hat and went to fetch a cup of coffee. It was not yet seven and quiet at headquarters. Lahnstein had been restless, wondering whether the file would be there, and had got to the office early. He sat down at his desk, gave his shoes a good rub, blew the dust off the file, fanned it away and turned to the first page. A friendly face looked out at him, round and clean-shaven except for a moustache that was split down the middle into two distinct halves. Thinning hair, low-set prominent ears with a slight kink to them, a powerful chin, a broad-bridged nose, and alert, narrow eyes that drooped slightly at the corners. It was the kind of face, Lahnstein thought, that you might have seen at the front, the coarse but not unappealing face of a forbearing and good-humoured trench soldier, who took things—even the shelling attacks—as they came.

Friedrich Heinrich Karl Haarmann, Lahnstein read, *born on 25 October 1879, the youngest of six children.*

In 1886 he started at State School 4 on Engelbostelerdamm in Hanover.

In 1895, he was accepted at the Training School for Non-Commissioned Officers in Neu-Breisach.

A soldier—well, that was no surprise.

Six months later, on 3 September, he was admitted to the garrison hospital with *hallucinations* and *signs of mental disturbance*. The doctors suspected sunstroke or concussion after a fall from the horizontal bar during drill.

Medical report on admission:

Average-strength patient with a flushed face and heated head; facial expression cheerful, occasionally anxious, sometimes childishly curious.

Pupils react to light, consistently dilated. Patient has no scars on head or elsewhere on body. Eyelids and bulbi mobile, eyes sometimes have a rather fixed look. Hearing and sense of smell normal, good general mobility.

7.9.: Patient has been calm, walking in garden and helping out with work.

11.9.: Status idem.

15.9.: Haarmann has been of consistently sound mind; he asks to be discharged.

18.9.: Patient discharged back to school in good health after closed observation.

On 11 October he was in hospital again: *epileptic equivalent.*

On 3 November he was once more sent home at his own request.

A few pages later, Lahnstein came across the first criminal proceedings against Haarmann in mid-July 1896, when he was seventeen. He had, on several occasions, been caught luring small children into doorways and cellars. *Acts of indecency.*

Lahnstein read the words again. *Acts of indecency.* He slammed his hand down on the table. It was unbelievable.

The criminal court sent Haarmann to the Provincial Psychiatric Hospital of Hildesheim to have his mental condition assessed. He remained there from 6 February 1897 until 25 March 1897 and was classified as *mentally ill.*

Innate imbecility, Lahnstein read.

On 27 March 1897, Division II b of Hanover District Court ruled as follows:

In the case against filius familias Fritz Haarmann of Hanover on charges of indecency with minors under fourteen years of age, namely schoolboys Willy and Fritz Ketil and Edouard Störmer, in Hanover in 1896, the request for a trial has been denied at the expense of the public treasury, because, according to the opinion of Medical Counsellor Dr Gerstenberg, Director of the Prov. Psychiatric Hospital of Hildesheim, the defendant was, at the time of committing the acts, in a state of pathological mental disturbance that prevented him from exercising free will.

Haarmann was admitted to the City Hospital in Hanover and stayed there until 28 May 1897.

Powerfully built, well-nourished person, very well-developed for his age, with a florid complexion. No abnormalities in skull, pupils or reflexes; no sensory, motor or vasomotor disturbances. No abnormalities in the large bodily cavities or their organs.

Penis well developed except for phimosis; no abnormalities in the anus. Urine free from s and a.

S and a? Sugar and albumen?

Patient appears imbecile and childlike with no understanding of his situation or the moral aspect of the acts with which he is charged. He says that in the summer of 1896, while in his father's cellar with several young friends, he played with his own genitals and those of his friends. Denies onanism etc.

Relates everything in naive and childlike tones, apparently very cheerful and often bursting into an imbecile laugh. Repeats himself frequently. Often traces circles on the doctor's hand during the examination. Cannot give the answer to 6 x 2/3, 10 x 10 or 7 x 6. Cannot list any of the Ten Commandments or say any of the Creed. Cites France and Russia among the continents. Asked to name the present Kaiser, he says William I, 'who had a birthday the other day'.

In a court medical report, city physician Dr Schmalfuss declared Haarmann an *incurable imbecile.* The Magistrate of Hanover sent him to Hanover Lunatic Asylum.

Lahnstein was tempted to skip ahead and look at the final entries to see what the latest verdict was, but he resisted. One thing at a time; he'd read the file like a book. He lit a cigarillo that he'd bought from Emma just before Christmas, before leaving for Bochum. He'd chosen a small box—and five cigars for his father, which she had wrapped for him, slowly, carefully.

'I was hoping you'd be here over Christmas,' she said, without looking at him.

'Then my father would have been on his own,' he said.

'Plenty of people are on their own.'

'Did you ever speak to your brother?'

'I told him not to do it again.'

'That was all?'

'He had a difficult childhood. We all did. A lot of rows and beatings…he was troubled.'

'What do you mean, *troubled*?'

'He once made a straw doll, dressed in our sister Anna's clothes and laid it on the front steps so that it looked as if she was dead. Mother got the shock of her life when she came home—it took her hours to recover.'

'Will you spend Christmas with your brother?'

'I have three brothers and two sisters.'

'But you'll spend it alone, just you and the boys?'

'Afraid so. We've all fallen out.'

'I'm sorry about that.'

'I'm a good cook,' she said, 'I'd have made you a nice dinner.'

'We'll make it up another time,' he said.

She'd finished wrapping the cigars and looked up at him. 'Do you mean that?' she asked.

'Yes. We'll have our own little Christmas when I'm back.'

'I'll leave the tree up till you've been.'

'Let's hope the French let me out.'

'Let's hope so. Otherwise I'll sit here evening after evening watching the needles drop until it's nothing but a skeleton. That would be sad.'

'Very. I'll be as quick as I can.'

She gave him the parcel and he pulled out his wallet.

'No, you mustn't.'

He tried to insist, but she refused.

'Off you go,' she said.

On 13 October 1897 Haarmann escaped from the lunatic asylum. Five days later the police found him in his parents' flat and had him admitted to Hildesheim. Not long before Christmas he was moved to another asylum in Langenhagen. On Christmas Day, he escaped again and for a few years he lived without drawing attention to himself. The only thing in the file from that time was a certificate of integrity issued by the police. Lahnstein took it out and studied it.

It is hereby certified that nothing adverse has come to notice regarding the integrity of the above-mentioned person.

A citizen of unblemished integrity?

At Christmas 1899, Haarmann's engagement to a certain Erna Loewert was announced.

Unblemished? Not queer? Lahnstein's spirits sank.

On 12 October 1900 Haarmann received a call-up order and was made a reserve recruit in the Hanoverian Hunters Battalion No. 10.

Personal Description

Height: 1.62m

Build: heavy

Chin: sm. dimple

Nose: ord'y

Mouth: –

Hair: d. blond

Facial hair: tash
Dist. features: scar on r. palm.

In September 1901 he collapsed during a march, suffered from subsequent fits of weakness and dizziness, and was admitted to the garrison hospital in Bitsch on 10 October. Diagnosis: *weak nerves (neurasthenia)*.

Lahnstein's mother had been similarly diagnosed: apprehension, nervousness, anxiety. Neurasthenia was suddenly a common complaint—and much ridiculed. Then war broke out and Lahnstein's mother felt vindicated. It was clear, she said, that neurasthenics were in fact healthier than most; unlike everyone else, they had sensed that dreadful times lay ahead.

'That's one way of looking at it,' his father said.

When Lahnstein arrived in Bochum just before Christmas, it seemed to him that his father had shrunk. Not the kind to elbow his way forward, he was standing in the third or fourth row behind the ticket barrier, and waved so that Lahnstein would see him. They hugged briefly and made their way out. A troop of French soldiers stood by their trucks outside the station. Father and son averted their eyes and hurried past.

As soon as they reached the flat, Lahnstein went upstairs to the Steukers, the only tenants in the building with a telephone. They agreed that he could leave their number with police headquarters in Hanover, so he put a call through, and then he and his father sat wrapped in rugs in the draughty sitting room drinking brandy—opposite them, on the sideboard, a picture of Lahnstein's mother.

He told his father as much as he could about the missing boys. It wasn't a lot.

'It's the fine gentleman,' his father said when he'd finished.

The 'fine gentleman' featured in the case of Richard Gräf. Richard, Number Seven, had lost his parents at an early age, but not to death. His mother had run off to America with her lover, and his father, a casual labourer, left his five children to fend for themselves when he got work in Eisenach. Otto, the oldest, had to support the family, though he was only twenty. His sweetheart helped him. In September 1923, Richard, the next-oldest, said, 'I'm going to America to find Mum,' and he, too, left home. Two weeks later, though, he was back; with neither passport nor money for a ticket, he hadn't made it on board a ship. He was worn out and hungry; his belongings had been stolen. But he didn't plan to hang around. He said he'd met a 'fine gentleman' at the station who was going to get him farm work, and if he earned enough he'd make another attempt at joining his mother. This time Richard set off never to return. A note in his file said: *Possibly in America.*

'I don't believe that,' Lahnstein's father said. 'Have you looked for this fine gentleman?'

'Yes, Dad, of course.'

He'd taken up all the old cases, questioned friends and family a second time—but it was no good. Apart from the one adjective, there was no description of the man.

'I can't tell you how many times I've scoured the station for fine gentlemen talking to boys. It's hopeless.'

'What makes a gentleman fine in your eyes?' his father asked.

'Good, smart clothes, clean shoes, well-cut hair—'

'That's your mistake,' his father said, interrupting him.

'What?' he asked, rather sharply.

'You're looking for your idea of a fine gentleman. A humble boy like Richard would have a very different picture in mind.'

Lahnstein fell into an annoyed silence; he knew his father was right.

'That makes it even harder,' he said at length. 'Looked at like that, almost any man could be a fine gentleman.'

'Yes. But the last person to see a missing person is always the first suspect. You know that.'

'I do. But here it's a fine gentleman and in the next case it's a detective.'

He was thinking of Wilhelm Erdner, boy Number Eight. Wilhelm was the son of a metalworker and rode to a machine factory on his dad's bicycle every morning. In his file was a statement made by a man named Lunghis who'd lost both arms in the war and was known as a drifter and not quite 'with it'. Lunghis, it seemed, had said to the boy's father, 'I know where your Wilhelm is. Detective Fritz Honnerbrock's taken him down to the nick. Honnerbrock's a regular at the Ham Hock Inn on Goethe Bridge and I often see him with Wilhelm—ran into him just yesterday. Wilhelm wasn't with him, so I asked where he was. "Oh, him!" he said. "I arrested him in Schillerstrasse and took him to police headquarters." Boy must have been up to no good.'

Wilhelm's parents went to headquarters and were told that there was no one there by the name of Honnerbrock and no Wilhelm Erdner in the cells.

Some time later, Lunghis met the supposed Honnerbrock again, and again he asked where Wilhelm was. 'Can't remember that case,' was the answer. 'I'm on duty at present. Come to the Ham Hock at seven this evening and we can talk then.' Lunghis went to the Ham Hock at the appointed time but Honnerbrock wasn't there and he never saw him again.

'Who says a detective can't be a fine gentleman?' Lahnstein's father asked.

They both smiled.

'Do you trust your people?'

'I don't think they're covering for a serial killer. But other than that, no, I don't. The monarchists—and they're almost all monarchists—refuse to believe that a democracy can provide security.'

'Well, clearly it can't,' his father said, 'not in Hanover anyway.'

'That has nothing to do with democracy.'

'Strange, this business with Honnerbrock,' his father said. 'A clue that leads to the police.'

'But we don't have a Honnerbrock.'

They were silent for a while. Lahnstein kept an ear out for the telephone.

'Dad, I'd like to ask you something.'

'Go on.'

'Did you ever—don't take this the wrong way...'

'Out with it.'

'Did you ever hit suspects, or torture them when you were stuck on an important case?'

'We boxed the odd ear.'

His father looked at his hands.

'It's nothing to be proud of.'

'I'm not proud of it, but sometimes it was the only way to get their respect.'

'How about torture?'

'Never.'

'I surprised some colleagues of mine beating up a suspect. Later it turned out that he was innocent. But if he had been the culprit and I'd prevented them from proving it, by whatever means, would I be to blame for the next missing boy?'

'There's no point worrying your head over such things,' his father said. 'Let's go to bed. I have to be up early to fetch the goose.'

He stood up abruptly.

Lahnstein stayed awake for some time. He lay on the sitting-room sofa where, one evening in another life, he and Lissy had first made love while his parents were at a concert.

On 14 May 1902 Haarmann was admitted to the psychiatric ward of Garrison Hospital I in Strasbourg.

Small man in good state of nutrition with florid complexion and well-coloured mucous membranes. Mildly depressed disposition; complains of pressure in cardiac region. Pupils equal in size, medium-dilated, reactive. Skull free from abnormalities, no tenderness. Tongue straight, minimal trembling; pharyngeal reflex good. Brisk reflexes in upper and lower limbs; direct muscular excitability present but not increased.

17 May: *Feels quite well; reports only occasional pressure in cardiac region when climbing stairs. Pulse at rest between 80 and 84, rising to 100 during exercise, but without dyspnoea, and soon steadying.*

7 x 21 = 147 (after much thought)
6 x 18 = 108 (after 1½ minutes)
94 x 6 = –
38 – 24 =14 (½ minute)
97 – 33 = 64 (2 minutes)

Alphabet incorrect. Months of the year correct. Lord's Prayer largely correct.

On 2 July 1902 Surgeon Major Pillath wrote a military medical report:

Results of examination: medium-sized man in moderate state of nutrition; complexion pale; chest 87/93 cm; weight 65 kg, as compared with 64 on admission.

Because of a past mental illness that has left him with a degree of imbecility, Haarmann is permanently unfit to serve in the civilian service and temporarily (2 years) unfit to work. This decision is in accordance with Supp. IIb No. 17 of the Regulations.

So he wasn't in the war after all. What a pity.

In Haarmann's discharge papers, his conduct was classified as 'fairly good'. A pension ruling granted him a monthly payment of twenty-one marks.

Müller came in, bright and breezy, wished Lahnstein a happy new year and sat down at his desk, pretending not to notice the file.

'How was it at your old man's?' he asked.

'One always reverts to being a child at home, no matter how long ago it all is.'

'I know what you mean,' Müller said.

'Apparently Haarmann was an imbecile,' Lahnstein said.

'Ah, so the file turned up?'

Müller shot him a charming smile—innocent, relieved.

'It was on my desk. You don't happen to know...'

Müller threw himself back in his chair and flung up his hands. 'Don't thank me,' he said.

'Haarmann committed acts of indecency when he was only sixteen. Did you know that?'

'I'd no idea. Really I hadn't. It's years since I last saw the file.'

'I can believe that,' Lahnstein said, returning to his reading.

On 5 April 1901 Fritz Haarmann's mother died and the six children sued each other over the inheritance. In 1902, Haarmann sued his father for maintenance although he was plainly living with him again. At any rate, they had the same address. Haarmann couldn't work because of heart and nerve complaints, and his military pension was meagre. His father protested that Fritz had malingered to get off military service and be with his fiancée; he was just too lazy to work.

In February 1903 old Mr Haarmann went to the public prosecutor in Hanover and brought charges against his son for threatening to kill him and his other children. It seemed that Fritz had also accused his father of murdering an engine driver called Schröder and tried to blackmail his uncle Adolf Haarmann. Fritz's father declared his son a lunatic and a public menace and petitioned to have him locked away in an asylum.

Nice family.

Lahnstein turned back a page. Hadn't Haarmann's dad accused him of malingering? Yes, that was what it said here. And now he was calling him a lunatic? Haarmann's brothers and sisters refused to confirm the statements made by their father, and the proceedings were dropped. Fritz Haarmann sued his father for calumny. That case was also dropped.

In an attempt to shed some light on Fritz Haarmann's mental state, police headquarters in Hanover asked district physician Dr Andrae for his expert opinion. Although, Andrae wrote, Haarmann was *morally inferior, not particularly intelligent, sluggish, coarse, irritable, vindictive and an utter egoist, he [was] not, properly speaking, insane, so that there [was] no reason to warrant committing him to a lunatic asylum.*

In 1904 Haarmann's pension was raised to twenty-four marks a month.

Lahnstein closed the file, leaving his thumb between the pages so that he could see how far he'd got. Not yet halfway. He leafed forward; the next pages were taken up with criminal cases. He resumed reading.

From 4 July until 19 October 1904 Haarmann was sentenced four times for grand larceny and embezzlement. In the following year he amassed a total of thirteen months in prison for a variety of offences. One of these involved buying a small disinfection device with which he called on the recently bereaved, whose names he had gleaned from the death notices. Claiming to be an officer from the council department for disinfection, he would announce that he had to clean the dead person's room and clothes to prevent disease, and after sending out the bereaved on the pretext that the disinfectant might get in their lungs, he would shut the door and clear out all the drawers and cupboards. If offered anything to eat or drink, he always declined, saying that it was against regulations for a council officer to accept refreshment.

This man was a serial killer?

On November 1906 Haarmann was sentenced to a month in prison for bodily harm. His father was the victim. Fritz had demanded that old Mr Haarmann finally pay out his share of his mother's inheritance. They had come to blows.

Hit one's own father? Lahnstein thought with mild emotion of the peaceful days he had spent in Bochum. On Christmas Eve, his father had gone out early to fetch the goose and a few other things. Lahnstein woke later when the phone rang. He leapt out of bed, slipped on his trousers, pulled on shirt, socks and shoes, and ran his fingers through his hair. But no one came. The ringing had stopped and after a while he went to the door and listened. All was quiet. He paced restlessly through the flat; he sat down and polished his shoes. Still no one knocked. He felt sudden relief.

In the bathroom he undressed again, washed to the waist

and shaved. He went to the corner pub where he and his schoolmates always met on Christmas Eve. There weren't many left. Nine out of twenty-five had fallen in the war, two had been carried off by the Spanish flu and one shot in a French POW camp. Of the thirteen survivors, two were invalids: one had lost an arm at the Somme and another both legs in the Ruhr uprising, when he was run over by a truck.

There were eight of them this year, but Lahnstein's one remaining best friend wasn't among them; he lived in Rhodesia and only came home every other Christmas. They sat at a round table with beer and bread and sausage and reported on another successful year. Ever upwards was the burden of their song; after such heavy losses, things could surely only get better. This wasn't necessarily an allusion to the war; *loss* was a word they associated principally with Versailles.

Lahnstein made up a case he'd solved, a little hero's tale. He didn't mention the boys. Nobody at the table would have appreciated the use of the word 'queer'.

The others began to complain about the French—the airs they gave themselves, their arrogance and condescension, their ridiculous rules, their brutal methods: thirteen Krupp workers shot dead. The stories were partly for Lahnstein's benefit—an attempt at consolation. But he didn't feel consoled. Looking at his watch, he got up abruptly and said he must be getting home to help his dad. They all understood. He endured the backslapping and hugs and made his escape.

His father was sitting in the kitchen plucking the bird he'd bought from a Polish coal-mining friend who bred geese in his garden. Lahnstein peeled potatoes. For a while neither spoke, then they both began to cry. Lahnstein's father got up, cut an onion in half and set it down in the middle of the little table.

'There,' he said. 'Now we're allowed to cry.'

'I don't think we need an onion for that.'

That afternoon, when the goose was in the oven, they walked to the cemetery with a bunch of flowers. Lahnstein slipped an arm through his father's at the gate. The lump in his throat began to swell, but this time he fought back the tears. They stood a while at the grave, images flitting though Lahnstein's mind—images of his caring mother who was always there for him, but also of his mother at the wheel of a motor car. Her father, a rich man, had owned one of the first cars in Bochum, and so she had learnt to drive early, and always took the wheel when they borrowed the car for a Sunday outing. Later, Lissy and August had been part of these excursions. Lahnstein was proud of his motorist mother. No one else he knew had a mum who could drive.

Her father had a Hispano-Suiza, a four-cylinder, pre-war model, and it was this car she was driving when she died in April. She was a nifty driver and the chances were that she'd taken the corner at quite a lick; she couldn't know that she'd get caught up in a shooting between French soldiers and suspected saboteurs. The roar of the Hispano-Suiza was so deafening that she wouldn't have heard the shots. She got a bullet in her head and must have died instantly. Lahnstein was sure of that, because the Hispano-Suiza had crashed into a lamppost and he knew that his mother would never have allowed that to happen if she'd been even remotely conscious.

After two days of helpless grieving, Lahnstein and his father went to the French commander and asked in their schoolboy French who had fired the deadly bullet—was it a French soldier or one of the supposed saboteurs? They didn't want to apportion blame, but it was important for them to know what had happened. It was being looked into, the commander said, but the day before the funeral they had heard nothing, and weeks later the matter still hadn't been cleared up. Lahnstein's father gave up in the end, but Lahnstein persisted. Twice a week he went to the French to make polite inquiries and each time, with increasing incivility, they turned him away. Eventually, like thousands of others, he was expelled from the Ruhr District. He was given three days to obey orders. The chief of police in Bochum recommended Lahnstein—'the best man I've got'—to his counterpart in Hanover, who was in urgent need of an inspector from outside.

When they got back from the cemetery they decorated the little Christmas tree in the sitting room—a job that had always been done by Lahnstein's mother. They tried to remember how she used to arrange the baubles and candles, but they couldn't get it quite right.

Lahnstein was only skim-reading now—a theft, a series of burglaries, a few months in prison, another petty crime, another stint in gaol. God, it was dull.

Royal Court of Lay Assessors, Hanover, the verdict from 22 April 1907:

On the grounds of a credible confession made by the accused, it has been established that on 22 October 1906, he took a pot containing 103 eggs belonging to his landlord, Mr Jorpsnuter, a decorator, with the intention of illegal appropriation.

An egg thief. He was wasting his time with this man. He turned page after page—more thefts, more sentences. He turned the pages faster—and then something caught his eye.

District Court of Hanover, the indictment from 20 January 1913:

On Thursday 14 November 1912, Otto Dörries, a schoolboy born on 3 October 1899, attended a cramming class at the Workers' Association in 30 Burgstrasse. When the class ended at 8 p.m., he set off for home and was accosted on the corner of Georgstrasse and Nikolaistrasse by a man unknown to him, the homosexually inclined defendant.

Asking the boy whether he had been to the cinema, the defendant engaged him in conversation, trying to draw him out by asking if he liked to smoke cigarettes, what his hobbies were, how much pocket money he received and so on. As they walked on in the direction of his flat—then in Tellenkampstrasse—he tried to solicit the boy for indecent purposes by making the following promises. If the boy visited him regularly, the defendant said, he could earn himself a tidy sum of money. His previous little friend, a secondary-school pupil, had moved away, so he was on the lookout for a new one. When it became clear that little Dörries had not understood, the defendant spoke more plainly and asked straight out whether he had good friends who played 'tickling' with him. The boy asked what he meant by this and he replied, 'Making love with your hands.' When the boy still did not understand, the defendant resorted to plainer language and said, 'It's when you say, "Show me what a big fat one you have."' He told the boy he would teach him. He could come home with him now, if he liked; he would give him fifty pfennigs, apples and pears, and a book to read.

When the two of them arrived at the defendant's flat, the defendant said, 'Next time you come to visit, you must knock at one of the ground-floor windows.' He opened the front door, saying, 'Come on in, it'll only take five minutes.' When the boy made no move to follow he put his hand on the boy's head and said, 'Come on, Otto, don't make a fuss.' At this point, the boy ran off home and told his father, who reported the incident to the police.

The verdict was delivered on 8 March 1913: five years and two months for unlawful assault and attempted crime under Section 176.3 of the Criminal Code.

'Haarmann has previous convictions for related offences,' Lahnstein said.

Müller didn't look up.

'Did you know that?'

Müller mumbled something.

'Is Haarmann queer?'

'*Queer*, what do you mean, *queer*?' Müller asked.

'Male love.'

'I know that. But is a man queer because he once fancied

a boy? Were the Ancient Greeks queer?'

Lahnstein shrugged.

'They were nice to each other. They were fond of each other. The boys learnt from the men—philosophy and what have you—but the men had their families and the boys would soon have theirs.'

'Does Haarmann have a family?' Lahnstein asked. 'It says here that he got engaged, but there's no mention of a wedding so far.'

'I know nothing of a family. But does that give us cause to suspect him? Do you have a family?'

'No,' said Lahnstein.

'Should we be suspecting you?'

Lahnstein bowed his head over the file again without replying, but he couldn't focus on the words. So the man's above suspicion? he thought angrily. Unequivocally innocent of killing those twelve boys? If it wasn't more by now. He glanced at the door and could have kicked himself for the nervous impulse.

All through the war, Haarmann was in prison. No front, no machine guns, no artillery, no airships. Fritz Haarmann spent the time of the mass slaughter behind bars, in safety. The great brutalisation passed him by.

Lahnstein wondered whether he too would rather have been in prison than fighting in the war—but then he and Lissy wouldn't have had August; they wouldn't have had the holiday on Lake Irr. The war would have separated him from Lissy soon after their engagement; there'd have been the odd visit, perhaps, but no skin, no lips—and by 1915 the engagement would have been over. He wouldn't have become a father. He'd never have rocked August in his arms—never have woken up to see him looking at him quizzically, toe in mouth, as if wondering what had brought them together and why. He'd have missed that flood of emotions—that second incarnation that comes with a first baby. But perhaps, he thought, that wouldn't have been such a bad thing; perhaps it would have been easier to bear than this plane that moved through his dreams, unable to land.

Not long before the end of the war, Haarmann was released. At around the same time, on 4 October 1918, war veteran Alois Rothe reported his seventeen-year-old son Fritz missing.

Presumably kept hidden by trader Fritz Haarmann, resident of 27 Cellerstrasse, who was allegedly seen with the boy. (N.B. Not correct.)

Why not?

Soon afterwards, human hands and feet were found in Hanover. On 7 November Rothe's mother went to the public prosecutor to examine the extremities.

Mrs Rothe did not recognise the hands she was shown as those of her son.

Further entries:

Admitted on 12.10.18 for luring young boys to his room and putting them up. Had fifteen-year-old Paul Braun in his bed last night. Acts of indecency with him.

Convicted on 28 April 1919 for two cases of unlawful assault. Inveigled two boys *into reciprocal onanism with him.*

An extract from the verdict: *The accused may be homosexually inclined and thus liable to be treated as inferior, but in view of his multiple previous convictions, all serious and one for a related offence, he is to be severely punished, as he presents a danger to young people.* Nine months' prison.

Inferior?

Friedel Rothe hadn't been found. Number One, Lahnstein thought. Rothe was the true first case. They'd all have to be renumbered.

In 1922 Haarmann applied for a larger pension. Once again he was called for a medical: *Age 42 years, good state of nutrition, healthy appearance, moderately developed muscles.*

Pulse 84, heart complaints 0.

Mental state: childlike, trusting nature, prone to tears when describing his life and at pains to stress his good descent. Grasps questions relatively quickly but answers circuitously without coming to the point. Mood—apart from emotional instability—moderate.

No paranoia or delusions.

Intelligence: 7 x 8 = 64, 7 x 15 = 105, 6 x 18 = 108, 7 x 8 = 52, 17 + 8 = 35, 47 + 36 = 83, 27 − 14 = 13, 32 − 17 = 0, 27 ÷ 3 = 0. Takes a very long time over the sums and is plainly under a good deal of strain. When he can't work out the answers in his head, he tries to do it on paper. His arithmetic aptitude has thus deteriorated considerably.

Cannot give the price of a cigar or a postage stamp. Reverse associations are severely disturbed; asked to list the months of the years in reverse order, he gets no further than October.

When his lack of knowledge becomes clear to him, he bursts out crying and says he used to know it all.

His pension is raised to 382 marks and seventy-five pfennigs.

Maybe he faked it, Lahnstein thought.

The last entry was a transcript from another file, that of Fritz Franke.

'Haarmann was involved with Fritz Franke,' Lahnstein said to Müller.

'The first missing boy?'

'The second. There was one before him, five years ago, called Friedel Rothe, but he seems to have been overlooked. Perhaps deliberately.'

Lahnstein returned to the transcript—a police statement. Soon after Franke had gone missing, Elli Schulz and Dörchen Mrutzek, both prostitutes, had turned up at the police station on Waterlooplatz with two pieces of supposedly human flesh which they claimed was Franke's.

Could his landlady be right?

The young women identified themselves as friends of Haarmann, and Mrutzek said that she sometimes cleaned Mr Haarmann's flat. It was there, in 8 Neue Strasse, they explained, that they had met Fritz Franke, a pretty boy of sixteen, a nice lad. They had sat and drunk together until Mr Haarmann said he had urgent business to attend to and threw them out. Then they went on to the rifle clubhouse, accompanied by a certain Hans Grans, who had also been present at the little gathering. Fritz Franke turned out to be a good pianist, and Mrutzek and Schulz danced with Grans. The statement mentioned that he was their pimp. When they were tired, they walked Franke back to Haarmann's flat because he was staying the night there. They did not go in with him.

The next morning, according to Mrutzek's statement, she went to Haarmann's flat to clean as usual. Haarmann opened the door and she saw Franke lying in bed, his half-bare torso 'all white'. Alarmed, she asked Haarmann what had happened to the boy. He covered Franke up and whispered, 'Shh, he wants to sleep. Go away and come back this afternoon.' She left and said to Elli, 'There's something funny going on there.' In the afternoon, she went back to Haarmann's, but he'd locked himself in and told her he was busy; she should come and clean in the evening.

In the evening, the flat had already been cleaned and all the windows were open. 'Dörchen,' Haarmann asked, 'is there a bad smell in here?' He was agitated, sweating. Fritz Franke's clothes were lying on the bed. Mrutzek screamed and asked again where Franke was. Haarmann said, 'He's gone to Hamburg. Must have been up to no good because he wanted new kit. I swapped him and paid the difference.' Elli Schulz and Hans Grans turned up. 'What's happened to the boy from Berlin?' the women kept asking. Haarmann and Grans reassured them.

Two days later, Dörchen and Elli went into Haarmann's room to clean. He had to go out and they took the opportunity to search the place. In the drawer of the table, they found Franke's cigarette holder and wallet. Behind the hatch under the stairs, they found a bloody apron and a big pan filled with chunks of meat.

'We took two pieces, all covered in hair. Here they are.' With these words, according to the statement, they presented Inspector Müller with two slabs of meat.

When Lahnstein and his father sat down to the goose on Christmas Eve, Lahnstein suddenly got it into his head that he was eating human flesh. He knew it wasn't possible; he'd seen his father pluck the bird and prepare it and put it in the oven. He'd seen him check the meat to see if it was done. He'd been there when he took it out and carved it. But when the phone rang as they started dinner, the thought took hold of him and he couldn't shake it. He cursed his gossipy landlady, swallowed the rising bile and forced himself to keep eating.

'Don't you like it?'

'Oh, I do, Dad. It's delicious.'

He drove his knife into a piece of breast, chewed doggedly, swallowed, made a moue of appreciation. His father gave him a funny look. No one came to call Lahnstein to the phone. Headquarters hadn't rung.

They didn't talk much that evening. After baked apples they played Chinese chequers, draughts, and fox and geese, each smoking one of Emma's cigars. Lahnstein's father had been pleased with the present and insisted that Lahnstein have one too. They hugged before going to bed.

In the days that followed, Lahnstein avoided going out more than was necessary. There were a lot of French soldiers on the streets and although he'd done his best to forgive them, the sight of them still churned him up inside. It had been an unfortunate accident, he told himself, his mother driving so fast that the gunmen had been taken by surprise and couldn't stop shooting in time. Nobody knew who had fired the fatal bullet; it might have been one of the so-called saboteurs. But the very presence of the French was provocative. It had all gone too fast, Lahnstein thought, and it was harsh, too—marching into the Ruhr just because the government was behind with reparations. Resistance seemed justified—even sabotage—and seen in that light, the French were to blame for his mother's death even if they hadn't fired the bullet. Lahnstein didn't want to think like that, but whenever he saw a Frenchman in uniform, his mind started to grind out the same old thoughts. And so he preferred to stay at home. It also made him easier to get hold of—or would have done if anyone had tried to ring.

On New Year's Eve they drank red wine from Baden-Württemberg. In the past Lahnstein's father had always drunk French wine from the Rhône, but he had poured his stocks away saying, 'I'm not going to drink my wife's blood.'

Roast meat, potatoes, sprouts. Then Chinese chequers, fox and geese, draughts—and another couple of Emma's cigars.

'Once,' Lahnstein's father said, an hour before midnight, 'we had a case of kidnapping in Bochum. A fourteen-year-old mine-owner's daughter; the ransom was huge. We soon caught the chap—a lone culprit, a psychopath. But he wouldn't tell us where he was hiding the girl. All we could get out of him was that he'd locked her up, and that she had nothing to eat or drink—he hadn't expected to be arrested, of course. We spent an entire day trying to convince him that it was all over in any case. That poor girl. We promised him a reduced sentence. But he only grinned. We deprived him of sleep, we beat him—a few slaps, a few punches. He just laughed. We considered torturing him, but I was against it and as I was in charge of the case, he was spared.'

'What happened?'

'We never found the girl. Now you know the real reason I retired early. It was nothing to do with my health; I'm as fit as ever. But I didn't think a man with a human life on his conscience should remain in the force.'

'But do you have the girl on your conscience?'

'It was my job to save her. And I botched it. Let's not talk about it anymore. Time to open the Sekt anyway.'

Music swelled from a neighbour's flat, a cheerful song; it was nearly midnight.

They clinked glasses and hugged again, though not as tenderly as at Christmas.

'I'm proud of you,' Lahnstein told his father.

By half past midnight they were in bed. Lahnstein thought about his father for a long time. During the Empire he had believed in the Kaiser; now he believed in Stresemann and the German People's Party; he was conservative, but in favour of reconciliation with France, despite—or perhaps because of— what had happened to his wife. He was a dependable father, never unjust, and although once strict, he had grown lenient with age.

'Are you the Inspector Müller in this file?' Lahnstein asked.

'Not impossible.'

'Why did you never tell me any of this? Why was Haarmann's name never mentioned?'

'They were a pair of hysterical females,' Müller said. 'Little good-for-nothing floozies. There was nothing to their story.'

Lahnstein studied the file again. The meat had been examined by forensic specialist Dr Schackwitz. Pork. A warrant had, nevertheless, been issued to search Haarmann's room, but nothing was found.

'What kind of an examination was it?'

'What do you mean?'

'How exactly did Schackwitz examine the meat?'

'Visual examination. The result was unequivocal.'

'A visual examination is hardly accurate.'

'Schackwitz knows what he's doing.'

'And why is his statement missing from Franke's file? It ought to be here.'

'I don't know. And I won't be grilled like this.'

'But you have to admit it's odd. We're looking for a culprit in the homosexual scene and here's a man who is clearly both homosexual and violent. And yet no one's ever mentioned him to me.'

'Do you think we didn't investigate Haarmann? Of course we did. Searched his room, had him watched, questioned him. We had nothing on him. He has nothing to do with the case.'

'I should have been informed.'

Müller shrugged.

'I forgot, I'm sorry.'

Lahnstein leant forward, elbows on desk, chin on hands. He looked hard at Müller.

'I'm going to speak to Haarmann,' he said.

Müller nodded.

—

His heart was pounding, but he had to be patient; he mustn't talk to the boy too soon; he must wait till he was tired and distressed, sore from sitting too long on the hard wooden bench, hankering for a bed. He walked back to the buffet, bought himself a small glass of beer, and went and stood at one of the tables, glancing now and then at the waiting room. Mustn't let his quarry escape. It had been known to happen. He sipped the beer slowly to make it last; he never had more than a small one. Constable Schöndorf sauntered over. That didn't worry him; he got on all right with Constable Schöndorf—though things were trickier since that new chap had started at headquarters; the pressure was rising. Had to watch out these days, even with Schöndorf.

'Evening, Constable. How's the family?'

Schöndorf liked talking about his family—the old lady, the little girl. A bit of a chat, a bit of blarney. There was the subject of meat, too, of course. Everyone was after cheap meat.

'Be having a delivery soon from Karl the Butcher; you're at the top of my list.'

That made him happy, the silly idiot—but wasn't it time he was moving on? A few minutes more and he did.

'Better get back to the beat.'

'Duty calls, eh? My regards to the missus.'

Schöndorf ambled off, his hefty backside swaying, his truncheon dangling. He could tell him where to stick it.

Just before midnight he went into the waiting room. The two women were still there—and the boy. He spoke to the women first, to show the boy that he checked on everyone.

'Everything all right, ladies?' He flashed his warrant card at them. Missed their connecting train, they had; be on their way first thing.

'Oh, dear me, yes, it's true, the hotels are expensive in Hanover, but you must take care; the waiting rooms aren't safe—a lot of shady customers, constant robberies.' He spoke loud enough for the boy to hear.

'Be seeing you then, ladies.'

He sauntered on to the boy who looked small sitting down— pale and fragile. Beside him was a checked suitcase.

'Evening. You stranded too, like the ladies over there?'

The boy nodded shyly—he did look sweet.

'These things happen, not the end of the world. Where are you headed?'

'Bremerhaven.'

'Ah, Bremerhaven. Not far to America from there.'

The boy threw him a wary look. He sat down beside him on the bench.

5

As the train drew into the station, the boy had a feeling he'd missed his connection. He hoped vaguely that there was a train he didn't know about, but when he asked at the ticket office his fears were confirmed: the next train to Bremerhaven didn't leave until 6.02 the following morning. That was eleven hours away. What was he to do in all that time? He looked about him. He'd never been in such a vast, high building. At first he felt awe, but then he was gripped by excitement at the thought that there was a whole city belonging to this station. He dropped his suitcase at left luggage and went to the lavatory to stow his watch safely with his money, in the pouch strapped to his body. Then he sauntered out. The light from the gas lamps astonished him; he hadn't realised that night could be so bright. He stood and stared at it all, not knowing which way to go, and in the end he simply struck out.

There weren't many people about. The boy crossed the station forecourt and turned into a broad street lined with shops that were all closed. There was a nip in the air. He thrust his hands into his pockets and felt his courage drain away. Everything was so big and high, but it was empty, too. He began to feel uneasy. Then he saw a street that was narrower but livelier and turned into it. He was reassured by the presence of women; if women were safe here, he thought, he'd be safe too. One of them came up close to him, took his hand and tried to make him go with her. Alarmed, he pulled away from her and quickened his pace. He'd heard about women like this, wicked women—though often, he knew, the victims of their fate. Fallen women. He thought of Monika, but pushed the thought away.

He was hungry and thirsty and though he felt queasy, he knew he ought to eat and drink, so he went into a brightly lit public house and ordered bratwurst and fried potatoes and a bottle of lemonade. No one took any notice of him.

One Saturday, Monika had asked him to join her on a boat trip. Her uncle lived on the river and had a boat he didn't use on a Saturday because that was his day for going to town. They took the boat out and the boy rowed it into a winding stream hung with weeping willows. Monika had brought a hamper and a bottle of wine, and after lunch they lay on the grass and told each other about their families. The vicar was strict, Monika said; he was forever finding fault and wouldn't stand for answering back.

On their fourth boat trip, they lay in the grass and kissed and the boy kept thinking that he really ought to stop; he mustn't carry on; he must get up and help Monika into the boat and row her home. He did mean to stop, but he couldn't—and neither could Monika. She said herself that they ought to, and each time he said, 'I know,' and they carried on. Once or twice he found himself thinking of Heiner but that made it even harder to stop. And so it had happened.

He paid for the food and lemonade and went back to the station, past the fallen girls. Maybe he wouldn't go on to Bremerhaven tomorrow, he thought; maybe he wouldn't go to Dunedin. In the station, he collected his suitcase and went to sit in the waiting room.

—

Lahnstein had been waiting for two hours. He'd climbed to the top of the stairs and knocked on Haarmann's door, but there was no answer. Back on the street, he leant against a lamppost and smoked one of Emma's cigarillos, thinking of her and of the aeroplane as he watched the smoke—then he threw the cigarillo to the ground, trod it out and went for a bit of a walk. There weren't many people about. Some children were crouched on the cobbles, turning over a dead or half-dead rat with a stick. Lahnstein stood on the bridge and watched the currents of the Leine. It began to rain. He returned to Rote Reihe and looked up at Number Two, a three-storey stucco-fronted building flanked by half-timbered houses. There were two gables; the one on the right belonged to Haarmann's room. On the ground floor there was a pub. Lahnstein went back into the building and tried Haarmann's door again, but there was still no answer. He returned to his post at the streetlamp and had another smoke.

When he had waited three hours, he saw a man coming towards him along the narrow road. Lahnstein couldn't make out his face because it was hidden behind a big bundle of what looked like old clothes. The man was clutching this bundle to his chest, lurching unsteadily, because he couldn't see where he was going. Outside Number Two, he stopped and dropped the bundle, opened the door and put in a foot so that it wouldn't fall shut. As he stooped over to gather up the clothes, Lahnstein caught a glimpse of his profile and thought it possible that it might be Haarmann. The man kicked the door ajar and squeezed his way into the house. The door slammed shut behind him.

Lahnstein lit another cigarillo to measure the time before he went in, but smoked hurriedly and decided halfway through that he'd waited long enough. He crossed the road to Number Two, stepped into the dark hallway and climbed the narrow stairs to the attic. There were cubby holes full of junk on the landing and a door to either side, one of which was Haarmann's. He listened out for a moment, but heard nothing. He knocked. The silence seemed to deepen. Seconds passed and then a surprisingly high voice called out, 'Who is it?'

'Lahnstein, Criminal Investigation.'

Silence again. Lahnstein heard a rustle, as if things were being moved out of the way.

'The new man?'

'So to speak.'

'What d'you want from me?'

'I'd like to talk to you.'

'Are there charges?'

'No.'

'So why d'you want to talk to me?'

Slurred words, swallowed sounds.

'No particular reason. I'm interested in the neighbourhood. You know the ropes; you hear what's going on.'

'You've no right to question me without charges.'

Downstairs a door slammed. Lahnstein heard footsteps on the stairs.

'I know that. Come on, I'll take you out to lunch. We'll have a little chat.'

'No time.'

The front door banged shut.

'I can summons you, if you'd rather.'

'Thought there were no charges.'

'That's never quite true of those born on the seventeenth of the fifth.'

Lahnstein was ashamed of these words, but he had no other way of getting anywhere. He heard footsteps and more rustling, and the door burst open on a broad man of medium height wearing a broad-brimmed hat. His eyes were narrow, his eyebrows straight lines, his small, cleft moustache rather unkempt. The same face as in the photograph, perhaps a little fuller. Haarmann jerked out his hand and Lahnstein took it—a fleshy hand, a limp grip. Then, avoiding his eye, Haarmann pulled away and silently led the way down the stairs and onto the street. He walked quickly; Lahnstein had to hurry to keep up with him.

'Why don't we go to the pub in your building?'

'Food's bad.'

'So where are we going?'

'The Golden Hind.'

'May I ask what was in the bundle that you were carrying into the house?'

'Old clothes.'

'You deal in them?'

'It's my trade.'

Haarmann flung out greetings left and right, and people smiled when they saw him; hands flew to hat brims; fingers shot out in salute. In a few minutes they reached the Golden Hind. Haarmann opened the door and waved Lahnstein in. The air was heavy with the smell of cabbage and tobacco and stale sweat. The windows let in little light. Dark wooden tables were flanked by dark wooden benches. Haarmann headed for a window table; they took off their hats and coats and sat down. Haarmann pulled a cigar from his jacket pocket—a surprisingly good, expensive cigar—and trimmed it. He was wearing a knitted tie attached to his collar with a pin. His hair was parted on the right and combed across his high forehead in a straight line.

'The horsemeat's good,' he said.

'Do you supply the pub?'

'You've done your homework.'

'I've heard this and that. You trade in meat as well as clothes?'

Haarmann lit the cigar, took two drags and puffed out smoke, examining the evenly burning ember with a satisfied nod.

'That's right,' he said, 'but I don't supply this pub. My competitor does that. Try the horse schnitzel.'

A waiter set down two big glasses of beer on the table with a brief nod to Haarmann.

'Anything to eat?'

'The horse schnitzel for the gentleman here—is that right?'

Lahnstein nodded.

'And the bratwurst for you, sir?'

'That's it, the usual.'

The waiter left. They raised their glasses and drank.

'Didn't you say the horsemeat was particularly good?' Lahnstein said.

'I don't eat horse.'

Lahnstein thought of the horses he'd seen from the air after the shellings at Verdun—twisted limbs, half bodies, bodies in shreds, severed necks, bloated corpses lying on their backs, legs in the air. They were scattered among the human corpses, but more visible from the air on account of their size—and often the human bodies had already been carted off, the horses left to rot. Some were still alive; they kicked their legs as he passed overhead, as if they were waving to him. He remembered one that had dragged itself along without any hind legs.

'What d'you want from me?' Haarmann asked, sucking on his cigar.

He looked at Lahnstein with interest but without concern, smiling faintly in a sly, almost patronising way. His voice was very high and slightly cracked, like an old woman's. He looked broad even without his coat, but there was something flabby about him—something rather feminine, Lahnstein thought—or did he only think that because he knew about his proclivities from reading his file?

'Where do you get hold of the clothes, if I may ask?'

'So this *is* an interrogation?'

'No, I'm only asking.'

'Dead people, mainly.'

Lahnstein felt his eyebrows shoot up and his eyes widen. Haarmann noticed and looked at him coldly.

'Dead people?' Lahnstein asked, feigning composure.

'Spanish flu. People dropped like flies; they didn't need their clothes anymore an' their families were desperate for money—specially when it was the men that died, leaving 'em without an income. That's how we started, with second-hand men's clothes. Did good business, too; no one had money for new things after the war.'

As he talked, his tongue flicked out, touched his lips, flicked back again. A disagreeably meaty tongue.

'Who is this *we*?'

As if he didn't know.

'Me an' Hans. Hans is my partner.'

'Hans Grans?'

'Can't help yourself, can you, Mr Interrogator?'

Haarmann laughed good-humouredly.

'I'm sorry,' Lahnstein said, 'It's in the file anyway.'

'No hard feelings.'

Lahnstein paused to collect himself. 'So is business slower these days?' he asked.

'People are better off, healthwise and moneywise. They're not dying as much an' they're not buying as many second-hand goods. We're starting to feel the pinch.'

'You and Grans?'

'Me an' Hans Grans, yes.'

The waiter brought two steaming plates of potatoes and a greasy, almost black gravy. The meat, drowned in the gravy, was barely visible.

'Luckily I have the meat trade, my second mainstay.'

'And who supplies you with meat, if I may ask?'

'Ask away.'

He sucked on his cigar, but said nothing.

'Where do you get your meat?'

'I've a supplier. In the country.'

'Karl the Butcher?'

'You're well informed. Please eat, you must eat while the gravy's hot. Nothing worse than lukewarm gravy, don't you agree?'

Lahnstein plunged his knife into the gravy where he supposed the meat to be.

Haarmann watched him intently, nodding as the morsel disappeared into Lahnstein's mouth. Then, still holding his cigar, he cut off a piece of sausage. His fingers were long, except for a stump on his left hand. They chewed in silence, Haarmann puffing on his cigar in between mouthfuls and blowing the smoke over Lahnstein's plate. Lahnstein tasted only a rather sour gravy, so hot it burnt his mouth.

'Is it good?'

'Yes, thanks.'

Lahnstein drank some beer. He didn't want to think of human flesh, but he couldn't stop himself. In the POW camp, there had been weeks towards the end of the war when they'd had hardly any meat and not much of anything else either. In their hunger, they fell to talking about cannibalism, recalling old yarns about shipwrecked sailors who'd resorted to eating dead members of the crew or even killing off the weaker ones for food. The hungrier the prisoners were, the more they talked of these things—for all the world, Lahnstein thought, as if they were preparing themselves to eat each other. Well, he wasn't going to touch Franz, that was for sure. After a time, supplies improved and the subject was dropped.

He went on eating. The gravy could have been worse and his mouth was so burnt that he could barely taste a thing anyway.

'In your file it says you also traded in guns.'

'Why d'you keep mentioning my file?'

'Because, naturally, I looked at your file.'

'It's not all that natural, when there are no charges.'

'What happened to your finger?' Lahnstein asked.

Haarmann put down his fork and studied his left hand.

'Chopped it off, cutting up a big animal.'

He brought the side of his right hand down on his fingers.

'Does that count against me?'

'Depends.'

Haarmann gave a sudden laugh, writhing and slapping the table with the hand that gripped the cigar.

'Now I've got you,' he said with a snort. 'I know what you're thinking. You're imagining the meat cleaver, the blood spurting—an' a big, *human* animal. Admit it.'

Lahnstein tried to look unfazed.

Haarmann grew calmer.

'You could at least admit it,' he said, pouting like a sulky child. Then: 'Don't worry. It was bitten off, in a fight.'

'What was the fight about?'

'Competition's tough in my business.'

Haarmann turned back to his plate. He squeezed off big pieces of bratwurst with the side of his fork and rolled them in the gravy, eating hurriedly, greedily, as if afraid someone might take the food away.

'I don't trade in guns anymore,' Haarmann said.

'Where did you get the guns when you did?'

'Almost everyone had a gun in those days—millions of soldiers back from the war an' they all had rifles. There was no officers left to return them to—none that anyone took seriously, anyway. Or maybe people were afraid of a counter-revolution. It was less of a risk to sell the guns to me.'

That meaty tongue again. Lahnstein wondered whether part of the reason it repelled him was that there was something erotic about it—something revoltingly, preposterously erotic. He pushed the thought away.

'Who did you sell the guns to?'

'Freikorps people, revolutionaries—whoever needed them. There was a lot of shooting after the war. And there's more to come, I can tell you.'

'Did you do any shooting?'

'Me? No, only in the army, before the war. I was a soldier then.'

'I know.'

'All in the file, eh?'

'All in the file.'

They ate in silence.

Then Lahnstein said, 'You've heard about the boys?'

'What boys?'

He asked innocently, his voice even higher than before.

'The missing boys.'

'Are they dead?'

'That's the question.'

'Everyone's heard about the boys.'

'What do you think happened to them?'

'Foreign Legion.'

'I think they were killed.'

'Comes to the same.'

'Not for me, it doesn't. If the boys lose their lives fighting somewhere in Africa or Asia, it's not my business. If they die here, it is. It might be murder.'

'War or murder. Makes no difference to the boys.'

'It makes a difference to me.'

'Were you in the war?' Haarmann asked.

'Yes, Verdun.'

Haarmann nodded appreciatively.

'Ah,' he said. 'The blood pump.'

'You know the expression?'

'Of course. Pump the blood out of the French till they're done for. Then march on Paris. That much trickled through to us prisoners. We were all for it. We didn't want the French and British to win; we were always for the Germans. They may not have treated us well, but the Frogs an' Brits weren't going to liberate us, were they?'

Nothing imbecile about that, Lahnstein thought.

'What do you think of when you hear the words *blood pump*?'

Haarmann looked at him uncomprehendingly. 'Lots of blood, what else?'

'It was a slaughterhouse.'

'An' you were right in the middle of it?'

'I was an airman.'

'Shoot any planes down?'

'Twelve.'

'What was your name again?'

You idiot, Lahnstein told himself. You bloody idiot.

'Lahnstein,' he said.

Haarmann puffed at his cigar and looked at him, chewing and nodding.

'You're lying,' he said.

'The lists aren't complete.'

'I know you're lying.'

Haarmann had finished his bratwurst. His lips were shiny with grease. He took a big slug of beer, licked his lips and wiped his mouth with his sleeve. Now his lips were clean and his sleeve was greasy.

'You've been involved with boys in the past,' Lahnstein said, hoping he wouldn't blush.

Haarmann shrugged.

'Aren't we all, in our youth? Nothing wrong with a bit of polishing.'

He *was* blushing, damn it.

Haarmann was looking at him, but if he noticed anything he didn't let it show.

'It's illegal.'

'Polishing isn't.'

'It's all illegal.'

'I like women. I was engaged.'

'I know. It's in your file. But you didn't marry?'

'Isn't it in the file?'

'No.'

'Then I can't have done.'

'Was it…' Lahnstein cleared his throat, '…because you realised you liked men?'

'Rubbish.'

His voice was sharp and somehow convincing.

'Erna'd been carrying on with a student. He knocked her up.'

Lahnstein thrust his fork into the last piece of horse schnitzel, wiped it in the gravy and popped it in his mouth. It was quite tender.

'Was it good?' Haarmann asked.

'Yes, thank you.'

'I'd like to go now.' He stubbed out his cigar in the ashtray and made to get up. Then he sat down again.

'Assuming I did like men an' boys, why would I kill 'em? It wouldn't make sense. Ever thought of that?'

'Even normal people commit murders of passion,' said Lahnstein.

'I'm normal. As normal as you, believe me.'

'I didn't want to offend you.'

Haarmann got up again.

'Have you never heard anything?' Lahnstein asked. 'You get about a lot in Hanover, selling your clothes and meat. You must hear things. Has nobody ever mentioned the boys?'

'No, never. An' now good day to you.'

He put on his hat and coat and left.

Lahnstein asked for the bill.

'The meat was good,' he said to the waiter out of politeness.

'Came from your friend,' the waiter said.

'From my—? He said it came from a rival.'

Lahnstein's throat tightened; he felt sick.

'Is that what he said?'

'Yes.'

'He doesn't have any rivals,' the waiter said. 'No one supplies meat as cheaply as Haarmann.'

Lahnstein thrust money into the waiter's hands, rushed to the lavatory, knelt in front of the toilet bowl, stuck a finger down his throat and retched and retched and retched.

That evening he went to a Social Democrat meeting. He hadn't been for a long time and felt a stranger among the workers, most of them rubber-works employees who banged on about working conditions and hourly wages. Intermittently, they also discussed the next steps into the realm of socialism, but with less enthusiasm, as if they were in no hurry to get there. In the POW camp, Social Democracy had meant something different. Sitting talking on the lawn in summer or in one of the barracks in winter, they had seen it as an officers' revolt against the monarchy and its war. Justice for them was political justice—the right to genuine participation, the right to form a government. That government would, of course, do something for the workers; it would ensure better conditions and higher wages. But its main task was to build up a republic.

Now, sitting here with workers who wanted to do something for themselves and considered him as much a stranger as he them, he wondered whether they hadn't made some mistake and in fact the SPD of the camp and this peacetime SPD had nothing to do with each other. Then again, Friedrich Ebert had made it to Reich President and with each new round of beer that came, they all drank to him. (The SPD was not, however, in government; Wilhelm Marx was Reich Chancellor—a man of the centre, despite his name.)

Lahnstein had gone to the meeting for the company and perhaps also for some sense of security—to be with people who saw eye to eye with him on a thing or two. There were a couple of dozen men attending, most of them still in their work gear, two or three who looked like professors or teachers, and three women, one of whom he recognised as Magda Hennies, mother of Number Twelve. She was the one who'd worked on the machines at Continental during the war and was now having to clean instead because the machines were being worked by men again. He felt awkward, meeting her here. The others knew he was a policeman and had accepted the fact with indifference, but they didn't know he was responsible for the missing-boys investigations. Magda Hennies was at the far end of the table with the other women and wasn't taking part in the discussion, most of which was about the Reich Banner Black-Red-Gold, a new organisation that the Social Democrats were planning to found with other supporters of the Republic. If Lahnstein understood correctly, the Reich Banner was to defend the Republic against her enemies—with weapons, if necessary—but there was a lot of muttering and whispering going on and Lahnstein had the impression that some of the men would rather he didn't hear what was being said. It was as if they knew what he was thinking: wasn't it the job of the police to protect the Republic?

'They can't even protect our boys,' one of the workers said.

'Now you sound like a Communist,' another said.

Lahnstein looked at them in horror. They were talking about his case, as if he weren't there.

'The Communists are exploiting the case to discredit Noske. Don't you read the papers?'

'Not the red ones.'

'It's their revenge for Luxemburg and Liebknecht.'

'It's time they stopped blaming Noske for that.'

'But they're right about the boys,' said one of the professor types.

'What does our comrade from the police have to say?' one of the workers asked.

Lahnstein glanced at Magda Hennies. She was looking at him intently—as indeed they all were.

It seemed easiest to blame Versailles, the lack of staff, the impossibility of proper investigations. But the response was sceptical. Lahnstein remembered, too late, that Social Democrat Hermann Müller had signed the treaty. Lambasting Versailles was the prerogative of the other side, of the Republic's opponents. They saw the treaty as a diktat imposed on German democrats by foreign democrats and held it up as proof of the Republic's failure.

Lahnstein broke out in a sweat. His voice began to shake and he strayed into rambling explanations that convinced no one.

Magda Hennies came to his rescue by insisting that they change the subject. Her son was one of the missing boys, she said; she couldn't bear to hear any more. No one demurred.

For the rest of the evening, Lahnstein kept out of the discussion, drifting off into thoughts of the boys and their murderer. Now that he knew what Haarmann looked like, he had begun to imagine him as the boys' attacker in various gruesome scenes, and although he couldn't be sure that Haarmann had killed them, he fitted the part; there was something disturbingly right about him in the role. This method of determining whether a lead was worth pursuing had seldom failed Lahnstein. If a face worked in a scene—if it didn't blur and fade when he tried to focus on it—he knew he was on the right track. He had sometimes been proved wrong, of course, but not often.

He was almost surprised when the meeting came to an end and people began to leave. Out on the street, he was approached by Magda Hennies.

'May I speak to you for a moment?' she asked.

'By all means.'

'I've been thinking,' she said. 'You asked me if Adolf is one of those, one of them—oh, I'll say it straight.'

She paused, searching for the right expression. He watched her struggling, her face twitching as she strained to find an acceptable way of putting it. Eventually she forced out the words. 'If he falls in love with boys.'

Lahnstein looked away, giving her time to collect herself.

'It's all right,' he heard her say and looked at her again.

Her face was relaxed now, smiling, with only a touch of embarrassment.

'I think he must be,' she said. 'Whenever I was out with him, he always turned to look at the boys—the girls never got a glance. I noticed a while ago, but I think I tried to convince myself the lads were just friends of his.'

'Thank you for telling me this,' Lahnstein said. 'It's very helpful to me.'

'Do you know what it means?' she asked.

'What?'

'He couldn't do what he wanted to do at home, in safety. He had to go out in the dark, where bad people prowl and loiter. There was no other way.'

She began to cry.

'Would you have let him bring a girl home and take her to his room?'

'Of course not, he was too young for that.'

'So it makes no difference. You're not to blame.'

'It does make a difference,' she said. 'I should have known he was putting himself at risk. The kids who put themselves at the mercy of men always have to take care, girls and boys alike. That's just how it is. I know what I'm talking about.'

What could he say?

She looked at him and shrugged. 'I just wanted to tell you, to set you on the right track,' she said.

Lahnstein gave her his hand, rather touched.

When he visited Emma Burschel a few days later, she had shut up shop and put the boys to bed. He knew he wouldn't sleep with her; he had decided as much on the way there, and only briefly hesitated at supper, because it felt so good talking to her, better than any other conversation he'd had with a woman since his return from the war—better, indeed, than any he'd had with a man. They ate roast meat with potatoes and red cabbage, and drank beer. He told her about Lissy and August; he had made up his mind to it.

There was a fir tree in the corner of the sitting room—six or seven baubles hung in its brown needles, and two or three angels with childlike faces. The candles had burnt down. Beneath the tree was a roughly hewn wooden crib: Mary and Joseph, Jesus in the manger, ox and ass. Emma had given him a box of her best cigars, wrapped up and tied with a ribbon.

He didn't mention the aeroplane. After a while, he broke off the story of Lissy and August and said abruptly, 'Your turn now. Tell me about your parents.'

'My mother was seven years older than my father,' Emma said. They were eating marble cake for pudding. 'She was a good mother. I'm afraid my father made her suffer.'

'What did he do?'

'Maybe he only married her for her fortune—a few houses, a small shareholding. He drank. Every day at noon he left the house and did the rounds of the pubs in the old town. He was always looking for a fight and he found plenty. Sometimes he'd come home bleeding. He was a little man.'

Lahnstein took one of the cigars and trimmed it as she continued her story.

'He brought women home too. Mother put up with it. What else could she do? After the birth of her sixth child, she was bedridden. Father carried on with his mistresses in the next room and she'd no choice but to lie there listening. Until he got sick himself—you know—and had to stop seeing women.'

She lit his cigar for him.

'Syphilis?'

'Please, don't say that word here.'

'Forgive me.'

He took a first drag; it tasted almost sweet.

'Not to worry. It was almost unbearable, the way he treated Mother. There she was, sick in bed and we'd hear him in his room, laughing. Used to hear the women squeal, too. The women squealed and Mother just stared at the ceiling. But it was worst of all for my little brother. He loved his mum; she'd always been the one who protected him. Father had regular fits of rage, and poor Fritz bore the brunt of them. Whenever Father was after him he'd run to Mother and hide under the covers. He spent a lot of time in Mother's bed; he was safe in there.'

She opened another bottle of beer and filled their glasses. Froth ran down the sides.

'It's no wonder he wet the bed and messed himself for so long.'

She wiped away the froth with her napkin.

'"Christened your trousers, have you?" That's what Mother always said when he shat a new pair.'

'I'm sorry,' Lahnstein said.

'What are you sorry about?'

He didn't know what to say and took refuge in a question.

'Why did your father have it in for him?'

'Fritz was a funny one. He used to knit and darn stockings. Our father didn't like that, but Fritz was always in Mother's bed, doing the things she'd have done if she hadn't been sick. Sometimes he played with a doll; if Father caught him at that, he took the poker to him. It's no wonder Fritz sometimes acts strange.'

'Such as when he breaks into your shop and steals cigars,' Lahnstein said.

She laughed this off. 'He says it's because I did him out of part of his share of Mother's inheritance. He says he's only taking what's his by right. Maybe he has a point.'

'When did your mother die?'

'Sometimes you sound as if you're interrogating me.'

'Forgive me, please, I didn't mean to.'

'Of course you didn't. She died on 5 April 1901. My father refused to split the inheritance with us. We sued him and we sued each other. It was a terrible time. I don't really want to tell you about it, but you're sitting there all quiet and attentive, smoking your cigar.'

'One of yours.'

'Do you like it?'

'Very much.'

'We sued each other over Father's inheritance too.'

You couldn't call her beautiful; her narrow eyes were too small for her round face. What he liked about her wasn't the fixed moment that a photograph would capture, but the movements of her face and body. There was, he thought, something fluid about them; they had charm, grace, poise.

On his first combat mission he had tucked a photograph of Lissy into the cockpit so that he'd see her whenever he looked at the dashboard, but it had fluttered away soon after take-off. He wanted to turn back and retrieve it, but instead he flew on. Afterwards, he wondered if it wasn't then that he lost her.

A photograph wouldn't do Emma justice; he wouldn't tuck her photo into the cockpit. The thought drew him up short; he hadn't intended a comparison. Having started, though, he would go on: Emma, he decided, would be better caught on film—except that films didn't capture people's natural movements; everything was so brisk and jerky.

'What's wrong?' she asked. 'You're so far away.'

'I was thinking,' he said.

'What about?'

'About your brother.'

'I love my brother.'

'Is Burschel your former husband's name, Mrs Burschel?'

'Won't you call me by my first name?'

He raised his glass.

'Robert Lahnstein,' he said.

'Emma Burschel.'

They clinked glasses and drank.

'And what's your maiden name?'

'No one's ever asked me that before.'

'I'm sorry. Forget that I asked.'

'Haarmann.'

It was out. She was Emma Haarmann and he was the inspector who was trying to convict her brother. He had suspected it for some minutes; now it was certain. He saw similarities he hadn't noticed before: the narrow eyes, the straight eyebrows, the round face. Why hadn't he seen it at once? Or had he seen it and ignored it?

'How did your brother treat you?'

'He was nice to me most of the time. Though he did tie me up sometimes.'

'That's not nice.'

'Once he made a straw doll, dressed in our sister's clothes, and laid it face-down on the front steps. Have I told you this before?'

'Yes, you have.'

'That's brothers and sisters for you. Don't you have any siblings, Mr Lahnstein—Robert?' She laughed.

'No, I don't.'

'Be thankful.'

'What does your brother do now?'

He was speaking like an interrogator again; he must be careful.

'He trades in clothes, meat, all kinds of things. He scrapes along. Steals from me, minds the boys.'

'Aren't you afraid?' he wanted to yell, but he restrained himself.

'Why all this talk of my brother?' she asked.

'Bashfulness,' he said.

She filled their glasses again.

'Bashfulness!'

He was wondering what to say, when one of the boys burst into the sitting room. Lahnstein had forgotten their names, but thought it was the older one. He stood in the middle of the room in his pyjamas, rubbing his eyes in the light.

'I can't sleep,' he said.

His mother stretched out her arms to him, but he didn't move.

'What's that man doing here?' he asked, pointing at Lahnstein.

'We're talking,' she said.

'Why?' There were tears in the boy's eyes.

Emma went and put her arms around him. They stood there for a while, as if frozen.

'He's asleep,' she whispered. 'How can I get him back to bed?'

'Would you like me to carry him?'

She nodded. Lahnstein got up, gathered the boy gently in his arms and followed Emma to the boys' room. The child was warm and smelt of sleep. They went into a small room with a bed on either side and a narrow aisle in between. Lahnstein laid the boy in the empty bed, brushed his hand over his head and followed Emma out again.

That night he lay awake thinking of Lissy and the way she had vanished from his life while he was in the POW camp. It had been a strange time. The war was over, but they weren't allowed home until there was a peace treaty. The English newspapers, which they now received regularly, reported street fights in Berlin and strikes and shootings in the Ruhr District. Lahnstein, who had just joined the Social Democrats, was horrified: Gustav Noske was having the workers shot at—his own people. In the camp, things were less tense than they had been. Those officers loyal to the deposed Kaiser also supported the Freikorps and gloated to the Social Democrats that the SPD government couldn't survive without the old forces. 'You owe us for this,' a colonel shouted. Lahnstein didn't reply. He was cold; it was a chilly winter that year in Yorkshire.

He looked forward to the letters with nervous anticipation, even more anxiously than during the war. August was growing, but he was a frail, skinny lad. Lahnstein, sometimes mad with worry, imagined him almost skeletal. 'Take him to Lake Irr,' he wrote to Lissy, whose letters remained reserved. The farmers would have plenty to eat, Lahnstein thought, and in the country Lissy and August would be safe from the shooting. 'Send them to Lake Irr,' he wrote to his parents—and then weeks passed before a letter came from his father with news of their departure. Lahnstein felt a rush of relief and went back to waiting. A letter—posted in February—came from Lissy in April: all well, plenty to eat, colds and coughs, nothing serious. This time the relief was even greater. But Lahnstein never heard from Lissy again. In May, his parents wrote that the strikes were over; all was calm once more in the Ruhr District. They didn't mention Lissy.

The POWs read about the Paris negotiations in the papers. Everyone was hoping for a mild treaty; all hopes were pinned on the American president Woodrow Wilson who promised to grant nations the right to self-determination. People had cheered him as he travelled through Europe. Now it was the Social Democrats' turn to gloat. 'What did we tell you? Only a democratic politician can save us.' Their taunts were greeted with silence.

The news from Paris grew worse. French demands were

tough. Germany was to lose large swathes of territory; Entente soldiers were to occupy considerable areas of land, far beyond the Rhine. And why weren't the Germans allowed to sit at the negotiation table? Why were decisions being made over their heads? There was anger in the camp. But there was also sympathy—and even affection—towards the guards. The French were calling for the Rhineland to be detached from Germany, but the Americans and British were against it. The POWs wrote a letter of gratitude to their guards which they all signed. It was handed over ceremoniously, together with a drawing of the king of England by an artistically minded officer. The guards' thanks were frosty; they remained aloof.

Still no letter from Lissy. Lahnstein wrote to her brother on Lake Irr, but received no reply. His parents hadn't heard from her either. He asked his father to go to the lake to find out why she hadn't written. His father hesitated, afraid to leave Bochum. The French were expected to march into the west of Germany at any moment—what if he were cut off and couldn't get back to Bochum and his wife? Lahnstein was torn between understanding and anger. And why did everything have to take so long? It was sometimes seven or eight weeks before he received an answer. Bloody war, bloody captivity, bloody peace conference.

In June the English papers printed the results of the negotiations. All the prisoners gathered on the lawn as the terms of the treaty were read out by a major who had grown up in Birmingham and spoke the best English. Alsace-Lorraine was lost—well, all right, that was to be expected, but why so much of West Prussia? Why Posen, the Hultschin district, the Rychtal area? One man, who must have been from the Rychtal, let out a wail. Eupen and Malmedy had gone too—fallen to Belgium. In some areas, residents were to vote on whether they wanted to join other states—Denmark, Poland, France. The French wanted to annex the Saarland. The men on the lawn grew quieter and quieter. Some of them cried.

Arms restrictions, reparations, all colonies lost. The blame for the war fell exclusively on the German Reich. When the major had finished, there was shouting and stamping; one man beat his head against the barracks wall and had to be restrained. A lieutenant who was careless enough to remark that they had been let off lightly found himself in the garrison hospital with a bloody nose.

Guards appeared with rifles. The German officers scattered. They spent the rest of the day sitting in small groups, talking in whispers. Lahnstein preferred to be alone, but then he went to the guard at the door and asked when he thought they'd be released. The guard didn't know.

'I want to see my family,' Lahnstein said.

The man nodded.

'Are there any letters?'

The man shook his head. 'Go back to your comrades,' he said.

Lahnstein took himself off. He read Lissy's last letter; he'd held it in his hands so often that it was falling to pieces. August was no longer afraid of the cows. They had snow, fresh snow every day. Her brother had to shovel it off the roof to keep it from caving in.

It was summer now.

At one point, he stumbled. Hang on, he thought, that's funny. He read the words again. 'Started on some mittens for the little one. Very easy pattern.' The first letters of four consecutive words spelt 'love'. His heart skipped a beat. Little One Very Easy. Was it Lissy's timid way of expressing her feelings to him? He read the words over and over until it seemed to him that the initial letters were written with more emphasis, that the letters were thicker, bluer. Then the impression vanished. It was all imagination—the madness of his fears and longing.

He went through all the boys in the village, saw them as they were in his memory, sitting by the fire in the lakeside inn, smoking, drinking, sounding off. There had only been a few, exempted from war service because they worked on the land. Now there would be more young men, back from the trenches; Lahnstein pictured them to himself, battle-hardened, heroic, attractive—or perhaps invalids, disfigured or crippled, or both. Didn't people say that pity kindled love? The Treaty of Versailles forbade the reunification of Germany and Austria, but it didn't forbid travelling between the two countries—and why should it? Stop this madness! He would go down to Lake Irr as soon as he was released.

The day came. They were taken to Dover and sent over the Channel on a steamer and across France in trains that stopped frequently, not always at stations. Lahnstein was returning to an unknown country; he couldn't imagine a German Reich without a Kaiser, a republic led by Social Democrats.

His train drew into Bochum. No one was waiting for him;

nobody knew he was coming. He had last seen the city on leave three years before and at first it looked familiar—but as he walked out of the station he was struck by the quiet. There were fewer motor cars, fewer people, less bustle. Clothes were shabbier and people moved more slowly or stood loitering—beggars, invalids, wretches. The Republic seemed greyer than the Empire; it was a shock. Lahnstein walked home with his little bundle. He found his parents safe and sound, but they had no news of Lissy and August. Lahnstein would have set off again immediately, but he came down with something and couldn't travel for months. It was January before he was strong enough to leave for Lake Irr.

'How did you get on with Haarmann?' Müller asked when he got back to the office.

'Your friend Haarmann?'

'Friend? Please.'

'He sends his regards.'

'I don't believe you.'

'Why not?'

'He has no call to.'

'But you know him?'

'I've questioned him often enough.'

'And now he's off the hook?'

'How do you mean?'

'He must have been a prime suspect right from the start. Why didn't you follow up the lead?'

'I could ask you the same.'

'The file was withheld from me.'

'Maybe you didn't make enough of an effort.'

Lahnstein restrained himself and said nothing. Then he said, 'You're right. He didn't send his regards.'

'Get anything out of him?' Müller asked at length, his tone conciliatory. 'Come to any conclusions?'

'We must keep an eye on him. I'd like you to see to it that he's watched around the clock.'

'Very original.'

'Excuse me?'

'All that's been done before—at least as far as Versailles permitted. But if you say so. We can do it again.'

Müller laughed mockingly and left the office. Lahnstein reached for the telephone and asked for Müller's staff file to be brought to him—at once.

Müller's career had been slow to take off; in the ten years leading up to the war, he was promoted only once, and he had a reputation for being lazy, often arriving late and twice taking more holidays than he was due. Disciplinary talks made no difference; he remained below par. There was some suspicion of corruption. The man who ran the queer cafe behind the opera house had clearly paid Müller small bribes to stay open; investigations were underway. But then Archduke Franz Ferdinand was assassinated by an irredentist in Sarajevo; Russia mobilised; Germany declared war on Russia. In August 1914, Müller volunteered to fight. After the war, things were different; the force was glad of every man in possession of all his limbs. (It had been the same in Bochum, Lahnstein remembered.) Müller's luck changed;

he had soon busted several gangs of gun-runners and a ring of counterfeiters. The chief of police rewarded him by promoting him twice in quick succession.

Coming back into the office, Müller spotted the file on Lahnstein's desk.

'Mine, I assume,' he said.

'If I were a cynic, I'd say you'd been saved by the war.'

'I prefer to say that I spent the war serving the fatherland.'

'Perhaps both are true.'

'I was fighting on the ground while you admired the countryside from on high.'

'I have no doubts about your wartime achievements for the fatherland. And since the war, too, your achievements are impressive. Before, on the other hand…'

'War brings out the best in some men—and rather less than the best in others.'

He grinned at Lahnstein, who said, 'Do you remember that cafe proprietor in the one-seven-fiver scene?'

'A liar.'

'Of course. But the case was never solved.'

Müller leapt to his feet and began to shout.

'Let me tell you something. I was at Verdun, sitting in the trenches as the shrapnel rained down and the ground shook and the earth sprayed up and half buried us—more than half buried some. I lay in the mud, surrounded by dead bodies. I heard the screams of the wounded and saw legs and heads flying through the air. I was hungry and thirsty and near to frozen. I pushed my bayonet into French bodies and got a few bullets in my own. You, meanwhile, were sitting in your little heated box, far from everything—and now you have the cheek to insult me with your ridiculous insinuations. The war wiped out what came before. None of that counts anymore.'

His face was puce. For a few seconds he stood at his desk in silence. Then he sat down again.

'All right,' Lahnstein said, 'let's say no more on the subject.'

Müller nodded.

'I'd like to talk about what's happened since. Haarmann was released from prison in April 1918; you returned from the war in December. After that you both went about your work in Hanover—each in his own sphere, but not, shall we say, without a degree of overlap. I think it's fair to state, is it not, that you were familiar with the one-seven-fiver scene in which Haarmann moved?'

'If you say so.'

'Even before the end of 1919, you had scored unusual successes.'

Müller gave a laugh. 'You mean I have Haarmann to thank for my promotions?'

'It's not impossible,' Lahnstein said, 'that he played a part. The odd tip-off from the scene can work wonders for a career in the force.'

'We all have our informants. It's the only way; you know that.'

'I do. The only question is what's the quid pro quo? This is where we get onto moral ground. To what extent is it acceptable to make concessions to a criminal in order to solve a crime?'

'What's your view on the matter? I'd like to hear it.'

'Letting an egg thief go who informs on a burglar—absolutely fine. Covering for a serial killer who helps you up the career ladder—out of the question. Now it's your turn. How do you see it?'

'I hope you're not insinuating that I'm covering for a serial killer?'

'I'm only asking.'

'That's what we say in interrogations.'

'And what's your answer?'

'I share your view exactly. The former is absolutely fine, the latter is out of the question.'

'Is Haarmann your informant?'

Müller looked out of the window. 'He gives us the odd tip-off,' he said. 'Has done since 1919. But he wasn't suspected of being a serial killer in those days.'

'That's true. But he was a suspect in the case of Friedel Rothe. That was 1919.'

'He was suspected by a couple of hysterical women, a pair of whores. There wasn't the slightest evidence that he'd killed Rothe. I've told you all there is to tell.'

Maybe not quite all, Lahnstein thought. He closed Müller's file and went out to return it to the staff office.

A woman was sitting in the corridor, mid-thirties, tear-stained eyes. Unlucky Number Thirteen—for real this time.

'Come into my office, please.'

Hermann Spicker was born on 15 June 1906, the result of a youthful love affair. They hadn't married, the woman said, but the young man's parents had offered her money.

There was an awkward pause before she went on with her story.

The money was given to her on condition that she didn't seek contact with her son's father. She agreed—what else could she do? They were both minors and she needed the cash. Before long, she met another man and brought Hermann with her into the marriage. He was a modest, hardworking boy, who ended up apprenticed to a master tailor. Good with his hands, he was, and quick with a needle. He had a glass eye from an accident.

On the evening of 4 January, Hermann came home from the shop with a handsome suit, a loan from his apprentice master because he was to testify in court the following day after witnessing a collision between a coach horse and a motor car. (The horse had died and its owner was seeking compensation.)

'He set off in the morning with his friend Siegfried Kurt,' the woman said. She had thin hair and looked unkempt; none of her clothes matched.

'His friend?' Lahnstein asked.

'Yes, Siegfried, a nice boy. They spend a lot of time together.'

'Do you have his address for me?'

'I can give it to you, but it won't be much use.'

'Why not?'

'Siegfried has emigrated to Argentina.'

'When?'

'Today. They went into town together yesterday. Hermann said goodbye to Siegfried outside the court and went on to Bremerhaven. His ship sailed this morning.'

'Are you sure?'

'That's what they told me. It was the plan.'

'Had they quarrelled?'

Lahnstein was almost disappointed. It sounded like a different kind of story altogether—a long-plotted murder and an elaborate getaway—jealousy, pent-up hatred or whatever. Or else they'd both skedaddled to Argentina.

'They never quarrelled,' the woman said.

'Did your son testify in court?'

'Yes, but nobody's seen him since. He didn't come home last night.'

Which meant, Lahnstein thought, that it had happened after he'd seen Haarmann. The man had a nerve. But it all seemed so unlikely.

'Is it possible that your son emigrated to Argentina with his friend?'

'Without saying goodbye? Without his things? I don't think so—no, I'm sure he didn't.'

He asked the usual questions and showed the woman out. As he opened the door for her, he saw the chemist's wife, Mrs Schiefer, sitting on the bench in the corridor. She glanced at the other woman but immediately looked away, making no move to get up. Lahnstein went over to her.

'Finish your other business first, please,' she said, waving a hand towards the mother of Number Thirteen.

'May I introduce you?'

Lahnstein made an expansive, inclusive gesture, but Number Three's mother had averted her eyes again. Three and Thirteen—there were nine missing boys between the two women.

The chemist's wife pretended not to hear and stared the other way down the corridor, as if lost in thought. Lahnstein saw Hermann's mother to the top of the stairs.

'Is she missing a child too?'

'Yes.'

'How long's he been gone?'

'Almost a year.'

She began to cry again. Lahnstein said goodbye rather brusquely. Tears of indictment were the last thing he needed.

'You must treat Richard's case separately,' the chemist's wife said in his office. 'I told you that the last time I was here.'

'I only wanted to introduce you.'

'But why? We have nothing in common.'

'Grief?'

'That least of all. There is a noble grief and another, lowlier variety. There can be no comparison between them.'

'I don't understand.'

'One man dies leading an assault. Another is shot in the back. Are they to be grieved in the same way?'

'Both are missed.'

'Don't be ridiculous. The other boys were quite possibly involved in unspeakable things. You don't mean to insult me, do you?'

'Of course not. What can I do for you?'

'Has there been any progress? Have you pursued the possibility of murder and robbery?'

'We have a suspect who trades in clothes.'

'Ah, very good. And is there a suspect for the other cases?'

He nodded. 'Indeed, we seem to be getting somewhere.'

'Wouldn't it be better to separate the cases altogether? You could take on Richard's case and that man Müller could look after the others.'

'We're very short-staffed—Versailles, you understand—there are limits.'

'Versailles is our tragedy,' the chemist's wife said. 'I can't understand why we lost the war; it makes no sense to me. Our soldiers were far into French territory; we didn't see hair nor hide of the enemy over here until we let them in, just like that, without putting up a fight—without so much as firing a shot. Now they're here destroying everything. I wasn't against the Republic, I'll have you know. We women have the vote now and that means a lot to me. All my life I've been nothing but the chemist's wife: I do the exact same work as my husband, but he went to university and studied and I had to teach myself everything in the shop. It would never have entered my parents' minds to let me study—and then I became a mother and I thought my son would be a great man. He was my son, after all; he took after me in so many ways and I taught him such a lot—but now there's the Republic and everything's so precarious, maybe because of Versailles, maybe because of the Republic itself, who knows. All these new liberties—everything's permissible, everything has to be tolerated, but we do need to be able to live in safety too, and we can't anymore. Our shop's forever being broken into; no one does anything to help us. My husband's planning to get himself a gun and I assure you, he will shoot. He won't hear any more talk of our son; he's had enough of all that.

Slinks off and mixes his potions and never a word to me. Sometimes I wonder if he isn't mixing himself poison.'

She got up to leave.

'I'll be back,' she said. 'I won't stop coming until you've found the corpse—until you can tell us how our son died. We shall have no peace before then. He may not be alive anymore, but it's your duty to return him to us.'

'Why are you so sure he's no longer alive?'

'If he were, he'd have come home.'

She left.

Maybe she doesn't want him alive, Lahnstein thought.

—

'When does your train leave?' he asked the boy.

'Six.'

'Crikey,' he said, 'you can't spend all night in the waiting room. You'll fall asleep and someone'll steal your luggage. Might even steal you.' He laughed and the boy laughed too, softly, timidly.

'Oh dear,' he said with concern. 'What hotel can we put you up in?'

'I don't have the money for a hotel,' the boy said.

'Go on with you, that's my lookout.' He pretended to think. 'It's a tricky one. The trade fair's on; most places are booked out and it's too late for the smaller hotels.' He looked at his watch and shook his head. 'They don't have night porters.'

'I can stay here,' the boy said.

'Oh no you can't, it's too dangerous. D'you have any idea what goes on here? Boys go missing all the time. I tell you what,

if we don't find anywhere, I'll put you up at mine.' The boy raised his hands defensively.

'Not frightened, are you?' he asked with a laugh.

'No,' said the boy.

'Here, I'll show you something,' he said and fumbled in his pocket for the warrant card. The boy looked at it and relaxed.

He got up and took the boy's suitcase. In the end, you just had to be firm enough.

'Come on,' he said. 'I'll buy us a round, then we'll work out what to do.' He led the way, knowing, without turning to look, that the boy would follow. They went to the Donkey, a bar he could depend on to be closed at that hour. As they walked, he quizzed the boy about his home, his parents, his brothers and sisters. He didn't much like the answers; it was clear that the boy would be missed. But then a lot of the boys were missed and no one had tracked him down yet.

'Got a girl?' he asked the boy.

'No.'

A boy? he wanted to ask, but swallowed the words. It would only frighten him. He'd known boys to slip his grasp on the doorstep. The lust rose in him, needing release; this mustn't go wrong.

He talked about the difficulties of police work, the cunning of the crooks. Boys like this were always fascinated by his stories and all he had to do was tell them about the things he did and saw every day—only from the other point of view. It was easy. And now they'd arrived at the house where he lived. This was the moment of truth. He'd also reached quite a cliffhanger in the story he was telling: would he or would he not catch the conman? The boy, like almost all the boys before him, was desperate to know, and so the two of them went into the house and up the stairs and into his little flat. He lit some candles to make things cosier.

'Sit down,' he said, pointing to the bed. He took out a bottle of schnapps and poured two big glasses.

They drank. 'I do have a girl,' the boy said. 'She's pregnant.'

6

Who was this man? The women seemed suspicious of him at first, but their faces brightened as he talked to them. Exhausted, the boy leant back on the wooden bench, fumbling in his pocket for the watch he'd filched. His father would be angry about that. But the watch would be the least of his worries if he returned home now, after knocking up the vicar's daughter and doing a bunk—unless they were so relieved to see him that they took mercy. Father was a soft touch, but Mother sometimes lost her nerve and clobbered him. And Heiner? What would he tell Heiner?

'Hello there, missed your connection?' The man had crossed the waiting room and stood over him, smiling down. The boy nodded.

'Easily done,' the man said. 'Your train gets in late, the next one's gone, an' then you're stuck here.'

'Yes,' the boy said. He felt ill at ease; the man—a hefty fellow

of medium height with a hat and a moustache—was standing so close. At the same time, though, there was something compelling about him, something disturbingly compelling. Stop it, the boy told himself.

'When does your train leave?' the man asked. He wasn't going to tell him that, the boy thought. What business was it of his? But he told him anyway. What harm could it do? He put a hand on his suitcase and, hoping the man wouldn't notice, craned his neck in search of the policeman who had sauntered past the waiting room a few minutes before.

He believed in policemen, just as he had once believed in the soldiers who were quartered in barracks at the edge of the village. They had everyone's respect. People gathered to watch when they turned out to do drill on their horses, the proud officers at the front with their swords, the squads behind them, no less proud. The village constable saw that no one went too close to the horses, the way he saw to everything. But as the war went on, the number of soldiers dwindled and the few who returned weren't quite as proud. Then the war was over and recently the barracks had stood empty. Because of Versailles, people said. But the constable was still around, still seeing to things.

A detective was higher up than a village constable—much higher. The boy went with him.

The Donkey was closed. They came to the house where the detective lived. On the ground floor there was a pub, also closed. The boy was surprised that the detective lived in such a small, shabby house. Some of the boards had been ripped out on the stairs.

'Go careful,' the man whispered. 'Got to keep the noise down; people are asleep an' the walls are thin.'

For a moment the boy thought of turning back and returning to the draughty waiting room with its hard benches—and perhaps he would have been free to go. But instead of leading the way, the man had let the boy go first, and he was following so close behind that the boy could feel him.

The last six weeks had been quiet. No more missing boys—but nothing new on the existing cases either. Questioning the boys' friends and families continued to yield nothing. Our son, a fairy? Bloody cheek.

At first Lahnstein was suspicious of the lull, but as time passed he felt less on edge. The lack of activity since Haarmann had been under surveillance suggested that he was their man. All the police had to do now was sit tight until the urge overtook him again. He was bound to slip up eventually. Once or twice Lahnstein trailed Haarmann himself. He saw him buying and selling old clothes; sometimes he met Hans Grans. The pair of them waved when they saw Lahnstein, then went on talking as if he weren't there.

He had questioned Hans Grans, though Grans hadn't made it easy for him, making a run for it when he stopped him on the street. A brief chase had ensued through the alleys of Little Venice—nothing wild; it felt more like a sport. Lahnstein closed in on Grans and was thrown off. Closed in on him again. Lost sight of him. Glimpsed him again. Sprinted. Caught up with him. He didn't jump on him from behind, but simply took him by the jacket and held him fast. The gentle way. Grans didn't resist.

At headquarters he went through Grans' file with him.

State primary, secondary modern. His parents ran a stationer's and bookbinder's in the old town with a small lending library.

'I did a lot of reading,' Grans said.

He was blond and delicate—rather girlish—and wore his shabby clothes with style. He was cocky and articulate.

After completing school, he apprenticed as a tradesman in Söhlmann's metal goods factory where he embezzled money from petty cash and forged receipts to claim money from customers.

Then he was in Berlin for a spell—worked at Bergmann's Electricity Company, helped out at a post office.

In 1918 he was called up to the Heuschel Mortar Assault Detachment.

'Were you at the front?'

'Didn't get there, thank God. Sometimes I say more's the pity.'

He grinned.

He was discharged for unpunctuality. Spent his days loitering at the railway station and his nights in dives. Started trading in old clothes.

'How did you meet Fritz Haarmann?'

'We called him "the queer package".'

'Tell me more.'

'He gave me twenty marks.'

'What for?'

Grans shrugged.

'He said I was hairy as an ape. I shaved myself for him.'

'You lived with Fritz Haarmann?'

'He took care of me—didn't want me getting into any more trouble.'

'Did he treat you well?'

'Yes, he did.'

'I mean, was he ever violent when he was…excited?'

'He sometimes got carried away, but I just had to stick my tongue down his throat and he'd behave himself.'

'Right.'

The first criminal charges against Grans came in 1920. A stolen bicycle and unnatural fornication.

'I'm not one of *them*,' Grans said.

Nor am I, thought Lahnstein, and then wondered with horror whether he'd inadvertently spoken the words out loud. He looked nervously at Grans, but there was no reaction.

'One of what?' Lahnstein asked.

'The one-seven-fivers. Really, I'm not.'

Nor am I. This time he knew he'd only thought the words. But he didn't even want to think them, didn't want to involve himself in any of this.

'So why the charge of unnatural fornication? Why the nights with Haarmann?'

'I needed the money.'

'I see. But Haarmann had promised to take care of you. Why didn't he keep you out of trouble with the law?'

'He was behind bars for most of 1921; he'd no control over me.'

On 5 March 1921 Grans was arrested for receiving stolen

goods and sentenced to three weeks in prison and three years' probation.

During the years of inflation he was caught in a raid and arrested again on the same charge. But although he'd been selling fake gold and silver on the black market, he was able to prove that it had been legally purchased: he may have been a fraudster, but he wasn't a fence. The judge let him go; the probation remained.

'Very clever,' Lahnstein said.

'Thank you.'

He smiled charmingly.

Next item: pimping. One of Grans' girls stole a wallet from an engineer and passed it on to him. He swore she'd given it to him as a present. The girl was punished; Grans got off scot-free.

There was a further arrest, but again, Grans got off.

'Were you living with Haarmann all this time?'

'I moved about a bit, couple of months here, couple of months there. Sometimes I put up at Haarmann's, sometimes at the Christian Hospice or the Prince of Lippe.'

'Did he have other boys up to his room?'

'Only when we gave parties. He didn't need other boys; he had me.'

That charming smile again. There was something disconcerting about it, but Lahnstein couldn't work out what.

After two hours he let Grans go. There was nothing useful to be got out of him.

Lahnstein waited. Sometimes the lull unnerved him. He was

still caught in the same old trap: on the one hand, something had to happen or he'd never get a lead—on the other hand, nothing must happen, because it was his job to keep the peace.

One evening, as he entered the lodging house, he saw his landlady through the door of the sitting room, asleep in her winged armchair. He took off his shoes and crept past her, but she called out after him.

'Inspector.'

He contemplated ignoring her, but turned and walked back to the sitting room.

'Have you noticed?' she asked.

'What?'

'The price of meat's going up.'

'What of it?'

'It means supplies are short.'

'I know nothing about the meat market.'

'But you know about the missing boys.'

'Good night,' he said. 'Go to bed; it's not comfy in that armchair.'

'Any more gone missing?'

He shook his head.

'What did I tell you?' she said.

'Sleep well.'

He went to bed and slept, but not for long, because Lissy and August were soon flying through his dreams again.

Lissy had visited Lahnstein during his months of training. He was in barracks on an airfield in the hills of the Rhineland

and she put up at a pension in Kürten and came to the airfield every day. The drillmaster lent her a pair of binoculars and she sat on a chair at the edge of the runway and watched the men fly circuits and practise war manoeuvres. Lahnstein had acquired something of a reputation for his ability to read the wind and his prowess with a machine gun. He was happy; he was where he wanted to be. He had his flying and when he wasn't flying he had Lissy. It didn't bother him that the German advance had been held up in the west; things were going swimmingly in the east and they would soon come to an agreement with their western opponents. They had to. Maybe the war would be over before he was called up, but he would still have his training, and when they started building up civil aviation—with regular connections, like the railway—they would need him to fly for them.

Wanting to reward him for his good work, the drillmaster suggested that he fly a circuit with his wife. Lahnstein was thrilled at the thought of uniting his celestial pleasures with his earthly ones. He made the proposal to Lissy after a flight exercise, going down on his knees to her, his voice as solemn as if he were proposing marriage. She pulled a face.

He thought there must be some mistake and was about to start over, because surely she ought to be looking at him in delight. But no, he was going to have to put up with the look of undelight.

'What's wrong?'

She said she felt queasy, maybe she was expecting a baby, and who knew what effect flying might have on an expectant mother. He tried to talk her round. Where was the harm in cruising a few hundred metres above the earth with the wind in your face? That couldn't hurt anyone. He'd fly carefully, just a small circuit, nothing risky. She shook her head.

He stood up. It would mean so much to him to fly with her, he said—all the more so now that she might be expecting a child. It would be a baptism of air for his son or daughter, who would one day be a master of the skies like him. Lissy refused. Lahnstein got cross.

That evening, as they sat in a restaurant in Kürten, she apologised for being short with him—but she couldn't believe, she said, that his passion for flying meant more to him than her fear of losing him in the war.

'You won't lose me,' he said. 'The war's nearly over.'

'So many are dead,' she said. 'Gertrud and Rosalinde have lost their husbands. How will they cope?'

Lissy would never look favourably on an element that put her husband's life in danger. That was her last word on the matter.

Three weeks later Lahnstein had a letter from her saying that she thought she really was expecting a child. Was he pleased? She joked about the landlady of her pension who had allowed visits from men because she thought the Reich needed soldiers. 'I'd rather have a girl, though,' Lissy wrote, and that was fine by him.

How unfair it was, Lahnstein thought, that Lissy had to fly through his dreams for evermore, when she had so loathed the skies. He tossed and turned for hours in his narrow bed, but eventually he slept.

It was still too quiet. No more missing boys—in fact, nothing going on at all. Then, on 15 January 1924, just as Lahnstein was beginning to despair, a man and woman appeared outside his office. At last, things were moving again. Maybe this time there would be a lead.

Number Fourteen—Heinrich Koch, eighteen years old, born on 22 September 1905, apprenticed to a slipper-maker called Otto Moshage. On 13 January Heinrich had told his mother and father he was going to a masked ball. He never returned.

The boy's parents were distraught, reproachful, tearful. Lahnstein said the usual things. He still spoke with warmth, but the phrases came a little too pat.

'Thank you for answering my questions. Let me see you to the door.'

'Will you find him—alive?'

'We'll do what we can.'

'Was Haarmann being properly watched?' he asked Müller when they were gone.

'We had to rearrange the shifts. There'll be round-the-clock surveillance again as of the day after tomorrow.'

They spoke to the boy's friends and family who fed them the old familiar lies whenever they tried to steer talk round to the subject of male love. It was like talking through a fog. Lahnstein came away with nothing of use—no lead, no clue, not a single piece of the puzzle.

—

There was a lull of almost four weeks before Number Fifteen went missing on 10 February. Hermann Speichert, born on 11 April 1908, was just coming up to his sixteenth birthday and apprenticed to an electrical engineer at Mühe & Co., in Linden. In January his parents had noticed that he was coming home from work in clean clothes, but when they quizzed him about this, he dodged their questions and they were left none the wiser. The boy's father drove to Mühe & Co. to speak to the apprentice master and was told that Hermann hadn't shown up for four weeks. After a good deal of pleading, he convinced the master to give his son another chance and begged Hermann to take his work more seriously. Hermann said sulkily that he wasn't interested in engineering. He did eventually defer to his parents' request, but only after his father had issued threats. On 8 January he didn't come home. Two days later his parents went to the police.

It couldn't be Haarmann, that much was certain. They'd watched him round the clock, hadn't lost sight of him for a second. Lahnstein himself had spent the occasional night outside the house. Haarmann sometimes wasn't home until long after midnight, but he was always alone—no boys, no women. The man had been under permanent police surveillance. Could there be a better alibi?

'Didn't I tell you?' Müller said.

'Maybe there's more than one culprit. Or maybe this boy isn't part of the series and simply did a bunk.'

Müller gave him a scornful look.

Lahnstein's colleagues groaned and cursed. He sensed their loathing. There weren't enough of them for an operation like this. He called off the round-the-clock surveillance and replaced it with hourly spot checks.

Things went quiet again. March passed with no missing boy. 'Prices are falling,' said Lahnstein's landlady. In Munich the November putschists came up before the People's Court. Lahnstein read every line in the papers. The verdict was delivered on 1 April: Ludendorff was acquitted of the charge of treason; Ernst Röhm and five other men were sentenced to three months' imprisonment and a fine of a hundred marks.

Three months, Lahnstein thought. A hundred marks. For a coup that might have wiped out the Republic.

Hitler and three co-conspirators were sentenced to five years' imprisonment and a fine of two hundred marks.

Well, that was something.

Then he read the court opinion: the defendants had been guided in *their actions by a spirit of pure patriotism and the noblest and most selfless motives.*

They believed *that they had to act to save the fatherland and that they did nothing other than what the Bavarian leaders had recently planned to do.*

Didn't that sound like an acquittal? A moral acquittal and pathetic punishments. He put the paper aside and stirred his coffee. It was only a little over a month until the next elections, on 4 May. The Nazis had been banned from standing, but they had formed an alliance with the German National Freedom Party and were leading an aggressive election campaign, concentrating, among other things, on matters of security.

Lahnstein hoped there wouldn't be any missing boys in the weeks leading up to election day; it might affect the results.

At about this time, he happened to meet Haarmann on the street. They tipped their hats to each other, smiled tersely, exchanged cursory greetings. Ought Lahnstein to feel guilty for wrongly suspecting Haarmann? He thought not. It hadn't been unreasonable to suspect him. And it was still possible that he was guilty—that Hermann Speichert had run away or drowned in a nearby lake. A few paces further on, he saw a face he knew from headquarters. Haarmann was being shadowed—and a good thing, too.

The tedium of it all. He fretted, not knowing what to do. Others in his place might have come up with new ideas and methods, but Lahnstein was at a loss and growing listless. He slept longer and sat around in cafes, reading about the election campaign—or went to see Emma Burschel for cigarillos and a chat. He sensed that she was waiting for him, but knew he couldn't bring himself to make a move. He thought of going to a prostitute; that had sometimes done the trick. A different world, sheer lust—nothing, he told himself, to do with Lissy. The plane didn't fly when he lay on sordid beds.

One woman, well-disguised and cleverly made-up, turned out to be a boy. He hadn't noticed in the dim light—or perhaps he hadn't really looked. When he did realise, belatedly, already excited and aroused, he didn't jump up and run off, but let it happen, waiting for release before leaving, hurriedly, shamefacedly. He had felt a similar shame after visiting women. Was there a difference of degree? He couldn't tell and wasn't sure that he cared.

Six months after their release from the POW camp, a letter came from Franz. He told Lahnstein that he was living in Bonn (where he had a good job on the city council) and reminisced about camp life (nothing suggestive, thank goodness). What did Lahnstein say to meeting some time? He'd be happy to come to Bochum if Lahnstein was still living there. The envelope was addressed to Lahnstein's parents; Franz couldn't know that he'd moved out and now had a flat of his own down by the steelworks—small and noisy, but with all mod cons. Lahnstein pondered his reply and then forgot all about it. A while later he remembered and wrote back, saying that it would be good to see Franz again. He also wrote, untruthfully, that all was well with him.

In their next letters they arranged a time and place to meet. When the day came, Lahnstein realised with annoyance that he was rather excited.

Franz had grown plump, dressed like a dandy and smelt of eau de Cologne. He spoke at length about his work at the city council, although there was clearly little to tell. Lahnstein could have entertained him with tales of atrocious crimes, but he kept quiet about his work and Franz didn't ask. They talked about the war, the camp, other former POWs Franz was still in touch with.

'When's your train?' Lahnstein asked, at eight in the evening.

Franz looked at his watch. 'Oh,' he said, 'I've missed it.'

'Was it the last?'

'I fear it was.'

'What will you do?' Lahnstein asked.

'I suppose you have a sofa?'

'My flat's very small,' said Lahnstein.

'I don't take up much room,' Franz said, and for the first time, Lahnstein thought he saw something suggestive in the way he looked at him.

'You can have the flat,' he said. 'I'll sleep at my parents.'

'I can't accept that.'

Lahnstein insisted and showed Franz to his flat—one bedroom, a kitchen-cum-sitting-room, and a communal lavatory on the landing. He put clean sheets on the bed and Franz stood in the door and watched, his arms folded; Lahnstein could feel his eyes on him. He thought he might have to put up a fight to get past him into the little hall, but Franz moved aside for him. Their goodbyes were brief.

Lahnstein spent a sleepless night on his parents' sofa. When he returned to the flat early the following morning Franz had already left. They continued to write occasionally for a couple of years, then the correspondence petered out.

He couldn't, he thought, go to a prostitute in Hanover—not possibly. He'd have to go to Hamburg or Berlin.

On 6 April, Number Sixteen went missing—Adolf Hogrefe, born on 6 October 1907, resident in Lehrte. He was apprenticed to a mechanic in Hanover; every morning at six he took the train into town and every afternoon at half past five he returned home. On Mondays he attended trade school—or should have done. In early April, his mother and father were informed that he hadn't shown up for three weeks. For the first two absences he had produced letters of excuse from his parents, but not for the third time. Mr and Mrs Hogrefe knew nothing of any such letters. It seemed they had a forger for a son.

The boy's father was an engine driver, his mother a housewife. They were just like all the others Lahnstein had seen in his office; he could no longer tell them apart. At first he questioned them eagerly, greedy for details, hoping that this time there might be a lead. Then he realised that everything was the same as ever and his interest waned.

Number Seventeen went missing eleven days later—Wilhelm Apel, born on 4 June 1908, son of a turner, also Wilhelm Apel, of Leinhausen. Wilhelm junior was an apprentice at M. Neldel's shipping company in Nikolausstrasse, took the train to work every morning at six and returned at eight every evening. Since the New Year, his mother said, he had seemed very low: he sat at his books without reading them, and couldn't look her in the eye anymore. In February his father had caught him smoking and given him a severe reprimand.

They sat in Lahnstein's office, crying and crying.

Get out of here, I can't stand this. I can't stand you.

He didn't say the words out loud. What he did say, though, was, 'Is your son queer?'

The question slipped out, bald and direct. Their faces registered horror. Outrage.

He apologised. 'I didn't want to... I have to...'

They calmed down a little and told him what Wilhelm had been wearing the day he went missing. Lahnstein sent them on their way with the usual words.

'We'll take care of things.'

He'd had only three weeks with his son; they'd had seventeen years. And they had the nerve to come here and make this silly fuss.

Lahnstein saw seventeen boys parade past him in black suits, top hats in hand, their eyes turned on him. One by one they vanished into a mincer, over and over, until he fell asleep.

A sound woke him. Müller was sitting with his feet on the desk, looking at him.

'Had a little kip?'

'I've been thinking.'

'Come to any conclusions?'

'We have a new case—Number Seventeen. I've just seen his parents.'

'There's no end to it,' Müller said, and for the first time since Lahnstein had known him, he sounded sad.

'What can we do differently?' Lahnstein asked.

Müller shrugged. 'Anything of note in the new case?' he asked.

'No. Same old story.'

In the days that followed they went through the motions. Lahnstein kept warning himself not to get too blasé—to act as if it were only the first case or the third. But he didn't make much of a fist of it. He couldn't think of anything new or original to ask, and what use was originality anyway?

He asked one of Apel's friends whether Apel had liked dressing up in girl's clothes.

The boy looked at him in bewilderment. Müller suppressed a smile.

'No,' the boy said, 'why would he?'

Lahnstein dropped the matter.

'Nice question,' Müller said in the car on the way back to headquarters. Lahnstein stared out of the window; he didn't want to see the look on Müller's face.

He was growing more nervous and agitated by the day, haring down the corridors, shouting at people, calling meetings that were over in five minutes because no one had anything new to say.

He hadn't been as tired even in the war. He went to bed early, at about nine, so as to be wide awake the next day, vigorous and clear-headed, but invariably he woke only a few hours later. At first he thought it was morning and felt relieved to have had such a good night's sleep. Then he saw the clock. It was a shock every time. He lay awake for hours, brooding, thinking about the boys, Haarmann, the mincer, Lissy, Emma, Franz. When at last he fell asleep he dreamt that Fritz Haarmann was chopping up an almost grown-up August, and woke drenched in sweat. Then he returned to brooding, drifting back off to sleep only an hour before the alarm went off. He dragged his way through the days, barely speaking in meetings because he could think of nothing to say. He suggested to the chief of police that they impound all the old clothes bought and sold by Haarmann and make a nationwide appeal; maybe some of the missing boys' parents would come and identify their sons' clothes. Then, at least, they would have something to go on. The suggestion was rejected outright. It would draw too much attention to the case, too much attention to Hanover.

'Don't want it to look as if we're panicking,' the chief said.

I am panicking, Lahnstein thought.

'We must have Haarmann watched round the clock again,' he said to Müller one evening. It was half past ten and they were sitting at their desks, going through interrogation minutes.

'Last time things carried on regardless.'

'Maybe we weren't thorough enough.'

'What are you insinuating?'

'I'm not insinuating anything!' Lahnstein shouted. 'I just want us to find the culprit, and Haarmann's our only suspect.'

'I wouldn't call him a suspect,' Müller said.

'Fritz Haarmann is homosexual, he has previous convictions for related crimes and there are charges against him for chopping up a boy.'

'But there's no proof, not even evidence.'

'We need to search his room. Let's do it right away.'

'What, now? Have you cleared this with a judge?'

'Yes, I was planning to do it tomorrow. But why wait?'

He put his gun in his belt and set off at a run down the corridor, only glancing back once to see if Müller was following. He wasn't far behind, fumbling to get his pistol into his holster. They jumped into a car and told the driver to take them to Rote Reihe.

'We'll never catch him unless we take him by surprise,' said Lahnstein. He was trembling inside from all the humiliation, the futility.

They pushed open the front door to the building and stormed up the stairs, three at a time. On the top landing, Lahnstein hammered at the door.

'Open up, this is the police!'

Silence, then the same rustling sound as before.

'Open up.'

'D'you have a warrant?'

Haarmann's voice.

'We have judicial approval. We don't need a warrant for a house search.'

'For a night search you do. Paragraph 106.'

'Did you know that?' Lahnstein whispered.

'Rings a bell,' Müller said.

'Pity it didn't ring earlier.'

'It's not as if *you* knew.'

'I'd like to get some sleep,' Haarmann said.

'Are you alone?' Lahnstein asked.

'Of course.'

'Won't you talk to us a bit?'

'No.'

Lahnstein slammed his fist against the door and turned to leave, then changed his mind and banged energetically at the door across the landing.

A woman in her forties opened up.

'We'd like to talk to you about your neighbour.'

'At this hour?'

'Yes.'

She stood there, bewildered. Lahnstein showed her his warrant card.

'Well?'

'He's a quiet neighbour. That's all I can tell you.'

She closed the door. Lahnstein went to stop her, but Müller pulled him away.

'Forget it. There's no point.'

Müller got the driver to take him home. Lahnstein went into the pub downstairs and inquired about Haarmann and meat supplies, but the waiter couldn't answer his questions. It was Mrs Engel, the boss, he wanted to talk to; he should try again the next day. The place was a dive—dingy and grimy. Lahnstein wouldn't have eaten there if you'd paid him.

He wasn't going to go home, that was for sure; he'd make damn certain that Haarmann had no chance of disposing of anything. Back out on the street, he paced up and down for a while; then he leant against the lamppost across the road, and saw the lights go off and the windows darken. It was drizzling. He returned to walking up and down, and at length he sat down cross-legged on the cobbles and stared at the entrance, battling sleep until he lost the fight at about four in the morning. A couple of hours later he woke when someone pulled his gun out of its holster. He made a grab for the man's arm—he could smell him, but couldn't really see him—and after a brief scuffle the gun was his again. Lahnstein let the attacker go and struggled to his feet, frozen through and filthy. There was no point in searching Haarmann's room now; he'd had plenty of time to dispose of things. Nothing for it but to walk home—the world's most foolish policeman.

Two days later, on his way back from work, he heard the evening newsboys cry out his name.

'Inspector Lahnstein Defies the Rule of Law'

'Inspector Lahnstein Defies the Rule of Law.'

'Inspector Lahnstein Defies the Rule of Law.'

He stopped one of the boys and saw his own face on the front of the paper—and beneath the picture, the headline he had heard.

He bought the paper, keeping his face turned away from the boy, so that he wouldn't notice he was selling to the lead story's main character.

'That you?' the boy asked.

'No,' Lahnstein said, grabbing the paper and hurrying away, without waiting for his change—far more than he would usually tip. He thought of reading the article in a cafe and washing it down with a glass of beer, but he didn't know who he would be when he'd finished reading and decided against it. He rushed home and up the stairs, almost knocking over his landlady, and then at last he was safe in his room and could lock the door and start to read. He didn't even bother to sit down.

When he had finished he dropped back on his bed and lay there with closed eyes.

...rarely turns up to work...

...has committed a breach of law...

...wastes his working hours on political agitation...

...behaves outrageously towards the bereaved...

...lacks the expertise to handle a big case...

...reputed to be an enemy of the French...

...suspiciously lenient towards crimes in the one-seven-fiver scene...

The first thing he wondered was whether his father would read the article. Although a regional paper, the rag was known throughout Germany for its trenchant commentary, but it was run by the populist Hugenberg Concern, and ordinarily his father wouldn't have touched it with a bargepole. Ordinarily. But what if someone told him that his son was described in it as 'suspiciously lenient' towards one-seven-fivers?

Nothing in the article was substantiated; apart from the occasional quotation of something an anonymous 'colleague' had said, it was pure allegation. But it wasn't complete invention—only an exaggerated version of the stories circulating at headquarters. Müller. It had to be Müller.

There was a knock at the door—his landlady, urgently wanting to speak to him. He sent her away. He wasn't leaving the room ever—not in the foreseeable future, anyway, not for days, or weeks. He couldn't. He no longer existed in the outside world as the man he was; only as the man described in the newspaper—a man he didn't want to be, a man who wasn't him.

It was true, though, that he lacked the necessary expertise. And although he wasn't a one-seven-fiver, he didn't share the general abhorrence of male love and even had a degree of exp—He pulled himself up short.

Could you tell by looking at him?

Of course not.

He was little troubled by what his colleagues might think. Since the article simply repeated what many at headquarters were saying about him anyway, it could tell them nothing new about him, but only confirm what they suspected or thought they knew. The few more well-intentioned among them would recognise the rumours and have a pretty good idea of the journalist's sources.

Lahnstein didn't leave his room to eat, and peed in the washbasin to avoid having to go along the passage to the lavatory. He lay down on the bed hungry and thirsty, without even undressing, fell asleep early and woke soon afterwards to the usual nightly terror.

The next day he got up as always and left his room at the accustomed time. His landlady waylaid him, waving a newspaper in his face.

'Are you mixed up in this smut?'

'What smut?'

'One-seven-fivers.'

He pushed her aside, left the flat and walked to headquarters. He never had visitors to his room, male or female. How dare she, the old hag?

He wondered whether Franz would read the article—and what he'd make of it if he did. Perhaps, he thought, with sudden fear, Franz would write to the newspaper and tell of their intimacy at the camp. He was already dreading that evening's paper.

Oh, for God's sake, stop it.

He got some scornful looks at headquarters, but not as many as he'd expected. It felt almost like an ordinary day; there was even a new case to deal with: Number Eighteen, Konrad Heidner.

He hardly listened to the boy's parents. Three dead boys in a month.

He left headquarters in good time because he wanted to know what—if anything—the papers were saying about him. If the worst came to the worst, he told himself, he could buy them all up, but even as he thought it, he knew it was ridiculous. He felt fear and panic. They could write anything. If it wasn't true, it became true the moment it was printed.

But the newsboys had other topics; they didn't mention him. Lahnstein bought a stack of papers to trawl through, found a cafe and ordered a big glass of beer and a chaser. Thus armed he began to read. He started with the anti-Republican, anti-democratic papers, because they were the most likely to launch another attack, but there were no reports on him or the missing boys. Relief welled up inside him. He was out of the news.

But still he walked the streets a one-seven-fiver, a lawbreaker, an enemy of the French, a corrupter of the Republic—not the man he was, but the man the papers had made of him.

What would Haarmann feel when he saw the article—if he saw it? Gratification? Delight? One of us, he'd think, chuckling to himself. Lahnstein decided not to go straight home, but to head for Haarmann's house.

It was a still, clear evening; the first warmth of spring was in the air, but Lahnstein was struck by the emptiness of the streets. He blamed himself. He'd failed to solve the case and so people preferred to stay at home when it fell dark, afraid of the killer. The whole city had come to a standstill. What effect would that have on the bars and pubs and restaurants? When would they notice a drop in sales?

Outside the house, Lahnstein stopped and looked about him. There was no sign of anyone, though he'd given orders for round-the-clock surveillance to be resumed. Maybe it was a good sign. Maybe it meant that whoever was on the job knew how to watch without being seen. Lahnstein walked the whole length of the street, peering into doorways, but still he found no one. He took up watch himself and stayed all night, this time without falling asleep. But he saw nothing out of the ordinary.

At five in the morning a colleague from headquarters showed up. He was surprised to find Lahnstein there.

'Someone has to do it,' Lahnstein said peevishly and went home. He would have to talk to Müller.

There was no sign of his landlady. He lay down on the bed and slept for two hours, dreaming of the plane. Then he freshened himself up and walked to work. Outside headquarters he saw a large crowd, hundreds of people brandishing placards and shouting something he couldn't make out. It was only as he grew closer that he could hear the words: 'Protect Our Children.'

'Protect Our Children.'

'Protect Our Children.'

'Protect Our Children.'

The same words were printed on some of the placards. Another, clumsily rhymed, read: *Better Investigation for a Safer Nation.*

He saw the Hannappels, Magda Hennies, Mrs Koch, the mothers of Numbers Two, Six and Fourteen. They looked at him and he averted his eyes and dived into the crowd, jostled and was jostled, worked his way forward.

'Bloody fairy.'

He heard the words clearly and looked about him. A man leered in his face. Lahnstein scrabbled on; he was sweating heavily by the time he made it into headquarters. The chief of police was standing in the foyer, wringing his hands.

'Do something!' he yelled at Lahnstein. 'For Christ's sake, do something!'

On 26 April, Number Nineteen went missing—Robert Witzel, born on 18 March 1906, the second son of foreman Georg Witzel from Linden. Father and sons all worked at the Excelsior rubber works.

'Such a good boy,' his mother said. 'Always at home when he wasn't working. Only treated himself to a cup of cocoa in Cafe Kröpcke now and then.'

'Kröpcke?' Lahnstein asked. 'Do you mean Cafe Köpcke?'

'Maybe,' the boy's father said—a small man, almost tiny, half a head shorter than his wife.

'Maybe,' she echoed.

'Anything about this cafe?' the man asked, a glimmer of hope in his voice, as if it might be somewhere a person spent several days.

'Nothing particular,' Lahnstein said. 'I just wanted to be sure we're talking about the same place.'

'Oh. I see.'

The hope had gone.

These people made Lahnstein want to puke, sitting there with their tear-stained faces, pretending the boy was the world to them. Why hadn't they taken better care of the stupid little fairy if they loved him that much?

He immediately felt guilty for the thought. The boy was eighteen. He had to take care of himself. And it wasn't right to call him names.

Eighteen years they'd had with him.

On 26 April his mother had given him fifty pfennigs to buy himself something in town. She noticed that he'd put on his best Sunday jacket, though it wasn't a Sunday.

They had brought a photograph of their son—a thin-haired, bright-eyed boy. Lahnstein kept the photo and asked them to tell him precisely what the boy had been wearing the day he went missing.

He mustered as many men as he could, but he'd been expecting eight and only five showed up. *Off sick*, he was told. *Out on the beat.*

'Cafe Köpcke,' said Lahnstein, ignoring the familiar objections. *Not again. No bloody use anyway.*

They piled into two cars and drove to the cafe. Four men got out. No one knew where the fifth was; he'd vanished without a word to anyone. 'Might show up later,' one of the others said.

'We're going in,' Lahnstein called. 'Three men at the front, two at the back, no guns.'

A few boys would get away, of course. He'd have needed eight men for a proper raid. They charged off to take up guard at the entrances, wide-legged, broad-shouldered. Five or six customers tried to get out; two succeeded. Hands flew as people flung drugs on the floor. Then all was quiet.

Lahnstein counted twenty-two men and three women—not bad for an afternoon. Haarmann wasn't among them. Lahnstein stepped forward, pulling the photograph from his pocket.

'I'm going to go round and show you a photo—boy called Robert Witzel, eighteen years old. We know he was here from time to time. I'd like you to have a good look at the picture and give me a sign if you recognise him. All right?'

A few of the customers nodded; others smiled. Lahnstein did the rounds with the photograph, describing the clothes that Witzel had been wearing the day he went missing: a dark-brown plaid tweed jacket, fawn trousers, tan laced boots. No one owned to knowing him, though a number of them studied the photo at length, feigning concentration, some better actors than others. One or two actually took the matter seriously—thought he looked a bit like someone they'd seen in the cafe once, though they couldn't say for sure. In the end, Lahnstein left without getting anywhere, humiliated once again.

The general nervousness was exacerbated by the election results. Lahnstein was shocked at the figures. The Social Democrats had dropped 1.2 points to 20.5 per cent—no great loss in itself, but with the Independent Social Democrats out of the picture, Lahnstein had expected the SPD to absorb the best part of their votes, and this hadn't happened.

It's all my fault. His mind rattled.

The Communists were 10.9 points up. A disaster.

All my fault, all my fault. Oh, don't be so stupid. You exaggerate your own importance.

The German National People's Party climbed to 19.5 per cent, which left them almost as strong as the SPD. The National Socialist Freedom Party, their ranks swelled by the supporters of the banned Nazi Party, won an alarming 6.6 per cent. That made almost 39 per cent for the opponents of the Republic.

All my fault.

On 20 May a police constable burst into Lahnstein's office and stood to attention in front of him, gasping for breath.

'Some kids...' he panted '...kids playing down by the river in the Pleasance...' He paused, still fighting for breath. 'They've found a...' Another pause, filled with heavy breathing. 'Found a skull. Looks to have been washed up by the Leine.'

'Male or female?' Lahnstein shouted, jumping to his feet. 'Young? Old?'

'Don't ask me,' the constable said. 'I'm not a pathologist.'

'Go down to the cars, I'll be right with you.'

He went to Schackwitz and told him to come—they had a lead.

A lead, we have a lead. The words pounded in Lahnstein's head all the way to the Pleasance. Schackwitz rode in the front of the car; he sat in the back with the constable.

Moments later the skull was in his hands and he clung to it as if he would never yield it. A cluster of onlookers had gathered, most of them children. The constable kept them at bay. There was horror on some faces. Lahnstein stared at the skull.

'What do you think?' Lahnstein asked Schackwitz.

'If you'd let me have a look, I might be able to tell you.'

Lahnstein stared at it again. The eye sockets seemed to see although they were empty. The incisors were missing. He passed the skull to Schackwitz.

Schackwitz turned it and tilted it, rolling it gently in his hands.

'A man?'

'Probably a young man,' Schackwitz said. 'Missing incisors, a drilled molar without a filling—and look at this: see these nicks here?'

He held the skull out to Lahnstein, pointing to some fine scratches, delicate as hair.

'It looks to me,' he said, 'as if someone applied a razorblade or a sharp knife to the bone here to scrape off the flesh.'

'Thank you,' Lahnstein said. 'That's helpful.'

He asked who had found the skull. A girl came forward.

'I saw it first,' she said.

Lahnstein gave her a few coins.

The boy's corpse lay on the bed; the sheet was stained red, the pillow too. He made himself a cup of coffee. It burnt his lips and tongue, but he didn't care. Fastidiously he spread a cloth over the floor and set beside it a bucket and an oil-cloth bag. He laid out two tea towels, a thick chopping board, two big kitchen knives— one smooth-bladed, one serrated—one small kitchen knife and a cleaver. Then he lifted the corpse from the bed, put it down on the sheet and—after a quick glance—covered the face with one of the tea towels. He didn't like to see the eyes when he was working on the corpse; they had a habit of looking reproachful, or even angry.

With the smooth-bladed knife he made two incisions to open the abdomen. He took out the gut and then the stomach and slipped them into the bucket. Now the boy's abdomen was filled with blood; he mopped it up with the second tea towel, and wrung it out over the bucket, taking care not to spill any. This he did until all the blood had been mopped up.

Next, he used the serrated knife to saw open the rib cage. It took three incisions. He reached inside the ribs, pushed them up until they cracked at the top, cut them away with the knife and put them to one side. He took a gulp of coffee; he was sweating.

Back to work. He reached into the body, ripped out the heart and laid it on the chopping board. He cut it into fine strips and dropped them into the bucket. The same with the lungs and kidneys. A short pause. More coffee.

Time for the meat cleaver. First he severed the legs from the body, then the arms. He separated the flesh from the bones and stowed the choicest cuts in the oil-cloth bag. The rest he wrapped in waxed paper. He cleaned the chest and stomach cavities with the tea towel, then he cut off the penis and laid it on the chopping board. Seeing it there, he felt a sudden rush of horror. He didn't want to do this again. But the urge was too strong and, stirred to arousal, he sliced it up and threw the pieces in the bucket.

Now he opened a cupboard and took out a raffia mat, a few rags and an axe, set them on the little kitchen table, and put his cup down beside them. He cut the head from the torso and placed it on the mat. He peeled away the hairy skin, like a Red Indian scalping his victim—the thought made him chuckle every time. He cut the scalp into strips and threw them in the bucket. He turned the skull so that it was lying on its side and covered it with the rags to keep the noise down. Then he brought down the sharp side of the axe on the skull, over and over, turning the skull each time until it split into four. The brain went into the bucket; the splinters of bone were gathered up and put in a box along with the other bones. His work was done. All he had to do was scrub the floor and table and wash the linen.

7

Only one room: a dirty bed, dark stains on the floorboards, pale stains on the walls. A kitchen dresser, a small table, a sloping ceiling. The man had locked the door behind him. Hanover was a dangerous place, he said. You had to watch out. He put a bottle of schnapps on the table. The boy pondered a means of escape, but the key wasn't in the lock and he wouldn't be able to kick the door down in a hurry. Actually, though, the man was nice and all this was quite exciting.

The man sat on the bed with the bottle and two glasses and raised his schnapps to the boy in a toast. They clinked glasses and drank. The boy thought of how everything had started with that bottle of wine. It was because of the wine that he was to become a father, and now here he was, drinking schnapps with this strange cove in this squalid room.

The man chattered away, talking of criminal cases he had solved, and soon one of his hands was on the boy's leg, and the boy let it happen because the man seemed to think nothing of it, but went right on talking. Then, out of the blue, he asked the boy if he'd ever done it—did he and the others ever do it with each other? At first the boy didn't know what he meant, but then it dawned on him and he smiled in spite of himself.

'Got a little friend?' the man asked and his hand slid slightly higher. You weren't allowed to talk about that, the boy thought. And anyway, he hadn't. Heiner didn't count. He sometimes liked thinking about what had happened, that was all. This felt a bit like it—like that time in Heiner's room when his parents were out. Never again, he had said to himself afterwards, never ever, ever, and then it happened a second time—and a third. But there was no fourth time. By then he'd met Monika, and Heiner only looked at him with his big, yearning eyes.

Suddenly the man pulled him down onto the bed so he was lying on his back, the wall on one side, the man on the other. Then he planted a kiss on the boy's mouth and laughed. The boy laughed too. But the next moment he was seized by a howling fear. He had to get out of this place.

'I'd like to go now,' he said. 'I'd like to go back to the waiting room.' The man looked grave and shook his head. His grip was tight and the boy was trapped between him and the wall. Nothing for it but to stay. What happened next might be nice, though. It had been nice with Heiner.

—

Lahnstein got out at Zoo Station, crossed the road and went into Cafe Romanesque.

He ordered a cup of coffee and apple cake with whipped

cream. It was four in the afternoon and he had the evening to himself, but the thought daunted him. What would he do with all that time? He was free here; nobody knew him in Berlin except Georg, a policeman he had met in the military hospital and was going to see the following morning. Until then, the city was all his. He fetched an evening paper from the newspaper rack and settled down to read about the new government. There was no mention of the missing boys.

Then the word 'Viking' popped into his head and he couldn't concentrate any longer. On waking that morning, he had looked out of the window and seen it chalked on the wall of the house opposite: *Viking.* Just the one word, written in a clumsy scrawl, as if its author had been in a hurry, afraid of being caught. What was it doing there? Lahnstein could only think that it must refer to the Viking League, the paramilitary group that had succeeded Organisation Consul—the men who had assassinated Rathenau and Erzberger; enemies of the Republic, anti-Semites, right-wing terrorists. Was it some kind of message to him? A warning? A threat? *We know where you live. Watch out. Stop.* But stop what? Pursuing Haarmann? That would mean that Müller was involved. It wouldn't surprise him if Müller were a member of the Viking League.

Lahnstein thought of the boys, of Haarmann. The skull had been a disappointment; they couldn't trace it to a particular boy because a hole in a back tooth was hardly unusual and, though no one could say why, it looked as if the incisors hadn't been broken out until after death. Most interesting were the tiny nicks indicating that the boy had been boned—and suggesting that the rumours about human flesh were less far-fetched than imagined. That brought them back to Haarmann, the meatman. They had found the skull only yards from his room.

But had this got Lahnstein any further? Not a bit of it. Müller was still refusing to follow his line of reasoning and—as Lahnstein had recently discovered during a spot check—the supposedly constant surveillance remained patchy. Now, on top of everything else, there were the election results to worry about.

Lahnstein laid the newspaper aside. Marx would be Reich Chancellor again—and once again he would have the support of the bourgeois centre. But he would have no parliamentary majority without either the Social Democrats or the German National People's Party. The shambles would continue— one emergency decree after another. At least Ebert could be trusted, Lahnstein thought, as he paid the bill and went out. Ebert would do the right thing. It was a balmy May evening; people had shed their coats and were sitting at pavement tables. Lahnstein left his bag in a nearby hotel and took a bus to Alexanderplatz.

He wandered aimlessly, skirting the square and then veering off down an alley and looking in shop windows. He bought an umbrella just for the beautifully grained wood of the handle; you didn't see them like that in Hanover. Afterwards he felt foolish, walking around with an umbrella on a sunny spring evening—but he should have thought of that earlier.

He went into a pub and ate goulash washed down with

two glasses of beer. His thoughts were with Lissy and, determined that they should be nice ones, he decided against a third beer, afraid it might make him maudlin. He had a cup of coffee instead and then took his umbrella and went on his way, making for the street where the prostitutes plied their trade. Wilma had shown him the place once, before the war—a little nervous, but also proud of the seedy possibilities of her native city.

'Hello, Umbrella Man.'

He walked on without looking up. Cajoling whistles followed. He ignored them too.

'Don't be shy, sweetheart.'

He took refuge in a bar and knocked back a third beer after all. Not for the first time, he found himself thinking a thought he particularly loathed: that his grief at Lissy's death was a mere excuse for his inability to get close to another woman—that he had discovered something at the POW camp that suited him better.

On the other hand, he had never lusted after a man before or since. It was just that he sometimes felt this vague desire that he couldn't, or wouldn't, name—not even to himself.

Another beer.

He took a long draught. What nonsense it all was. Pure hysteria. He drained his glass and walked back to the hotel, realising when he got there that he'd left his umbrella in the bar. Never mind. He lay down, meaning to pleasure himself with thoughts of Lissy, but it was hopeless; he kept imagining her up in the plane instead of in bed with him, and eventually he gave up and fell asleep.

—

Lahnstein had arranged to meet his friend Georg in a cafe not far from Hackescher Markt. As he sat there waiting for him, he saw Verdun again—Verdun from the air: the churned-up earth, the shell-ravaged Fort Douaumont, the observation balloons, the smoke following an explosion. When visibility was good, Lahnstein had taken the plane up to watch the movement of the French troops behind the frontline; later he had dropped bombs, without much effect.

Georg had been two beds away from Lahnstein in the military hospital. Between them lay a man who was so thoroughly bandaged that they considered it no breach of etiquette to talk to each other over his white gauze head. They had no way of knowing whether he could hear them, but he certainly never complained.

Georg had been present at the capture of Fort Douaumont and then stayed on to man it. For weeks he was under constant fire from heavy artillery.

'Weren't you pretty much safe in the fort?' Lahnstein asked.

'The fort was constructed to ward off attacks from the east,' Georg said. 'From us Germans. But of course the French shot at us from the west, and that side wasn't anything like as well fortified.'

During one artillery attack, Georg didn't make it to the bunker in time and, though not critically wounded, he was hit by shrapnel in several places. It was then that he ended up in the military hospital. He was in the force too, so he and Lahnstein were able to swap police stories over the mummy's head.

When he arrived at the cafe, ten minutes late, they greeted each other warmly. Lahnstein was fond of Georg, though he never saw much of him when he was in Berlin. Georg had four children and avoided making appointments that would keep him away from his family outside working hours. And Lahnstein liked to take advantage of the big city (and usually managed better than he had the previous evening).

He brought up the situation in Hanover. Georg had a fair idea of what was going on from the papers.

'I need your help,' Lahnstein said. 'Can you spare me a couple of men to watch Haarmann for a few weeks? I need people I can rely on and I can't rely on anyone in Hanover. They're all in cahoots with Müller.'

'But why would Müller cover up for Haarmann? What does Haarmann have to offer?'

'I think he gives Müller tip-offs that allow him to pull off some pretty big coups. It's done wonders for his career. He won't want to risk losing that.'

'But can a man really be so cold-blooded as to accept tip-offs from a serial killer for the sake of his career? How many boys is it now? Eighteen?'

'Nineteen. You're right, but you have to think of his history—our history.'

'You mean the war?'

'Exactly. At first I thought I was looking for a former front soldier, someone who'd lost all sense of proportion and come to see death—even mass death—as a matter of course. During the war, people forgot that everyone has a right to life; they lost their sense of life's value.'

'That's true,' Georg said. 'But it is possible to recover that sense, Look at us. Look at most of the men we fought with. We've stopped killing.'

'We have, but not everyone succeeds. Think how they were at each other's throats in the election campaign.'

'Yes, all right. But a serial killer is of a rather different calibre.'

'I'm not so sure. As I said, I started off assuming that the culprit was an ex-serviceman, and because Haarmann had been in prison all through the war, I didn't pay enough attention to him at first. My mistake. But in a sense, I think my hunch was right. Only it isn't the culprit who's been brutalised by the war; it's his friends at headquarters who've lowered their standards and forgotten the value of life. They'll stop at nothing for their careers. And they were almost all at the front. We think the war's over, but it lingers on.'

'Possible. And in Müller's case plausible. But what about the others? Has Haarmann given them a leg up the ladder too?'

'I haven't worked it out yet, but I assume Müller's pulled one or two up with him. They're quite clannish at headquarters—almost all monarchists. Vote for the German National People's Party, if not worse.'

'You think they vote Nazi?'

'A few. Not many. Most of them would rather have the Kaiser back than this Hitler.'

'Well, he's safely behind bars for the next five years, thank God.'

Lahnstein thought of mentioning the Viking League, but

decided not to bother. He didn't want Georg thinking him paranoid. It was bad enough thinking it himself.

'Not half long enough. A scandalous verdict. Ridiculously lenient when you think that he tried to overthrow the state. Did you read the court opinion?'

They discussed the political situation for a while longer and then Georg had to get back to work. He said it wouldn't be easy to spare two men, but if the chief of police could be made to understand the urgency of the matter, he ought to agree.

Three days later two policemen arrived in Hanover from Berlin. Lahnstein had found them a room in lodgings and arranged to talk things through with them there, because no one was to know they were working for him. They agreed to spend most of their time at the railway station, disguised as tramps. Many of the missing boys had arrived in town on the train and Lahnstein thought the station might be a good place to track Haarmann down. He showed the Berliners the photograph from Haarmann's file and warned them to steer clear of the local police; no one was to be trusted. He came away feeling hopeful.

On 27 May, Wilhelm Mayhofer, a metalworker by trade, and his wife Therese, widow of the late Mr Abeling, came into Lahnstein's office to report the disappearance of Ferdinand Abeling, Therese's son.

'How old is the boy?'

'Eleven,' said Therese Mayhofer. 'Born on 14 March 1913.'

Number Twenty.

'Eleven, really?'

'I think I ought to know.'

'Forgive me, of course you do.'

'Anything wrong?' the man asked. 'With his age, I mean?'

What could he say? Was it wrong to go missing at the age of eleven—any more wrong, say, than at the age of twenty-two? It was an absurd notion, but the low age had outraged him; none of the other victims had been that young (if victims they were—but he no longer had any real doubts on that score). A mere child—and he mustn't even begin to think about whether an eleven-year-old's flesh was particularly tender—tenderer even than a sixteen-year-old's—but of course it was too late; the thought was there. Such horrible thoughts came unasked in the world he now inhabited.

'He asked me for twenty pfennigs before he left for school,' the woman said. 'I gave it him, but I didn't ask what he wanted it for. I regret that now, because it might have given you some clue as to what he did last. Before he went missing, I mean. All we know is that he went to school, same as every day.'

He wondered why she spoke so coolly and mechanically, her voice all on a level, without a trace of grief. What was the matter with her? All the others had been sad or distraught. Her husband sat impassively at her side.

Lahnstein asked the usual questions. He was annoyed that Georg's policemen hadn't managed to prevent the boy's disappearance—but then, they'd only been on the job for two days. At least he now knew that the culprit was still active; it surely couldn't be long before they had him.

'Have you forgotten anything that might be important?' he asked.

They thought for a moment and the woman shook her head.

'May I ask you one last thing?' Lahnstein said, though he'd sworn to himself he wouldn't.

'What?'

'You don't seem sad.'

The woman looked at her husband; he looked at her.

'We're very sad,' the woman said. 'When my first husband, Ferdinand's father, was dying, I promised him I'd take good care of the boy, and now he's gone. I ask myself where he could be. Maybe with the other boys. Do you think they're all together somewhere, all in one place? They might be, mightn't they?'

The same mechanical tone.

'I think it's unlikely. What kind of place do you have in mind?'

'I don't know. You're the policeman. You know about these things.'

'But we've never had a case where a lot of people disappeared and all turned up in the same place.'

'Maybe this time,' the man said.

'Who knows.'

Müller came in. He looked annoyed to see the two of them there, as if he didn't need another case just now—but then, who did? I do, Lahnstein thought, not for the first time. I need new cases to keep coming until Haarmann slips up and I can solve them all.

'Anything of note?' Müller asked, when the couple had left the office and Lahnstein was back at his desk.

'The boy was only eleven.'

'Pretty young. Someone's acquired new tastes, has he?'

'At least you've come round to the idea that we're dealing with a homosexual aggressor.'

'It would certainly be a solution.'

'I beg your pardon?'

He looked sharply at Müller; Müller smiled at him.

'I said, it would certainly be a solution.'

'But what do you mean by that?'

'I don't mean anything. I simply said it would be a solution.'

'I grasped that much. I just wonder what you mean by *solution*. A solution to the case? To homosexuality? To the situation in Hanover?'

'Take your pick.'

Lahnstein got up and planted himself in front of Müller's desk. 'I know exactly what you mean,' he said. 'It's out at last. You think it would be the best solution for this city—and maybe for the entire world—if as many one-seven-fivers as possible were to disappear. Because you hate their guts, because you think they're scum—loathsome creatures that deserve to be stamped out. You're jolly glad someone's made a start on the job, and you're damned if you're going to break your back trying to stop him. As far as you're concerned, he's doing the right thing; he has the solution for the one-seven-fivers. That's why we aren't getting anywhere.'

Müller rose from his chair and stood facing Lahnstein.

'Now it's my turn to tell you something. You were called to

Hanover more than six months ago to solve this case, because apparently we couldn't manage on our own; we needed this genius from Bochum to come and sort us out, speed things up a bit. And where are we now? Not a jot further. Things are going on just the same as before. But that has nothing to do with me. You're the boss here. You're responsible for this disaster, not me and not anyone else here.'

They faced each other for a few seconds, then Lahnstein turned and walked back to his desk. He sat down and stared at the notes he had made on the Abeling case. Müller had said nothing that he himself hadn't already thought in some form or other—nothing, that is, except the one sentence: *But that has nothing to do with me.* Those words were a lie.

He looked up. 'By the way,' he said to Müller, 'were you a member of Organisation Consul?'

Müller looked at him in surprise. 'That's illegal,' he said.

'That's why I asked if you *were* a member. Before the organisation was banned.'

'No, never.'

'Do you approve of what they do?'

'Do I approve of the part they played in helping to overthrow the Bavarian Soviet Republic? We've been through all that. I don't need to repeat myself.'

'And Erzberger's assassination?'

'I am, as you can probably imagine, no great admirer of Erzberger. He signed the Armistice of Compiègne though we hadn't even been defeated. For four years our men sacrificed themselves at the front to hold off the enemy, and then along comes the Republic and forces this disgraceful peace on us.

That's as much as I need say on Erzberger.'

'He signed because Ludendorff and Hindenburg were too cowardly. They knew that the front couldn't hold any longer and left it to the Democrats to seal the defeat of the German Reich.'

'Nonsense.'

'That's all you have to say? Nonsense?'

Müller was silent.

'Rathenau. What do you say to Rathenau's assassination? He didn't sign the armistice.'

'How should I know why he was assassinated?'

'Because he was Jewish?'

'Maybe.'

'Organisation Consul was anti-Semitic. It was also anti-Social Democrat.'

Lahnstein looked at Müller. Not a hint of emotion.

'Noske,' Müller said, 'had no objection to the part played by Organisation Consul in helping to put down the Soviet Republic in Munich.'

Lahnstein saw triumph in Müller's eyes. He searched for a response, but could think of nothing that wouldn't have discredited Noske. There was a short silence. Then he said, 'When Consul was banned, their people founded the Viking League. Are they active in Hanover?'

'What do I know? I've nothing to do with them.'

'It's possible that they're threatening me.'

He hadn't meant to say that; it had slipped out.

'It's also possible that you're sick—thinking that every last thing that happens in this country has to do with you. Do you know what that's called?'

He waited for an answer, but Lahnstein said nothing.

'Megalomania.'

Müller stood up, put on his coat and left the room without another word.

That evening Lahnstein went to confer with Georg's policemen in their lodgings. They were dismayed at their failure to prevent the boy from going missing, but were at least able to report that Haarmann had been sighted at the station. He had shown up quite late one evening, shortly before eleven, chatted to a few people, including the constable on duty, had a look in the waiting room and then sauntered off again.

'That's our lead,' Lahnstein said. 'This is where we get him.'

He bought two bottles of wine and went to see Emma.

'There's something I'd like to ask you,' she said, when they were eating.

'You can ask me whatever you want.'

'There was an article about you in one of the papers.'

'You read it?'

'My brother gave it me.'

'Does your brother know about us?'

'What is there to know? That you buy cigarillos from me? That I have you to supper?'

'Did you tell him that?'

'All I told him was that there's a detective from Bochum who comes here for his cigarillos. A nice man who once helped me out of a disagreeable situation.'

'You mean the time I saved you from that cove who kept making you get up on the stool?'

'Yes, it was thanks to him that we met.'

'So what is it you want to ask?'

But he knew.

She put down her cutlery. Then she picked up the fork and played with it, pressing the prongs into the heel of her left hand and examining the tiny dents in her skin. Eventually she looked him in the eyes.

'They write a load of filth, I realise that. Those rightists are out to wear you down.'

'The Reds too. But...'

'No but. I have a question, that's all. Please don't be cross with me.'

'Are you queer?'

It was Lahnstein, not Emma who put the question. He almost spat the words and Emma looked at him in alarm.

'That wasn't what I wanted to ask, really it wasn't. Not like that.'

'I'm sorry,' he said and the regret was genuine. 'I've been under a bit of strain lately. All these boys going missing, it's dreadful.'

She remained sullenly silent.

'Do you worry about *your* boys?' he asked after a while.

'You mean because there are so many going missing? They're all older than mine.'

'One was eleven. Your eldest is eight.'

'Don't scare me. They're not alone much. I take them to

school in the morning and shut up shop in the afternoon to pick them up. My brother helps out if I can't make it. I manage.'

Don't say anything, Lahnstein told himself. For God's sake, hold your tongue—but he knew he wouldn't be able to restrain himself. 'Do you really trust your brother?' he asked.

'He once told me about a boy called Friedel Roth or Rothe or something.'

Friedel Rothe, Lahnstein thought. The first missing boy. The one who wasn't given a number.

'It was in the war, soon after Fritz came out of prison. He said he was very fond of Friedel and was going to spend a lot of time with him. The way he said it, I knew he was trying to tell me he was fond of boys—fond in general, I mean. You know what I'm saying.'

'Yes.'

'I don't mean you know because you yourself…oh dear, it's too complicated.'

'It isn't really,' he said. 'It only gets complicated if you try to fight what's inside you.'

'I often asked about this boy, but after a while my brother said he'd gone, done a bunk. Then I read in the newspaper that the boy's parents were looking for him. But maybe he turned up later, I don't know.'

'And now, with all these boys disappearing, don't you wonder whether your brother isn't involved in some way?'

'Of course I do. I'm frightened. On the other hand, I trust Fritz. I see him here with my boys, playing so nicely with them. He dotes on them—and never a word or gesture out of place. I can't believe it of him.'

Silence.

'Is Fritz your main suspect?'

'I'm afraid he is.'

'And you visit his sister and don't mention it to her?'

She stood up.

'Get out,' she said.

'I didn't know at first that you were his sister.'

What a pathetic thing to say, he thought, as soon as the words were out. But it was the truth.

'Stop lying. You could have told me.'

He, too, stood up.

'You just wanted me to split on my brother.'

Say something, he thought, don't let her get away with that. Don't be cruel to her. She isn't even necessarily right.

'Get out.'

He went over to her and put a hand on her shoulder, but she shook it off and pointed him brusquely to the door.

At the weekend he took a cab to the small airfield outside town. His hands were clammy and more than once he was on the point of telling the driver to turn back, but each time he stopped himself.

Wooden barracks. Three warplanes, one an Albatros, unarmed.

He settled himself at the edge of the airfield and waited. For a long while nothing happened; he sat in the grass, the sun beat down, insects flitted about. He thought of his last flight.

—

An unsettled day—looming clouds broken by patches of deep blue and rays of dazzling light. Lahnstein was under orders to locate British reinforcements. There were two German planes in the air. British planes spotted in the distance had disappeared from sight, causing some alarm.

He didn't notice the attack until his tail rudder was hit. The British plane must have been invisible in the glare. Lahnstein's plane tipped, spun and plummeted towards the ground. His first attempts to steer failed; then the rudder began to respond again and he was briefly able to stabilise the plane. He couldn't prevent it from crashing, but the manoeuvre did at least save him from freefall, and he managed a kind of emergency landing before the plane overturned. When he came to, he was trapped in his seat. He saw farmers coming towards him, carrying rakes or pitchforks. Then he heard a strange rumbling sound and a tank rolled out of a wood, accompanied by British infantry. He was relieved; he'd been afraid the farmers would lynch him, but as it turned out, they were perfectly friendly, helping him out of the plane and smoking with him until the Brits arrived. *You lucky bugger.* His war was over.

A familiar sound jolted him from his thoughts and he jumped up and started to run. Then he stopped. It was the throb of an Albatros engine, the whirr of a propeller, but it wasn't war anymore. Lahnstein shaded his eyes with his hand and watched the plane roll onto the airfield. There were two men on board and another two standing next to the barracks. Lahnstein sat back down on the grass. He sized up the wind and issued silent instructions to the pilot. Not that the man didn't know what he was doing—and the chances were, he'd shot down more planes in the war than Lahnstein. But that's over now, Lahnstein told himself. None of that matters anymore.

The airfield was bumpy and the Albatros quivered and wobbled as it rolled into position for take-off. Then it stood there, the propeller belting round, the noise of the engine swelling, and at last it set off, lumbering at first and then faster. Lahnstein leapt to his feet again, throwing up his arms as if to stop it, but the wheels lifted off the ground, the machine rose, climbing rapidly, flying towards the sun.

Keep an eye on the sun, Lahnstein thought. No, nonsense, keep an eye out for Lissy and August. Bring them back if you can. He sat down again and stayed there on the grass, his head cradled in his arms, until the Albatros returned an hour later. He watched it land in safety, despite a strong crosswind, then got up and went to the barracks.

The pilot was young and didn't have the bearing of a military man, which made him more approachable. Lahnstein asked if he might fly with him some time—not for long; half an hour would be plenty. This puzzled the pilot—why should he take a complete stranger up in his plane? But Lahnstein told him of his passion for flying and had no need to pretend; the old yearnings were still there, waiting to be called up— his love of the skies, his longing to fly with the birds. The pilot was unimpressed, but he muttered something about the cost of flying and after that it was easy. Lahnstein named a price, and when the pilot looked sceptical he named a higher one. They set a date for the weekend after next.

Lahnstein walked all the way home because there were no cabs out at the airfield.

On Monday he was summoned to the chief of police again, and again he prepared himself to be sacked.

This time, too, Noske was there. A brief how-do-you-do and he pitched straight in. 'We are the adversaries everybody wants. No one has anything to fear from us, while we have everything to fear from them. Do you follow me?'

'I don't know that I do, quite.'

'Look at it from the point of view of a kidnapper,' Noske says. 'It's an interesting scenario. Just imagine you're a kidnapper and you get caught—who would you want to catch you? Democrats, monarchists, Communists, Nazis?' He leant forward. 'Well? What's your answer?'

'I don't quite understand…'

'What I'm asking is, who do you think would treat you fairly—or even leniently? And who wouldn't?'

'Luxemburg and Liebknecht were arrested in a republic…'

'Well, of all the…' Kogel snorted.

Noske made a calming gesture.

'…a republic,' Lahnstein continued, 'governed by Social Democrats.'

'You have a point there. But that was an exception. There had just been a revolution; they'd brought chaos on their own heads. All that aside, though, what do you say? Who would make the fairest adversary?'

Lahnstein thought of his time as a prisoner of war in the

hands of the Brits. They'd been fair on the whole.

'Democrats, of course.'

Noske clapped his hands together. 'Of course,' he cried, 'democrats. Obviously. Not everyone, I am afraid to say, is a democrat, but everyone would choose a democrat as his adversary. Even a criminal. Because Communists are ruthless. We know that from the Bolsheviks; they don't hang back.'

He fired an imaginary rifle.

'And judging by what I've heard about Mr Hitler and his friends, I wouldn't expect mercy from the Nazis either. As for the monarchists—well, it would depend whose hands you fell into. Some stick to the law; some don't.'

'I wouldn't want to fall into the clutches of the Viking League either,' Lahnstein said.

'Indeed, indeed, they're a nasty lot. First the Ehrhardt Naval Brigade, then Organisation Consul and now the Viking League. Different names, but the same old rabble.'

Kogel made a fierce, but furtive, gesture, which Lahnstein took to mean that he should change the topic.

'You didn't mind conniving with them in Munich,' said Lahnstein, a slight quiver in his voice.

'We've been through all this,' said Noske. And then, after a pause: 'No one could know that they'd back the Kapp Putsch and turn terrorist.'

They're threatening me, Lahnstein wanted to say, but didn't.

'The only dependable ones are the democrats,' Noske said abruptly. 'Do you see what I'm getting at now?'

It took Lahnstein a few seconds to remember what they'd been talking about before they got on to the Viking League.

'Of course. But method aside, we have no suspects to interrogate at present anyway.'

'I know, I know. I meant in theory. Do we have what it takes to solve the more difficult cases?'

'Are you thinking of torture?' Lahnstein asked.

'That,' cried Kogel, 'is an unacceptable insinuation.'

'It's all right,' said Noske. 'It's all right.' He turned to Lahnstein. 'What do you mean?' he asked.

'Let's say we have a kidnapper who has a child in his clutches, locked away in some hole, hungry, thirsty, afraid. There's only one thing the child wants—to get back to his mum and dad. And there's only one person who knows where the child is.'

'The kidnapper,' Noske said.

'Exactly, the kidnapper.'

'We've strayed rather far from the subject,' cried Kogel, wringing his hands.

'No, no, it's all right,' Noske said. 'It's an interesting case.'

'Do you torture him or don't you?' Lahnstein asked.

Silence. Lahnstein thought of his father's decision.

'No answer,' Noske said.

'That's your answer?'

'Yes.'

'But isn't that—with all due respect—cowardly? Aren't you shirking responsibility?'

'In a sense, but there's no other way. The question can be posed, but not answered—not before the fact. You just have to do the right thing when the time comes.'

'But what is the right thing? How do I know?'

'You just do, believe me. We had no plan for the revolution; we had no plan for dealing with the Bolsheviks. But when the time came, we did the right thing. And please, don't bring up Luxemburg and Liebknecht again.'

'Might the right thing entail torture?'

'Stop banging on about torture. Think. What can you do to find the culprit?'

'What do you want me to do?' Lahnstein asked. 'Make constant raids? Pick out people at random and harry them until they give me a tip-off? And then, if that leads me to a suspect, torture him until he confesses to the crimes because he can't take the pain anymore? What would be the good of a confession obtained like that?'

'Oh, for heaven's sake, that isn't what I said at all. You're misapprehending me.'

'That is indeed a gross misapprehension of the governor's words,' Kogel said sternly.

'Then I really don't know what you mean.'

Noske leant back in his chair. He propped his elbows on the armrests and his chin on his folded hands.

'Don't be over-fastidious; use the full latitude of the law. There are grey areas; not everything is regulated to the last detail. Be pragmatic. That's all I'm saying. The rest will become clear in the circumstances.'

He stood up, followed by Lahnstein and then Kogel.

'But you have to create the circumstances,' Noske added.

'We have a lead,' Lahnstein said.

'Good, good. Never forget what we, your comrades, did in the early days of the Republic. We provided liberty, but also security. Believe you me, both are essential. Without security, liberty reverts to its opposite. But we know what we're doing; we managed then and we can manage now. We mustn't let the side down. We must show everyone that we can take care of security—that it's not the prerogative of other parties. I'm depending on you.'

He shook Lahnstein's hand with a kindly look.

Kogel gave Lahnstein a nod. 'I'll speak to you later,' he said.

On 5 June another boy went missing—Friedrich Koch of Herrenhausen, born on 4 May 1908. He was a metalworker's apprentice and the son of a decorator, also Friedrich Koch.

Why did they insist on passing their names on to their sons? Why were they so vain? Why did they want copies of themselves?

Lahnstein looked at Friedrich Koch senior. He was dressed in his work togs—a white jacket and trousers of a coarse material, daubed with a bright, Kandinsky-like pattern, the jacket straining over his belly. What made you want a doppelganger? Lahnstein thought—and then pulled himself up short: You've got to stop this, you'll have to get yourself transferred, you can't carry on like this. You hate these people who've lost their sons and it's no good hating. You'll have to go.

The boy had caught the train to Hanover on 5 June to go to trade school with his friend Paul Warnecke who was also a metalworker's apprentice. On the way there, on the corner of Tiefental, a gentleman had come up to Friedrich, tapped his boots with his walking stick and said, 'Well, boy, don't you remember me?' A moment later, Friedrich had gone off with the man. That, at least, is what Paul told the decorator.

'Have I understood this right?' Lahnstein said. 'A man approached your son?'

'Yes.'

'Tapped his boots with his walking stick?'

'That's what Paul said.'

'Asked, "Don't you remember me?"'

'Those were his words.'

'And Friedrich went off with this man?'

'Do you think he was a bad person?'

'Did Friedrich ever mention a man?'

'Don't think so—did he?'

The decorator looked at his wife. She shook her head.

'Do you know where this Paul Warnecke lives?'

'The Warneckes are neighbours of ours.'

'Good, then we'll go and see them now.'

'What? Right this minute?'

'Right this minute.'

'But Paul'll be at work, at the garage.'

'Then we'll drive to the garage. Do you have the address?'

'5 Lindensteig.'

He took the woman's coat down from the hook and helped her into it.

Paul Warnecke was a sturdily built boy of medium height, broad-shouldered as an athlete. When Lahnstein arrived at the garage with the Kochs, he was fiddling around with a car, his dark-blue overalls stained, his face smeared with oil, his hands almost black.

'Would you mind leaving us alone for a moment?' Lahnstein asked the foreman who had shown them over to Paul. The man toddled off reluctantly.

Paul seemed shaken—guilty, almost. Lahnstein sketched the encounter with the man with the walking stick.

'Can you confirm that?'

'Yes.'

'Do you know the man?'

'No.'

'I'm going to show you a photograph and I'd like you to tell me if the man in the photo is the man with the walking stick, all right?'

He held out Haarmann's picture. Paul didn't take it, but said quickly, clutching his wrench, 'Don't know him.'

'Are you sure?'

'Yes.'

Lahnstein felt boundless disappointment.

'Look again closely, please. Don't you see any likeness? It's an old photo; the man may have changed. Look at his eyes. Do they remind you of anyone?'

The boy looked for a moment, but shook his head.

'They're piggy eyes, can you see that? Proper little piggy eyes. Do you know anyone with eyes like that?'

'No.'

'No one at all?'

'Only one person.'

'Who's that?'

'Fat Lutz. Boy I knew at school.'

'All right, lad, pull yourself together, you're to take this seriously. I'd like you to go over to that sink there, wash your hands and then come back, take this damned photo in your clean hands and have a jolly good look at it. Have you got that?'

He had raised his voice. The Kochs looked up in alarm; the foreman glared at him from the other side of the garage. Paul obeyed instructions and, after studying the photo at some length, returned it to Lahnstein.

'No idea who it is.'

The boy's intimidation had left him. He was defiant now, Lahnstein thought, as if, standing at the sink, washing his hands, he had come up with a strategy to save himself. My mistake, Lahnstein said to himself. You can't let the pressure off for a second. Not one second.

He put the photo away and said, 'All right, we'll move on to the next question. And no lies, please.'

He turned to the Kochs. 'Would you mind leaving me alone with the witness for a few minutes?'

'Not at all.'

'Thank you.'

They retreated to the edge of the garage, looking faintly offended.

'Have you even been in Cafe Köpcke?'

The boy's eyes registered alarm and then indifference.

'No.'

'Really?'

'Never.'

'How about the Queer Kettle?'

The hint of a grin, followed by the same look of indifference. No, he'd never been there either.

'But you know what goes on in Cafe Köpcke and the Queer Kettle?'

'There's only men there.'

'That's right. There are only men there. And you know, too, don't you, that those men are fond of other men?'

'They kiss.'

'That's right. They kiss. Was Friedrich ever in Cafe Köpcke or the Queer Kettle?'

'Never mentioned it.'

'Did you ever see him go in one or other of those places?'

'No.'

It might be the truth; it might be a lie. Lahnstein could guess Paul's state of mind: it hardly made a difference to him anymore whether or not he told the truth; all he was interested in was giving what he thought were the right answers. If it was right, it was true. Once someone was in that state of mind, you couldn't keep him from lying. Nevertheless, Lahnstein made one last attempt.

'You know that a lot of boys have gone missing?'

Paul nodded.

'It's possible that terrible things were done to those boys— maybe for days or weeks or even months on end. Anything could have happened to them. All you can imagine and worse.'

Paul looked uncomfortable.

'You and Friedrich are very good friends, aren't you?'

'Not with kissing, though.'

'No, I know, not with kissing. But Friedrich may be in trouble just now; it's possible that he's being tortured, starved, raped—made to suffer all kinds of imaginable and unimaginable things. And it's possible, too, that when his tormentor has had enough of him, he will kill him. You know we found that skull—it was in the papers. Now, I'm going to tell you something else, that we didn't tell the papers. It's a secret and I'd like you to keep it to yourself. Do you think you can do that?'

Paul nodded. Lahnstein took a step towards him and lowered his voice.

'There were scratches on the skull. Do you know what that means?'

He shook his head.

'It means someone scraped the flesh off the cheekbones.'

He ran a hand over Paul's cheek. The boy started back. The foreman and Friedrich's parents turned to look.

'Why would anyone do that?' Lahnstein asked.

'Dunno.'

'Think about it. If someone scrapes the flesh off, it's because he wants it for something. What do you think that something might be?'

He saw the horror on Paul's face.

'You know the answer. He wants to eat the meat, or sell it to others to eat. You're the only person I'm telling this. We didn't tell the press, because we didn't want to cause panic. Do you understand?'

'Yes.'

'What I'm getting at is this: it's possible that your friend

Friedrich will soon be butchered—that his flesh will be scraped from his bones and sold as pork or beef or horsemeat, or what have you. It's possible that this meat—your friend Friedrich's meat—will soon be on sale in the butcher's where your mother goes for her sausages and her Sunday joint. So if you don't tell me what you know pretty sharpish, you might find yourself eating a piece of your friend Friedrich for dinner.'

'I don't know nothing.'

He whispered the words, his eyes filled with horror.

Lahnstein grabbed Paul's arm.

'I don't believe you. You know the man in the photo. You know that Friedrich is a regular at Cafe Köpcke—and maybe you are too. You just have to bloody well admit it.'

The boy gulped. Lahnstein let go of his arm.

'Well?'

'It's not true, what you're saying. Leave me in peace; I've got to work.'

He made a sign to the foreman who hurried over.

'I won't finish my work if this copper keeps me any longer.'

'Are you done talking?' the man asked Lahnstein, glad to be able to take control again.

'Yes, we are, thank you.'

'I'll be back,' he said to the boy.

He instructed the driver to take the Kochs home and returned to headquarters on foot. On the way he saw 'Viking' scrawled on two walls, but nowhere near his digs.

Bloody Section 175. It was the cause of all his problems. No one dared speak the truth because they were afraid of being thought queer—of running into trouble with the law, attracting scorn.

When he got to Little Venice he marched straight to the Golden Hind, flung open the door and stormed into the kitchen. The waiter followed him; the cook barred his way and asked what he thought he was doing. Lahnstein flashed his warrant card in their faces, then made for the ice chest and began to take out pink and red and grey slabs of meat.

'Here,' he yelled, holding up handfuls of the stuff. 'Animal or human? We're going to find out.'

Waiter, cook and cook's boy stared, uncomprehending. Lahnstein looked about him at the squalid kitchen: cockroaches scuttled across the floor; mould was growing over the sink.

'Filthy hole,' he shouted. 'I'll send in the hygiene officers to take care of this place.'

He stormed out, his hands still full of meat, and charged through the dining room, knocking down a woman so that he had to stop and help her up. People looked on in alarm. At last he made it onto the street and raced off to headquarters, where he tore up the stairs and along the corridors, calling out Schackwitz's name long before he'd reached pathology and could thrust the meat into his hands. Was any of it human? He needed to know. And not just a visual examination, please. He had to be absolutely certain.

He fetched himself a cup of coffee and took it back to the office. A glance at Müller's face told him that word of his dramatic entrance had already got about.

'I'm going to get that Haarmann of yours,' he said to Müller. 'Depend upon it.'

'I won't have you refer to him as *mine*.'

'Yours or not, I'm going to get him.'

'Not with that pair of scarecrows on the job.'

'Who are you talking about?'

'Those pathetic-looking coppers loitering in the station like a couple of down-and-outs. That's who.'

'It wasn't your business to blow their cover.'

'I wouldn't have dreamed of it. They blew their own cover, with their ridiculous carrying-on.'

Oh well, Lahnstein thought. Another wasted chance. He'd wait for the results from pathology, talk to Paul Warnecke again, and if none of that yielded anything, he'd hand in his notice.

'I have a witness,' he said to Müller. 'Just you wait.'

'And who might that be?'

'I'm not telling you. I can't trust you.'

'If you say so.'

Lahnstein went to the railway station to tell Georg's men that they could abandon their observation posts and keep an eye on Paul Warnecke instead, but he found them gone. Surprised and angered by this, he continued to their lodgings, a little uneasy in his mind. Perhaps it had been foolish of him to tell Müller he had a witness; he might work out who it was.

There was no answer when Lahnstein knocked at the door of the lodging room, and the door was locked. He knocked again and said it was him, Inspector Lahnstein. There was a mumble and the sound of someone heaving himself out of bed and shuffling across the room, then the door opened and Lahnstein found himself looking into a swollen face, battered blue and red. The man turned away and hobbled back to bed. In the other bed, his mate was in a similar state.

'What happened?' Lahnstein asked, though he had a pretty good idea.

'Five men,' said the man who had come to the door. 'Dragged us into a doorway. They were armed with truncheons and coshes.'

'Police truncheons?'

'Could've been. We put up a fight, but we didn't stand a chance.'

'Do you need a doctor?'

'I think we'll be all right.'

'Is there anything else I can do to help?'

'The landlady brings us food.'

'Go back to Berlin when you're well enough,' Lahnstein said and left the room.

The following day, Lahnstein was in the news again. He came across the article by chance, as he perused the papers in a cafe after work, and it came as a shock. The photograph caught his eye first. It showed a fighter plane on an airfield, surrounded by German soldiers, one of whom, in a pilot's cap, was singled out by an arrow. It was a moment before Lahnstein recognised himself, and only after that did he take in the headline: *Coward Hunts Serial Killer.*

They had done some research into his wartime career, speaking to airmen from his squadron who had agreed to be anonymously quoted.

He was no ace.

The fellow was always being shot down.

He didn't exactly beg for missions.

The French could be glad when he was in the air.

Only two planes, it's laughable.

There followed an extensive report on his mendacious habit of 'flaunting' a much higher number.

Müller.

The paper deplored the recklessness of entrusting someone who was *not a proper man* with the task of *catching our children's murderer*. The governor of the province mustn't tolerate that. After all, *despite his failings*, Noske *was at least man enough to stand up to the left-wing extremists and prevent Bolshevism from getting a hold in Germany.*

The article ended with the words: *Detective Inspector Robert Lahnstein is a disgrace to Hanover, a city famous for its association with war heroes Ernst Jünger and General Field Marshal Paul von Hindenburg.*

He looked about him; no one was paying him any attention. He got up and put his coat on, then, sitting down again, carefully unscrewed the newspaper from its wooden stick, rolled it up as quietly as he could and concealed it inside his coat. The wooden stick he slipped under the chair. After counting coffee money and a large tip onto the table, he left the cafe and tossed the newspaper into a litter bin. He looked at the sky, wishing he were up there with Lissy. Ten more days.

—

Crossing the bridge over the Leine the next morning, he saw people standing by the water, and stopped to investigate. Fifty-odd men and women armed with fishing nets and rakes were poking around in the water, plunging their tools into the river, pulling them out again and looking to see if they'd made a catch.

Lahnstein went down to the bank to watch. A dead fish in a net, a scrap of cloth on a rake. It was warm; he lit a cigarillo. An old man pulled a gasmask out of the water.

'Might be my son's,' he said, not speaking to Lahnstein, but loud enough for him to hear.

'Was your son in the war?'

'Saw it through to the end.'

'I hope he made it home.'

'He did. Only lost an ear; he got off lightly. Even his gasmask survived. Don't know where it's got to, though.'

The man studied the mask, threw it back in the Leine, dipped his rake in the water and drew it through the shallows; the bottom of the river was invisible in the murk.

'What's going on here? What are you looking for?'

'Bones.'

'What kind of bones?'

'Boys' bones.'

He'd known all along, of course, but had hoped for a different answer all the same. He smoked in silence.

'A lot of boys gone missing,' the old man said. 'Nobody knows where or why. It's a mystery.'

He pulled out his rake. Nothing.

'A lot of boys,' Lahnstein said. 'Any of them relations of yours?'

'Not directly. Friend of mine's missing his grandson. I wanted to help. The cops do nothing.'

'Who's organised this?'

'A woman.' He gestured vaguely at the other side of the river.

'A woman?'

'Mother of one of the boys. Her son's been missing a long time.'

'Dreadful,' Lahnstein said.

'It's like the war. I know how it feels.'

'But your son came home.'

'One of them. Not the other.'

'I'm sorry.'

'You wait for the next letter—wait and wait. Sometimes the letters take a while. You tell yourself not to be afraid, not to panic, but you can't help it. Then a letter comes and it's the one you've been dreading.'

'I'm so sorry.'

They were both silent.

'I'm going to go and speak to that woman,' said Lahnstein.

'She's a good woman,' the man said. 'Soldiers on, doesn't give up.'

'Goodbye and all the best.'

'Good day to you.'

He crossed the river at the next bridge and walked along the bank until he saw a woman he knew.

'Magda, what are you doing here?'

'You might say I'm doing your job, Comrade Detective.'

She had on wellington boots under her long skirt and was wearing a white blouse. Her hair was loose. She was leaning on a long fishing net.

'I'm sorry,' she said. 'I didn't mean to turn on you like that. It slipped out.'

'Not to worry. What's all this in aid of?'

'We need to know for sure that the boys were murdered. Because until then, you're going to think they're with the Foreign Legion, or with their girls, or—' she paused briefly '—young men.'

She seemed glad the words were out. 'We need proof of crime to get you to make more of an effort. The one skull wasn't enough.'

'We're doing all we…'

'I know, I know. It's all right. Don't take it personally.'

He threw his cigarillo into the water and looked at the people on the bank. For a moment they seemed to have found a common rhythm and were moving their poles through the water in sync, like dancers in a comic ballet. To taunt me, Lahnstein thought.

'This isn't about Adolf,' Magda Hennies said. 'Really it isn't. Though I'd do anything for him. I just can't bear to hear those Communist pigs attacking our comrade governor because he supposedly can't provide security.'

'I can't bear it either,' he said, after a while.

'Have you read that rot, too?'

'Yes, I have.'

'All that tripe about traitors of the working class looking on as the working class bleeds—working-class children, in this case. What do the Communists know about the working classes? In Russia they're stamping them out and here they lure gullible halfwits with promises no one can keep—they least of all. All talk, they are.'

'Halloa,' somebody called.

'I won't let anyone speak ill of Noske,' she said.

'I've got something.' The same voice. On the other side of the river, a man was brandishing a net, in which something white glinted in the sun.

Probably a skull, Lahnstein thought, curiously indifferent. And he crossed the bridge with Magda Hennies to inspect the find.

On 14 June, Number Twenty-One went missing—Erich de Vries, born on 4 May 1908, fifteen years old. He was apprenticed to a trader in Hanover. His parents shouted at Lahnstein.

Almost as soon as they were gone, he began to tidy his desk, making a pile of things he would take with him and a pile of things he would leave behind. The meat he'd asked Schackwitz to test had turned out to be mutton, beef and pork. The mutton was old and well-nigh uneatable; the landlord would get into trouble. But the skull from the Leine was human and, like the previous skull, showed signs of scraping, probably with a sharp knife. It was most likely that of a boy or a young man. There was no doubt that they were dealing with a serial killer, but it was no longer up to Lahnstein to solve the case. He was out of here. He had a new name at headquarters: the Butcher.

The chief of police called him to his office. For once, Noske wasn't present. Lahnstein was given an insistent though not strident lecture, a long list of things to do. He barely listened.

There were people demonstrating outside headquarters again, almost a thousand this time. Placards, chanting, bitterness. Lahnstein saw no chance of getting into the building unscathed and was on the point of turning away when a fist hit his right ear. The blow came slantwise from behind; he didn't see it coming and took it full on. A sharp pain stung him and he stumbled, failed to catch himself, came down hard on the cobbles and passed out.

The evening papers printed a picture of him being carried into headquarters on a stretcher.

The right-wing paper titled it: *Republic Hunts Killer.*

The left-wing paper: *Noske's Best Cop.*

He went into Emma's tobacconist's. He was out of cigarillos—and besides, he wanted to talk to her. The last time he'd tried, she'd turned him away. She was standing behind the counter, serving a customer. Their eyes met for a second when he walked in, but she said nothing and immediately averted her gaze. The customer paid and left the shop. Lahnstein stepped up to the counter.

'The regular?'

'Emma, let's talk.'

'The regular?'

'Emma, please.'

She reached up to the shelf for his usual cigarillos and set them down on the counter.

'They're for free,' she said. 'And now, please leave my shop.'

He took them and went.

When he drove out to the airfield at the weekend, he asked the cabbie to wait for him. The pilot was already there and had got the plane ready. Lahnstein was afraid he would tremble, but he remained calm. He walked once around the plane, checking it the way he had checked planes in the war. All in order.

'Are you a pilot too?' the pilot asked.

'I was, in the war.'

'Do you want to steer?'

'No, I just want to be up there again.'

The pilot threw him a suspicious look, but didn't ask how many planes he'd shot down; Lahnstein breathed a sigh of relief.

'Temperature?' he asked.

'Twenty-seven degrees.'

'Wind?'

'Light north by northwest.'

Sitting in the plane as the propeller turned, a little jerkily at first and then smoothly, Lahnstein thought he was going to faint. He saw black spots and felt lightheaded. The plane rolled off. Lahnstein groped for the pistol inside his jacket, as if it could protect him.

Pull yourself together, he told himself. Your wife and son

are up there. You can get up there too. He began to feel calmer.

The plane rumbled along the runway into the take-off position. As it stood there, faintly swaying, the pilot turned and held up a thumb questioningly. Lahnstein responded in kind, the pilot opened the throttle and, with that slight time lag that Lahnstein remembered so well, the Albatros accelerated and took off. She wobbled a little at first, but soon there was sufficient airflow over the wings and she was cutting a straight line through the sky.

Lahnstein got through the first few minutes by concentrating on the ground, the countryside, the earth. Then he risked lifting his eyes to the bright, cloudless blue. He forced himself not to keep looking at the sun, and after a while he felt himself relaxing, yielding to the plane's rhythm, the steady quiver of her body, the little dips and rises caused by thermal currents. Now and then he looked down and saw flat fields, farms and villages, waving children.

It was lovely up here; he felt no fear, only a great peace. Perhaps, he thought, it wasn't so awful for Lissy and August to have to keep on and on flying. Perhaps it felt as good for them as it did for him at this moment—the plane sliding easily through the air over green pasture, yellow cornfields, red roofs. It was quiet, too, once you were used to the throb of the engine and the roaring of the wind—and by now, he supposed, they must be. Lissy and August.

They flew through some minor turbulence, then it grew calmer again. The pilot pointed out a plane on the right, flying the other way, a little distance above them.

No, thought Lahnstein, it's not possible. After a while it

had no longer mattered to him whether Lissy and August were really flying in a plane for all eternity. He rather supposed they weren't. But since they flew in his dreams and his dreams were a part of his life, such common sense was hardly relevant. In his reality they flew; the rest was neither here nor there. This plane, though, was a shock to him. He stared and stared. It was another Albatros with two people inside. Lahnstein couldn't make out more than their silhouettes against the sun, but it seemed to him that the person in the back was smaller than the one in the front.

His heart pounded. Then the pilot of the other plane waved and he saw that it wasn't a child in the back of the plane, but a man. The pilot was a man too. Lahnstein waved back.

He had forgotten, he thought on the taxi ride home, how lovely flying was when you weren't at war. Even if Lissy and August really were trapped in an Albatros, they had a pleasant enough existence in the sky; they didn't have to suffer. It was a comforting thought.

On 22 June Lahnstein sat at his desk, arranging his pencils into squares and triangles. He was alone in the office. At 6 p.m. Müller's phone rang. At 6.04 p.m. it rang again. This time Lahnstein walked over to Müller's desk and picked it up.

'Hello. Müller's phone.'

It was the railway police. They had Haarmann and a boy at the nick; apparently there was some confusion.

'Fritz Haarmann?'

'That's the one.'

'With a boy?'

'Yes. Haarmann wants to talk to you.'

'To me?'

'Yes. You are Inspector Müller, aren't you?'

'I'll be right there. Tell him I'm on my way.'

At the railway police station, Haarmann was sitting at one end of a bench and a young man of about sixteen or seventeen at the other end.

'What are you doing here?' Haarmann asked.

Nothing about him had changed since their last meeting. He was wearing the same clothes and sucking on a cheroot, his hat on his lap, his walking stick propped against the wall.

'I thought Müller was coming,' he said accusingly to the station policeman.

'So did I,' said the policeman.

'Inspector Müller is tied up, but the matter interests me. What exactly's going on?'

'This boy here has forged papers,' the policeman told Lahnstein.

'Let's have a look.'

A blatantly forged identity card in the name of Kurt Fromm, twenty-one years old.

'What's your real name?'

'Kurt Fromm,' the boy said.

'But you're not twenty-one.'

The boy said nothing.

'Seventeen,' Haarmann said.

'Fifteen,' the boy said.

'Where do you live?'

'In the welfare home,' Haarmann said.

'I'd like the young man to answer the question himself,' Lahnstein said.

'It's the truth,' the boy said.

'All right, so you live in the welfare home. And what's the young man doing here with Mr Haarmann?' Lahnstein asked, turning to the policeman.

'Haarmann reported him for carrying forged papers.'

'Why did you do that?' Lahnstein asked Haarmann.

'I like to assist the police where I can.'

'He does indeed,' said the policeman.

'How do you two know each other?' Lahnstein asked the boy.

'We've been hanging around together for a few days.'

'He's a wicked one, that boy,' Haarmann said. 'Lies and steals.'

'What do you mean by *hanging around*?'

'I treated him to a glass of juice.'

'I'm asking the boy.'

The boy sat slumped on the bench, his hands between his legs, his head bowed.

Then he raised his head and told Lahnstein that the gentleman here had approached him at the station four days ago and he'd gone back to the gentleman's digs with him because he needed somewhere to sleep and was sick of the home, and the gentleman had started doing funny things to him...unnatural fornication.

'Stop lying!' Haarmann yelled, leaping to his feet.

Lahnstein planted himself in front of him. 'Sit down and let the boy finish,' he said.

Reluctantly, Haarmann sat down. Müller came in.

'Heard we've caught a little fraudster.'

'We're listening to what he has to say first,' Lahnstein said. 'You said *unnatural fornication*,' he said, turning to the boy. 'How do you know the expression?'

'Heard it in the home.'

'And you know what it means?'

The boy nodded, grinning.

'Go on then,' Lahnstein said.

'Haarmann kept me locked up for four days.'

'But you could have shouted. I'm sure Mr Haarmann wasn't at home all that time.'

'He's lying,' Haarmann said, furious. 'You can tell he's lying. Are you just going to stand there and let him lie?' he asked Müller.

'Let the boy talk,' Lahnstein said. 'Now then, why didn't you yell for help?'

Shrugs.

'Did this man force you into fornication?'

'He seduced me into it,' the boy said.

Haarmann burst out laughing. 'Honestly!'

One morning, the boy said, he woke up because Mr Haarmann was holding a sharp breadknife to his throat. It gave him a real shock. Then Mr Haarmann asked if he was afraid of death.

'I said I was,' said the boy.

'And then?'

'He took the knife away. And when he was gone I legged it.'

'With my money!' Haarmann cried.

'All right,' Lahnstein said. 'Between you, you are under suspicion of various offences, one of them serious. Mr Haarmann, you're coming back to headquarters with me.'

'You've nothing on me.'

'That's what I'd say,' Müller said.

'We'll see about that,' Lahnstein said. 'Inspector Müller, may I ask you to walk on Mr Haarmann's left; I shall secure his right. And you,' he said to the policeman, 'accompany the boy, please. We'll walk to the car and drive to headquarters.'

But Müller was right, of course. There wasn't enough evidence to convict Haarmann—not even under Section 175.

The boys were always keen for it. Hey, Fritz, *they'd call out, when they saw him by the theatre,* take me home with you, Fritz. Let's do some polishing. I want a go too. *Most of them, a hundred, for sure, he'd sent on their way, knowing what might happen—though it didn't always happen; plenty of times it hadn't.*

What would they do with him now? What could they do? They had nothing to convict him on, no corpse, nothing. He'd taken care of that—made sure they wouldn't find anything. Six or seven trips it took him to get rid of one of those boys— four to the privy with the bits and pieces, and two to the river, under cover of darkness, with the bucket of bones. He quite liked standing by the water, throwing the bones in. Like feeding ducks. Some nights there was a moon.

Hey, Fritz, can you put me up? Got nowhere to kip tonight.

The detective would ask him a lot of questions—he knew all about that. But he'd be on his guard and wouldn't give anything away.

Eight thirteens are a hundred and four. Oh yes.

Wasn't so uncomfortable, the plank bed—you got used to it. But the irons chafed his arms and legs.

When he was out of here in a couple of days he'd wait a bit. Even if the dolly boys did call out to him—Hey, Fritz, let's do some polishing—*he'd leave them be. There was no knowing what might happen once he had a boy in his bed and they started cuddling. Lovely it was. The boy up against the wall so he couldn't get away. Such pretty boys, too. And they were still there when he woke in the mornings, alive and wanting to cuddle some more. Except when he'd bitten their throats—then they were all pale. But what could he do? It wasn't that he wanted it to happen; it just did. Caused him no end of bother.*

If they were still alive, they came back. Hey, Fritz, take me home with you.

Go away. Get lost. Give me a rest.

Thirty-six take away eleven is twenty-five.

Eighteen divided by three is six.

Fourteen sevens are...

Hey, Fritz.

Emma was good to him; she might pay him a visit. But was it worth her while? A couple of days and he'd be out. They wouldn't keep him just on account of a few dolly boys. That would be going too far. Just a few dolly boys.

He hoped they wouldn't hurt him—beat him and such. It wasn't allowed, but he'd heard that didn't stop them. The dolly boys weren't worth the trouble, though. No one cared about them.

...ninety-eight.

8

Sometimes she stood on the hill outside the church and watched for him. She didn't know whether or not to hope he would come back. In fact, she did know: it was better if he didn't. She wouldn't follow him either, though it would be easy enough to find him— he'd be in Dunedin, with the penguins. But what would she do out there?

Father was strict, but there was an understanding between them that she liked: if she worked hard, she would go to Göttingen to study law. And she did work hard: music lessons, reading, general education lessons—every afternoon after school, every evening. No slaving away over a stove for her; she would be a woman with a profession and one day she would be a successful lawyer. They were agreed on that, father and daughter. He didn't have a son. Thank heavens, she thought—but maybe that was unfair. He might have given her a good education even if there had been a brother.

She felt nauseous and was constantly throwing up. But it would soon be over. It wasn't a bad thing, she thought, if Father believed she was sickening for something. After tomorrow, she might be sicker still for a few days. She had made much of her ailments, so that Father wouldn't be unduly worried when she had to take to her bed. He was concerned enough as it was, though for the wrong reasons.

Maybe she shouldn't have told Martin; she should simply have seen to things and then slowly broken with him. She had been wanting it keenly for some time—and then there he was in church, taking pews out, putting pews in. A pretty boy. In the books she read with Father, her favourite heroines were those who did what they wanted: Emma Bovary, Anna Karenina. He had probably intended the books as warnings, but she saw a challenge in them. Though Emma and Anna followed their desires, they were submissive rather than assertive; there was, she felt, room for improvement.

Too bad that the boy hadn't taken care. She hadn't either, of course; she'd needed his release for her own, so it had been inevitable. But bad luck all the same. It needn't have been one of those days; it was just the way things had turned out. She only hoped it wouldn't hurt.

If she hadn't said anything to the boy he wouldn't have run away—wouldn't have had to go to Dunedin. But he'd wanted to go anyway; all she'd done was give him an excuse. That was one way of looking at it, at least. It was sad for his parents, though. They spent hours shut away in Father's study with him and didn't miss a single service—as if that could bring him back. Even Father didn't believe that.

She'd made the doctor's appointment herself. Independence—that was another thing Father had taught her. It was a pity, of course, but she'd made up her mind. Just had to hope it wouldn't hurt.

—

He climbed the stairs to the fourth floor until he was once again at Haarmann's door, only this time he had the key. His heart raced as he turned it in the lock. The door stuck. He gave it a shove and it sprang open. The room was about seven or eight square metres. A narrow, iron bedstead with a thin mattress, the striped ticking flecked with stains. Lahnstein paused for a moment, thinking of the agonies suffered in that bed.

Beside the bed stood a table with turned legs and a chair; a small shelf above the table held a clock; a cooking pot hung from the ceiling. The floor was stained and beneath the pot it was singed black; presumably Haarmann lit a candle under it when he wanted to cook. There were pictures on the walls, one of Major Schill and his troops, others in oval frames. A three-legged washstand jostled for space with another table and chair; you could hardly turn around. Lahnstein went to the little window and looked out between the floor-length curtains at the street below, the synagogue, the lamppost where he had stood watch.

He opened a small cupboard and found knives and a wooden-handled cleaver with a slight curve to the blade. Was that rust or blood?

—

He went across the landing to the neighbours' flat. A dog barked when he knocked, and a woman came to the door— the same woman he'd seen before.

'You again. We've nothing to tell you.'

She made to shut the door.

'I wouldn't do that,' Lahnstein said. 'Circumstances have changed. Mr Haarmann is in custody on strong suspicion of murdering at least twenty-one boys. We're going to have to find out if there was any complicity on your part.'

She let him in. The flat was about twice as big as Haarmann's and consisted of two rooms. The woman introduced herself as Mrs Lindner. Mr Lindner, a glassworker, was in an armchair, drinking beer from a bottle. Another woman emerged from the second room in a dressing gown; she looked as if she probably received the occasional male visitor to keep herself in pocket.

'Our lodger, Mrs Lapaschinski.'

Leaning against the doorframe, Mrs Lapaschinski pulled a cigarette from her dressing-gown and put it in her mouth without lighting it.

Lahnstein stepped over to the wall abutting Haarmann's flat and knocked on it.

'Flimsy,' he said. 'Must let a lot of noise through.'

'We hardly hear a thing,' Mrs Lindner said.

They had got the idea that Haarmann took in waifs and strays.

'Brought them home and gave them a place to sleep. A good man.'

'They were a peaceful lot,' Mr Lindner added.

'No screaming?'

'Screaming? Go on with you.'

'Sometimes gave us a bone for Fuchsia,' said Mrs Lindner.

'He was always taking bowls of meat down to the Engels,' Mrs Lapaschinski said.

'And carting bundles of clothes up and down the stairs,' said Mr Lindner. 'Must be an old-clothes man.'

'When he moved in,' Mrs Lindner said, 'he told me he was a bit of a hermit, so he wouldn't be using the privies in the yard; he preferred to use a bucket in his room.'

'We'd see him on the stairs with it,' Mr Lindner said.

'Covered with a cloth.'

'He was up and down an awful lot with that bucket,' Mrs Lapaschinski said.

'Like a dose of salts,' Mrs Lindner said.

'Bowels, I expect,' said her husband.

'The privies are permanently blocked,' Mrs Lapaschinski said. 'It's a disgrace.'

'That's all we can tell you,' said Mrs Lindner with a shrug of her shoulders.

The three of them looked at him, dazed, frightened.

'What'll happen to us?' Mrs Lindner asked.

'Have a good think,' Lahnstein said. 'Try to remember as much as you can, and come to headquarters around noon tomorrow. Then we'll see.'

He went downstairs and into the pub, where news of Haarmann's arrest had already arrived. Elisabeth Engel, the landlady, sat down at a table with Lahnstein and launched into her life story. Only one of her eight children had survived childhood—Theodor, the young man over there behind the bar. Eighteen he was and sometimes helped out here, though actually he worked for Continental. Her husband was a steward for the Social Democrats; both men were committed members of the Cyclists and Gymnasts Association 'All Hail'. She herself had Communist leanings. In times such as these, Communism was the only solution.

'Don't you agree?' she asked Lahnstein.

'Tell me about Haarmann,' he said.

She gulped and sighed and told him that she'd met Haarmann at the wholesale market soon after the war. She'd gone there for horsemeat, but there was hardly any to be had—or only at a ludicrously high price: sixty pfennigs! Haarmann's was going for thirty-five, so they were soon doing business—clothes as well as meat. She'd sold on old clothes for him; they'd done a lot together.

'He's a good fellow, if you ask me. Honest, decent.'

'The clothes were probably stolen,' he said.

'Begged, that's what he told me.'

She described how he would come into the pub kitchen with great slabs of meat and set about making sausage and brawn. Pork meat, it was. He'd dice it and plunge it into boiling water, then pour off the fat and bottle it. Or he'd put the meat through the mincer, season it well and stuff it into mutton guts.

'It was delicious sausage,' she said. 'Everyone loved Haarmann's sausage.'

'Haarmann, too? I mean, did he eat his own sausage?'

'Of course. Many an evening he sat here with us over sausage and beer.'

But in April, she said, they'd taken ill after eating Haarmann's meat and hadn't touched it since.

'But you still sell it?'

She shrugged.

'Do you have any here?'

'Not at the moment.'

'Are you aware that it might be human flesh?'

'Oh, no, I don't think so. No, never. I'd have noticed.'

'How?'

She looked as if she might burst into tears.

'Listen, this is what I want you to do: you'll gather up all the clothes from Haarmann that are still in your possession. Then you'll make a list of all the names and, where possible, addresses of the people to whom you have sold or given clothes that came to you from Haarmann. Later today, a constable will call, and you'll give him the clothes and the list. Is that clear?'

She nodded.

'Those trousers were from Haarmann,' she said, pointing at her son.

'Off with them then.'

'What, now?' the young man said.

'Yes, right now.'

'Just a moment, I'll go upstairs.'

'You'll do nothing of the sort. You'll give me those trousers at once.'

He took them off standing behind the bar, wound a

greasy towel around his hips and emerged from behind the counter with the trousers over his arm. They were made of coarse, brown cloth. Lahnstein rose from his chair.

'I'll take what meat you have, too.'

He followed the young man into the kitchen and watched him package it up.

'Were you ever up at Haarmann's?'

The boy looked at him in embarrassment and nodded.

'You were lucky.'

He nodded again.

The first time Lahnstein interrogated Haarmann, he only laughed. Müller was present, but silent throughout. The only way to get a confession out of Haarmann was to amass enough evidence to push him into a corner, give him a good rattling. Negotiation was impossible because he had nothing to gain by confessing; the death penalty was inevitable. Instead, Lahnstein appealed to his conscience. He talked of the parents' suffering, of the people of Hanover who had a right to know the truth and needed to be assured that there would be no more killings. And so on.

The chief of police had, at last, given Lahnstein a free hand in the search for clothes, and he issued two appeals. One called on people to deposit at headquarters any clothes they had bought from Haarmann, Grans or their intermediaries. The second was addressed to all parents whose children had gone missing, asking them to come to Hanover police headquarters in two days' time, to examine clothes that had possibly belonged to the missing boys. Lahnstein had both appeals delivered to the telegraph office. That evening all the local papers led with the same news: Fritz Haarmann had been arrested on suspicion of serial murder.

When Lahnstein arrived at headquarters the following morning, there were three frightened-looking boys outside the office. Eyes downcast, voices trembling, they introduced themselves as Hermann Wiese, Konrad Farin and Karl Köhler. Lahnstein showed them in, but didn't ask them to sit down. He was as nervous as they were. This might be the breakthrough.

'What brings you here?'

'We're friends of Adolf's,' Farin said. 'Adolf Hogrefe.'

Lahnstein looked out the file and skimmed the first page: Number Sixteen, born on 6 October 1907, son of an engine driver, missing since 6 April 1924.

'We read about Haarmann in the newspaper and we'd like to make a statement.'

'Fire away.'

Wiese told Lahnstein that he'd bumped into Adolf at Lehrte Station on 2 April and found him in quite a state, because of trouble at home. His father was very strict and always yelling at him, so he'd decided to run away. But he was skint—wouldn't Wiese buy his bike from him? Wiese bought the bicycle at a good price. The following evening he ran into Adolf again, this time at Hanover Station. Adolf proudly showed him an imitation-leather suitcase he had bought with the money from the bike. Wiese asked him where he'd slept. In the station, Adolf said. Then he asked if he could spend the following night in the Wieses' hayloft.

'My parents have a small farm,' Wiese explained.

'Had he changed his mind about running away?' Lahnstein asked.

'Yes, he was homesick. But he didn't dare go home because he was afraid of what his dad might do.'

'Because he'd lied and hadn't gone to trade school?'

'Exactly.'

'The rest of you never skive off, of course.'

They shook their heads earnestly.

Then Farin spoke. He introduced himself as a tailor's apprentice and said that he too had met Adolf at Hanover Station—on 4 April, the day after Wiese had last seen him. Adolf had told him all about the bicycle and the suitcase, which by this time was in left luggage. He also said that a gentleman had promised to put him up for the night—a detective who lived in Neue Strasse.

'A detective?'

'That's what he said.'

'What was the detective's name?'

'I can tell you,' said Köhler, the third boy.

'That's why we're here,' Farin said.

Köhler in turn had met Adolf at the station and heard his story. Adolf had proudly shown him the left-luggage ticket for his new suitcase and told him the latest news: his dad had chucked him out.

'The next evening,' Köhler said, 'I saw Adolf with Detective Fritz; they were sitting at a table in the waiting room.'

'Just a moment, please, who is this Detective Fritz?'

'Fritz Haarmann,' Farin said.

Silence.

'And you knew that?'

'We didn't know he was called Haarmann,' said Farin. 'We only saw that yesterday in the evening paper. That and the fact that he's a serial killer.'

'There's one more thing I have to tell you,' Köhler said. 'I met Adolf again two days later; we walked a short way down Heuschelstrasse together from the station. He told me he was seeing quite a bit of Detective Fritz.'

'You mean Fritz Haarmann?'

'Yes. And that was the last any of us saw of him.'

'Hang on a moment,' Lahnstein said, getting up. 'Are you telling me that your friend disappeared at a time when the whole city was in turmoil with all the missing-boy cases, and you saw him several times with the same man before he went missing, but none of you thought to inform the police? Have I got that right?'

Sheepish faces, clenched, white fists.

'He said he was going away.'

'He had a suitcase.'

'I saw the ticket.'

'I saw the suitcase.'

Lahnstein sat down again.

'What makes you think Haarmann's a detective?'

'That's what everyone thought.'

'He had a warrant card.'

When they had left, Lahnstein sat on his chair at a loss. Haarmann had gone in and out of the railway station, openly associating with boys, in full view of passers-by and station police, and nobody had noticed or owned to noticing anything. Adolf Hogrefe's father was an engine driver, for God's sake, and surely knew some of the station workers— yet he, too, claimed to have heard nothing?

Lahnstein didn't know whether to feel outrage or relief. He'd never solve the case at this rate. The whole city had conspired to turn a blind eye and let Haarmann get on with his dirty work, unimpeded.

He asked to be shown the things that had been taken from Haarmann when he was admitted to custody: clothes, a cheroot, a pencil stump and a warrant card bearing the name of a detective agency. It really did look like a police warrant card. On the way back to the office, Lahnstein passed a line of people in the corridor, all holding bundles or pieces of clothing in their arms. At the end of the queue was Emma. He stopped, but she averted her eyes. He stood there for a moment, then went on his way.

When he got to the office the next morning, there were four skulls on Müller's desk. Müller was fiddling around with red paper and a pair of scissors.

'What are you doing?'

Müller explained that they were skulls that had been found in the river. He was sticking red paper in the eye sockets and planned to light them from within like jack-o'-lanterns and hang one in each corner of Haarmann's cell. He was thinking of putting a sack of the boys' bones in with him, too. Haarmann was a simple soul and deep down he was afraid. He'd scare him a bit by telling him that the spirits of the dead were going to return to their bones and would give him no peace until he'd confessed.

Lahnstein burst out laughing.

'He isn't childish enough to be taken in by such hocus pocus.'

'Oh, but he is. It crops up in his file again and again.'

'If you say so.'

It was a rainy day when they opened the doors of the big meeting room. Four hundred exhibits were spread out on tables and draped over chairs—clothes for the most part, but also bags, keyrings, wallets. Everything could be traced back to Haarmann. Things that had been bought or sold as a job lot were grouped together, tagged with a note marking the date—or approximate date—of purchase. All the lights were on. A smell of must and old sweat hung in the air. Rain beat against the windows.

Haarmann stood off to one side against the wall, his hands and feet in irons. Two policemen held him by the arms in a tight grip; half a dozen more were scattered about the room, heavily armed—not because it was necessary, but to convey a sense of security. A couple of women from the Red Cross sat in a corner of the room, ready to minister to anyone who fainted. Schackwitz was in the building and on call in case of a heart attack or a stroke.

The first people showed up in the early hours of the morning. They waited in the foyer and when that became too crowded, they spilt out onto the stairs and into the corridors. At nine o'clock, they began to edge towards the meeting room, glancing about them apprehensively. Lahnstein stood at a window, his gaze flitting back and forth between the new arrivals and Haarmann, eager for any hint of what was going on inside him. Haarmann saw him and winked.

Soon the room looked like a church bazaar; people moved from table to table, examining trousers, jackets, shirts, ties, rubbing fabric between their fingers, peering at labels. They spoke in hushed voices. More church than bazaar. Some cast stolen glances at Haarmann—looks of fear, hatred or scorn. A sudden scream made everyone start. Lahnstein saw a woman pressing her face into a jacket. A man took her in his arms. They wept. No sign of emotion from Haarmann.

A policeman approached the couple and led them to a table at the edge of the room to take their details. Lahnstein went over to them; it was the parents of Erich de Vries, the last missing boy. His mother had recognised his suit by a hole in the trouser leg.

Lahnstein returned to his post, one eye on the boy's relatives, one on Haarmann's face. He saw the Hannappels, the Kochs, Magda Hennies; most of the others were strangers to him. He heard dialects from all over Germany. It seemed to him that pretty much everyone who was missing someone had come. Around noon they had to close the doors because the room was too full. From then on, groups formed.

He, too, was given contemptuous, angry looks.

'My brother shot down thirty-six planes before he was fetched by God,' one man muttered to him. 'Unlike you, he didn't survive.'

'I'm sorry,' he said.

The man waved this aside scornfully and went on his way. There was another scream—and another.

'Is that the murderer?' a child asked in a loud voice, pressing himself against his father's legs. That, too, Haarmann received with indifference.

A policeman presented Lahnstein with a shabbily dressed couple.

'They want to speak to the boss,' he said.

A peroxided woman and a boorish-looking man with huge, calloused hands. The man clutched a brown coat in his hands, the woman a tie.

'What can I do for you?'

'This here is our Willi's,' the woman said, holding out the tie.

'What was your name again?' Lahnstein asked.

'Senger,' the man said. 'Willi's our youngest. The tie was a present from his brother Heinrich.'

'Made it himself,' the woman said.

'You'll have to help me,' Lahnstein said. 'I can't place you just at present. Did you come to me to report your son missing?'

'No.'

'Then he must be one of the earlier cases.'

But I know all their names, he thought.

'We never reported him missing,' the woman said. 'He said he was going travelling. And then suddenly he was gone.'

'When was this?'

'Early February.'

'Number Fifteen.'

'Beg pardon?'

'Nothing.'

Number Fifteen, Lahnstein thought—and the others would have to be renumbered.

'How old is your son?'

'Nineteen.'

'And you thought nothing of it when he went missing? Despite the rumours? You must have heard there was a serial killer at large?'

Shrugs.

Dull-witted, Lahnstein thought. Thoroughly dull-witted.

'Come to my office at ten tomorrow. I need all the details you can give me.'

He turned his attention back to Haarmann who stood there indifferently, watching the goings-on.

Twenty-two.

A woman collapsed, slumping soundlessly to the floor, inches from Haarmann. He saw it and quickly looked away. The Red Cross nurses hurried over to the woman, propped her up and led her to a chair. Haarmann kept his eyes averted. It was Hermann Speichert's mother; her daughter was with her. The girl was holding her brother's case of compasses in her hands. It had been found at Hans Grans'; the boy's clothes had been at Haarmann's.

The Hannappels, who had travelled up from Düsseldorf, came to Lahnstein with a wooden crate and a big pile of clothes.

'This is all Adolf's,' Mr Hannappel said.

They had grown thinner since Lahnstein had last seen them. He went through the things with them.

A khaki hat with a dark-green band.

'How do you know it's his?'

'It was me sewed the sweatband in,' Mrs Hannappel said.

Two Marrakech shirts.

'The cuffs are new; I ran them up myself.'

A pair of braces.

'I mended the leather trim on the back straps. Here, see.'

A pair of laced box-calf boots.

'These have had some repair work done on them,' Mr Hannappel said. 'That was me did that.'

Breeches, best quality.

'Here's a scrap left over from when we had them made.'

A black sock.

'We've another pair like that at home. I can send you them.'

A pair of grey-green corduroy work trousers.

'I did some mending work on these,' Mrs Hannappel said, pointing to the left pocket and the fabric beneath one of the back buttons.

A blue sweater.

'There's a patch here that I darned with wool from our other boy's jersey.'

A khaki waistcoat.

A black coat.

'I've nothing to show you,' she said. 'But I'm positive it's his.'

A box of carpentry screws.

'I gave him them to make a rabbit hutch,' Mr Hannappel said with a sob. His wife, who had gently stroked each piece of clothing as if she were stroking her son, remained composed.

The following day there was less of a crush, but items of clothing continued to be identified and things continued to arrive. One man, who introduced himself as Raupus, told Lahnstein he was a bicycle dealer and presented him with a brake lever. He said he knew Haarmann; he'd been to his digs once with Grans. Haarmann had told him that Grans was selling his bike because he was strapped for cash.

'I took it. It was an old model, dark blue, crank pedals, no freewheel. I tarted it up a bit and sold it on. The brake lever's all I have left; it's aluminium bronze.'

He handed Lahnstein the lever. Later that day it was identified by the brother of Richard Gräf—the boy who'd talked of meeting a 'fine gentleman'. He also identified a pair of khaki trousers and a suit.

They were about to lock up at the end of the second day, when a well-dressed man presented himself. He was late, but they let him in.

'My name is Schiefer,' he told Lahnstein.

'You're the chemist?'

'We haven't met, but I believe you've spoken to my wife.'

'I wasn't expecting you. Your wife's theory is that your son can't be one of Haarmann's victims, because that would put him in a series with the others. Also, we're assuming that the murders had more to do with lust than robbery and there again, your wife has her own ideas.'

'We don't quite see eye to eye on the matter,' said Schiefer.

'You mean you're not such a snob as your wife.'

That was harsh, he knew. Had he reacted that way because he suspected Schiefer of voting for the German Nationalist People's Party? They were the worst, in his view—jingoist, populist, capitalist. Their newspaper had clobbered him.

'You must understand the pain she's going through,' Schiefer said. 'Richard was our only child. The thought of… of rape is unbearable to her. That's why she's so adamant it was robbery.'

'I understand very well,' Lahnstein said gently. 'Please, have a look around.'

They had cleared away all the items that had been identified; the tables and chairs were still full, but no longer piled quite so high. Schiefer went up and down the rows, pausing occasionally. Lahnstein wondered whether he hoped to find something and thus put an end to the uncertainty— or to find nothing so that his wife could be proved right.

He found a duffle coat and a pair of velveteen trousers that had been discovered in Haarmann's stash. His face twitched as he handed them over. Lahnstein wanted to say something, but Schiefer waved him aside and hurried out.

When Lahnstein got back to his lodgings late that night, his father was in the sitting room, talking to the landlady.

'What on earth are you doing here?'

He was so surprised, he sounded rude.

His father got up and embraced him.

'I thought you might be needing a little advice.'

Lahnstein glanced at the landlady.

'Come, let's go up to my room; it's not exactly spacious, but...'

'I'll leave you,' the landlady said, and she did.

Father and son sat down. They talked about what had happened since Christmas. Lahnstein didn't need to tell his father much; he'd read all about Haarmann in the papers.

'That's why I'm here,' he said. 'I fear you need a confession.'

'It's what the examining magistrate wants.'

'I'd like to tell you something,' Lahnstein's father said. 'Because I didn't give you the whole story last time.'

'About the missing girl? Why not?'

'I was too ashamed.'

Lahnstein looked at his father. He seemed to have shrunk even further since he'd last seen him; he was a tiny, skinny person and very, very old.

'I know it can be a burden when your father's held up as an example to you, and I don't by any means consider myself an example in everything. But in some things, maybe—and possibly in this case.'

'You've always been an example to me, you know that.'

'Thank you, my boy. But if your old dad's going to be an example to you, it had better be the real man and not some illusion.'

'I don't understand what you're getting at.'

'I wasn't honest with you. I want you to make up your own mind. You shouldn't feel constrained by what your father did or didn't do. Did do, in my case. Because the truth is that I didn't do nothing; I did something.'

'Now I understand even less.'

'When we had the kidnapper in custody we knew, of course, that a person can survive for three to four days without water. After he'd kept silent for two days, we began to slap him, deprive him of sleep and so on. He only laughed. We poured icy water over him, repeatedly. He shivered, but he still refused to speak.'

The old man paused and Lahnstein wasn't sure that he wanted him to go on.

'On the morning of the third day, I told my colleagues to leave me on my own with him. Two younger colleagues said they'd do the job for me, but I wouldn't hear of it. It was my case. I took a razor into the interrogation cell. I...'

'Dad.'

'I cut...'

'I don't want to hear.'

'I cut his arm, but when I saw the blood I couldn't go on. It was no good. It wasn't right. We carried on with the sleep deprivation and all that, but we didn't hurt him again. We weren't able to save the girl.'

'Did Mum know about this?' Lahnstein asked.

'I told her.'

'What did she say?'

'She said she'd have done the same, but seen it through to the end.'

'Mum. What became of the man?'

'We had to let him go. We hadn't even found the girl's body. Sometimes I think she might still be alive—that it was all a set-up, to allow her to run away to America or Australia, maybe with some boy. It's a comforting thought. The worst is the uncertainty. I went as far as hurting him, but wasn't tough enough to finish the job. Now I'll never know—maybe I could have saved her if I hadn't been so squeamish.'

'And if you'd flouted the law even more seriously,' said Lahnstein, not looking at his father.

'That too.'

They were silent.

'What am I to do with this story of yours?' Lahnstein asked.

'I can't decide for you,' his father said. 'But I didn't want to stand in your way. I didn't want you thinking you're the son of a man who did the right thing in a similar situation.'

'Instead I'm the son of a man who did the wrong thing and achieved nothing by it.'

'Probably because he didn't see the wrong thing through to the end.'

'We don't know.'

'No.'

'And now?'

'I trust you. Whatever you decide, you'll have my blessing and approval. That's what I came to tell you.'

'Thank you.'

He let his father have the bed and slept on the floor with his coat as a blanket. The following morning, his father returned to Bochum.

'Well,' Müller said the following morning, 'was the enterprise worth it?'

Lahnstein turned the aluminium bronze lever in his hand.

'It certainly was. A hundred and fifty items of clothing were identified as belonging to one or other of the missing boys. There are still questions, of course, and some tenuous claims that will have to be looked into. But I think we'll end up with well over a hundred identified items.'

'A tidy number. What's it worth?'

'Trust you to ask that.'

'I'm sorry, but one of us has to defend the rule of law.'

'Well, there's a turn-up for the books,' said Lahnstein. 'Since when have you'—he pointed the brake lever at Müller—'been an advocate of the rule of law?'

'Since today. We know the clothes passed through Haarmann's hands, but that doesn't mean he met the boys they belonged to. He's an old-clothes man; he has a licence to trade. He buys and sells old clothes—and, yes, all right, he sometimes steals them. But that's not enough to convict him and you'll never get him to confess, because of the death penalty. You know that.'

He did. The bloody death penalty.

'I can use the new information to turn up the pressure on him.'

'Good luck to you.'

Lahnstein didn't look at Müller; he could imagine the grin on his face.

'How about your hocus pocus with the skulls?' he asked. 'Did that get you anywhere?'

'You know it didn't.'

They were silent for a while. Lahnstein went back to turning the brake lever in his hands and stared out of the window, thinking. Then he heard Müller get up and start to pace the office. Eventually he stopped in front of Lahnstein's desk.

'Let's be sensible,' he said.

Lahnstein turned to look at him. 'I'm all for that.'

'All right. I'm going to make a suggestion.'

'A sensible one?'

'Please. I think we want the same things.'

'I'm not so sure.'

'How about this? First I help you out with Haarmann, then you leave him to me.'

'What do you mean, *help me out with Haarmann*?'

'You have three more days. If you don't have a confession from Haarmann by the end of that time, the examining magistrate will release him. The hurdles for a second arrest are much higher. And you know what the papers will say.'

'Indeed—especially if you're planning to feed them their lines again.'

'Oh, come on.'

'I thought,' Lahnstein said, 'that it was in your interest that he walk free.'

'He's out of the running as an informant. Everyone knows him after all the to-do here. One of the papers has already suggested he might be a police spy.'

'So now you drop him?'

'You won't get a fellow like Haarmann without a bit of brute force. I know him, he only speaks one language. I realise it isn't easy for you to accept that, as a democrat and so on, but I'll do it for you—that's my offer.'

'You're asking me to hire you as a torturer?' Lahnstein laughed.

'If that's what you want to call it.'

'And what do you mean when you say I should *leave Haarmann to you*?'

'I'll have a word with him once he's confessed.'

'What about?'

'It's in your interest too. We don't want Fritz Haarmann blabbing about his collaboration with us in a court full of journalists—reeling off a list of all our cock-ups. It could get embarrassing, don't you agree?'

Very, Lahnstein thought.

'But it needn't,' Müller said. 'I'll talk him out of it. He'll be all praise for the police.'

'Talk him out of it?'

'Leave him to me.'

'You're crazy, Müller. I'll never agree to a deal like that.'

'Then Haarmann will walk free and the odds are, he'll carry on murdering. The people of Hanover will thank you—especially the ones with pretty sons.'

That night Lahnstein dreamt he was flying again. The plane took off and rose slowly into the air, flying over battlefields and then over green, undamaged countryside—until Lahnstein realised with a start that there was a fox in his way and swerved to dodge it. Why a fox? The question woke him and he looked at the clock. It was a quarter past three. At least he'd been alone in the plane this time—no Lissy and August. It felt like progress. Then he felt guilty for driving them out of his dream, and turned his thoughts to his last trip down to Lake Irr.

The country seemed calm and empty on the journey south. He sometimes had to wait half a day for a train. The carriages were lined up in the station, but there was no engine. Word in the waiting rooms was that a lot of trains had been destroyed in the war, and the French were seizing German engines as reparation.

'They wanted war,' a man yelled, 'and now they blame everything on us and expect us to pay up.'

There were curses of agreement. Lahnstein kept quiet and looked about him at the gaunt bodies and haggard faces. This was in Stuttgart. He had to sleep on the waiting-room floor, because the benches were occupied by women and children. Contrapuntal coughing, all night. One man didn't get up in the morning. Everyone was talking about the flu epidemic and how it was going to rage on and on.

'Worse than the war,' somebody said. Hadn't Lissy mentioned a cough? Lahnstein pushed the thought away. The following morning he boarded the Munich train, but there was no engine again and they were stuck in the station for two hours. His compartment was hellishly crowded. After a while people stopped talking and slept or dozed. Then an engine steamed up to the platform and after that the journey went smoothly.

In Salzburg, Lahnstein haggled with a cab driver until he'd talked him down to a fare he could afford. His parents had given him money for the journey, but not a lot. He'd pay them back as soon as he was earning again. He counted notes into the cabby's hand. So many crooks around these days, the man said, he had to take the money up front. They drove slowly to Lake Irr, very slowly; it was snowing slightly and the car skidded every time the driver braked for a bend. Once it slid off the road into a field and got stuck in the snow; the wheels only spun. Lahnstein and the cabby gathered twigs to put under the wheels; it was cold on the hands and the car didn't come free until the third attempt. They drove on in silence. Dusk was falling; the mountains were grey shadows; faint lights showed in farmhouses. They crawled through deathly quiet villages, past Lake Mond and Lake Irr. At about eleven the cab stopped outside Lissy's brother's house. There was no light; everyone here was asleep at this hour. Lahnstein asked the driver to collect him and his family in two days' time.

Me and my family. He spoke the words loud and clear. If he said it with enough conviction, it would be true. He paid half the fare in advance. The driver said he wouldn't come out in a snowstorm.

'Then come after the snowstorm,' Lahnstein said.

The cab drove off.

Lahnstein stood at the door and knocked, though he knew no one was awake—and not likely to wake if he knocked so feebly. He also knew that the door wasn't locked. He listened out. Not a sound, not even a cow snorting in the cowshed. That was unusual, but it was snowing hard and snow swallowed sounds, didn't it? He pushed the handle down and stepped into the house.

Inside he called out, softly at first and then louder. He

groped around for a candle and found one in the kitchen. In the dim light everything looked neat and tidy, but Lahnstein was alarmed to see that the table was bare; he'd never known his brother-in-law's wife go to bed without laying the table for breakfast. The bedrooms were empty and chilly; the whole house had a chill to it as if it hadn't been heated all winter. The cowshed was empty too, except for a bit of rotten straw. Lahnstein went back in and lay down on one of the beds. There were so many possible explanations; it needn't mean anything for Lissy and August. But he couldn't sleep all the same.

The following morning at about half past five he heard the neighbour moving about in the barn next door and got up and went over to him.

'They're all dead,' the neighbour said. 'Killed by fumes. Last March, when it suddenly turned so cold, the family took to sleeping in the kitchen; it was the only warm room in the house and they were all poorly with the influenza. But the stove can't have been working properly, though it was one of those modern ones. Something wasn't right with the flue.

'I'm sorry,' he said. He tugged at a cow's udder and milk spurted into a pail. 'The man who serviced the stoves fell in Galicia, and his assistant on the Eisack.'

He got up and poured the milk out of the pail into a big vat. 'The war claims its dead everywhere,' he said. 'Even here, even in times of peace.' He took a beaker from a shelf, dipped it in the vat and held it out to Lahnstein.

'Get that inside you,' he said awkwardly, as if to say: I know a beaker of milk won't help, but it's all a man has to offer in a barn at dawn. Lahnstein took it and drank and the farmer moved on to the next cow.

After a couple of mouthfuls, however, Lahnstein dropped the beaker and staggered out into the fresh air. When he got to the road he turned left and tramped briskly through the snow. It wasn't deep; it couldn't have snowed for long and was already beginning to thaw. Lahnstein walked and walked, past stirring farms, the frozen lake to his right. He thought of Lissy and August—saw them on holiday with him by Lake Irr; imagined their last days, their death. He supposed it had been a gentle one and found the thought at once reassuring and disturbing. He saw them lying there peacefully, without suffering, August in Lissy's arms—a tranquil picture, and yet it filled him with horror. He struck off to the right across a sloping field, slipped in the snow, slithered a little way downhill, but struggled to his feet and carried on to the edge of the lake. Hesitantly at first and then more firmly, he stepped out across the ice, heading for the opposite bank until, without realising it, he began to walk in a circle. The same pictures repeated themselves over and over in his head, and sometimes he heard a scream. *No, no, no.* He stopped. The ice creaked, but he didn't care. Eventually he collapsed in exhaustion.

At eight o'clock, two ice anglers found him lying unconscious not far from the shore. They carried him to their hut, made a fire and plied him with homemade schnapps. They knew a second cousin of Lissy and took Lahnstein to his house in their cart. This cousin was trying to sell Lissy's brother's farm, but couldn't find any takers—not enough men left. Lahnstein asked why he hadn't let him know when Lissy and August died. He hadn't had an address to write to, the cousin replied.

'But there were letters from Bochum, from the POW camp.' Lissy's cousin shrugged. Maybe he couldn't read—not all the locals could.

Lahnstein walked to the cemetery in Zell am Moos, to the family grave. A small, plain gravestone was marked with the names: Lissy's parents, her brother and his wife, their three daughters, Lissy and August. Nine dead in one night. He bought flowers and laid them in the slush. All around him was a soft splashing as thawing snow dripped from the trees; the whole place was awash with puddles and brooks and rivulets—a shifting, liquid world. Lahnstein didn't return to his brother-in-law's farm, but took a room by the lake. In the evening he sat in the lounge with the green-tiled stove, a little apart from the others. He sensed that the landlady knew who he was and supposed she also knew what had happened to his family, but she said nothing. No one said anything and Lahnstein was glad. He kept pace with the locals, ordering beer and schnapps whenever they did, and once they'd gone home, he went on drinking on his own. At midnight he asked for the bill, but the landlady refused to take his money.

The next morning he got up early and walked down to the crossroads where one of the roads branched off to his brother-in-law's farm. The cab soon came. Lahnstein gave a wave, climbed in and asked to be driven to Salzburg railway station.

'Galicia is where the Austro-Hungarian army caved in,

isn't it?' he asked the driver. 'The Germans had to come to their rescue.'

The driver turned round to him. 'What makes you say that?' he asked.

'I don't know,' Lahnstein said.

They were silent for the rest of the journey.

'Makes no difference anyway,' said Lahnstein as he got out of the cab. It took him three days to get back to Bochum. Two weeks later he resumed his police work.

He didn't fall asleep again, but turned the light on and smoked in bed for the rest of the night. At five he got up. By six he was at headquarters and asked for Haarmann to be woken and brought to the interrogation cell.

Haarmann sat opposite him, yawning.

'Tell me about Willi Senger,' Lahnstein said.

'Willi? Willi from the railway station?'

'You know him?'

'Course I know him, good-looking boy, but not my type. Tall, sturdy, shoulders like this—' he held his hands apart. 'Rough fellow. You want to take care with him. Violent.'

'How did you meet him?'

'Oh, he was always knocking about the station. I'd see him on my rounds an' we'd get talking.'

'Did Senger go home with men for money—or to hotels?'

Haarmann tugged at his fingers. Again, Lahnstein was struck by the white flabbiness of his hands.

'Yeah, maybe, he was probably that kind. But I can't say for sure.'

'Did you ever take him back to your digs?'

'Me? No. I told you he wasn't my type. I don't care for rough fellows like that.'

'But you took other boys home?'

'I told you all this last time: I had them round for parties. We always had good parties at my digs. I know you don't believe me, Inspector, but the boys like coming to see me. You think old Haarmann's always after the boys, but that's not true. It's them runs after me all day long—can't leave me alone, they can't: *Hey, Fritz, how about it, Fritz? Take me home with you, Fritz. What'll you give me for it, Fritz?* Never leave off—such pretty boys, too, I can tell you.'

He made a strange rolling movement with his shoulders as he talked, lunging forwards and then shooting back.

'And every now and then you took one home and killed him. How did you do it? Strangle them? Stab them? Beat them?'

'Oh, no, Inspector, you've got the wrong man. The boys are nice to me an' I'm nice to them.'

Müller came in, sat down on a stool in the corner and folded his arms.

'Morning, Inspector Müller,' Haarmann called.

Müller didn't respond. Haarmann looked confused and licked his lips.

'We found Senger's coat and tie in your stash of old clothes,' Lahnstein said.

'In my digs? No.'

'Oh, yes we did. His parents have identified them.'

'I don't believe 'em. They're lying.'

'Why would they do that?'

'I must've bought the coat somewhere.'

'Why would Senger sell his coat? It was nearly new, it was his only coat and it was winter. Can you explain to me why he'd have wanted to sell it?'

'You'll have to ask Senger that.'

'We're assuming that Willi Senger is no longer alive.'

Haarmann shrugged, tugged at his fingers, licked his lips.

Lahnstein jumped up. 'We're also assuming that you killed him.'

'Balls.'

Lahnstein walked around the table until he was standing very close to Haarmann. He laid a heavy hand on his shoulder.

'Stop lying to me. We know it was you.'

'But it wasn't.'

Avoiding Müller's eye, Lahnstein returned to his seat.

'Another name: Adolf Hogrefe.'

'Never heard of him.'

'A complete set of Hogrefe's clothes has been found, some in your rooms, some at Mrs Engel's, some elsewhere.'

He read aloud from his list: 'Jacket of grey marengo wool, imitation astrakhan coat, fustian shirt, et cetera. Eight items altogether.'

'Must have made quite a killing,' Haarmann said, 'then told his ma someone nicked his things at the swimming baths.' He laughed delightedly.

Lahnstein pushed a photo of Adolf Hogrefe across the table to him.

'Don't know him,' Haarmann drawled. 'I already told you that, yesterday or the day before.'

'But you sold eight pieces of clothing belonging to him?'

'I don't know him.'

'Are you familiar with the name Detective Fritz?'

Haarmann grinned with pride. 'That's me. They all call me that.'

He looked at Müller, seeking recognition.

'It's you, yes. Where did you get this handsome warrant card?'

'Oh, that's from Olfermann, he has this detective's office. I used to work for him sometimes.'

'All right, now I have a little surprise for you.'

'What?'

'Three witnesses have told us that shortly before Hogrefe went missing, he was in contact with Detective Fritz and said he was going to spend the night with him.'

'Not that again. How many times do I have to tell you: I don't know this Hogrefe and I never took him home with me.'

He folded his arms and pouted.

Like a child, Lahnstein thought.

'You do and you did. We both know that.'

'Prove it.'

This went on for hours. Lahnstein could get nothing useful out of Haarmann—not even when they got on to the subject of Hans Grans. The story was that he'd met Grans at the station in 1919.

'He hassled me for money,' Haarmann said.

He took pity on Grans and began to help him out here and there—sometimes giving him as much as twenty marks at a time. Haarmann was hazy about whether he'd got anything in return.

'I had a thing about him,' he said.

Before long he was taking Grans home with him, because he had nowhere to sleep. Grans was 'hairy as an ape' and was later persuaded to shave himself for Haarmann.

'He's not a one-seven-fiver, though,' Haarmann said. 'He likes girls.'

For the first time Lahnstein saw real emotion on Haarmann's face. He looked sad.

'I know,' Lahnstein said.

'But he cuddled with me,' Haarmann said, and his face lit up.

Together they got the old-clothes business going. Haarmann pretended to be a wounded soldier and limped his way through the more genteel neighbourhoods, going from door to door, saying that he was buying unwanted clothes for his old man or for a dosshouse called the Homeland Hostel. Most people gave him things for free. Grans sold them to the junk dealers in Burgstrasse and they made about thirty to sixty marks a day. Sometimes they blew it all on drinking sprees, though as a rule it was only Grans who drank; Haarmann spurned alcohol. He would help Grans home in the early hours of the morning, sometimes even carry him.

Then their swindle was exposed. The papers warned of the fake war invalid and Haarmann had to resort to sneaking into backyards and filching washing from lines. This, too, Grans sold in Burgstrasse.

'I wanted someone I was everything to,' Haarmann said,

tugging at his fingers. 'Hans often made fun of me because he thought I was daft an' he'd read all these books from his parents' shop. But I couldn't keep away from him. I was mad about him.'

Grans had another friend, Hugo Wittkowski. He wasn't homosexual either, but Lahnstein had the impression that Haarmann saw him as a rival. When Haarmann was sent to the prison workhouse for stealing washing, Wittkowski moved into Haarmann's flat to live with Grans. The parties got so out of hand that Haarmann's landlady sent him a letter of complaint. By the time he was released, Grans and Wittkowski had moved out, but they had taken all the furniture with them.

'I forgave him,' Haarmann said with a sigh—and then, suddenly flaring up: 'But I didn't forgive Wittkowski. He never paid me back the money I lent him.' He made a fist.

Haarmann bragged endlessly about his curious relationship with Grans—at once that of punter and rent boy, father and son, devoted husband and uncaring wife. He giggled, screwed up his eyes, licked his lips with his meaty tongue, rubbed his forehead as if thinking, and then burst out laughing. It didn't sound as though Grans still gave him sex, but he evidently allowed Haarmann to hope that he might again some day.

'Does Hans Grans know that you butcher boys?'

For a moment Haarmann looked shaken. Up to this point he had seemed an almost effortless actor. Comic rather than heroic, provincial rather than progressive—but he had stuck to his role; he hadn't floundered. Now that changed.

His shoulders twitched, his eyes darted about, unable to settle.

'I'd have to do it for him to know about it.' His voice was very high, almost treble.

Lahnstein persisted, but Haarmann had recovered; there was no more shaking him.

After six hours, Lahnstein broke off the interrogation.

He was tired. He fetched himself a cup of coffee and drank it in the canteen because he wasn't inclined to be in the office with Müller after his defeat. It was hopeless; he had another thirty-six hours, but no idea how to crack Haarmann. Half an hour later, he changed his mind and returned to the office. Müller wasn't there. Lahnstein looked through the reports on the day's findings. More items of clothing had been identified—and a dictionary that one of the boys had been carrying on his last day. More witnesses had come forward who had seen Haarmann together with one or other of the missing boys. But none of it was the breakthrough Lahnstein needed—and what was he hoping for anyway? He saw Haarmann swaggering out of headquarters with a grin on his face. He saw the next boy's blood.

Müller came in and sat down at his desk.

'You did well today,' he said.

Lahnstein looked at him in astonishment.

'Especially towards the end. Did you notice? Grans is his weak point; that's where we'll get him. Even a monster has someone he loves—and just now he's so deeply wounded he feels something more like hate. The monster's sensitive;

this is our chance.'

Lahnstein felt pleased—and a little ashamed that he was so susceptible to Müller's praise.

'Just imagine,' Müller said, 'questioning him about Grans' role in the murders when he's very tired and his defences are down and all he wants is to sleep.'

Lahnstein turned back to the files, but couldn't concentrate. He yawned.

'Go home,' Müller said. 'You're tired yourself. Get a good night's sleep. I'll make sure you're dealing with a very different Haarmann tomorrow morning.'

Lahnstein folded his hands behind his head and stared out of the window. Then he gathered up his things, locked the files away, put on his coat and left.

He spent the evening at the pictures, hoping for distraction. It was a comedy, but he didn't join in the laughter, and half an hour into the film he fell asleep. When he came to, woken by a man with a broom, the cinema was empty. Lahnstein bought himself two bottles of beer in a pub and took them back to his room to drink as he pondered what Haarmann must be going through. He imagined his surprise at being kept awake, his protests, his childlike anger, his pouting lips, his treble voice. After a while, he got up and put on his shoes, thinking he'd go to headquarters to override Müller's instructions, but he changed his mind before he'd even tied his laces. He slipped out of his shoes again, gave them a good polish and went back to his beer. Then he fell asleep and slept until half past seven.

The next morning he glanced at the papers. There was some excited anticipation, though expectations were rather more moderate on the right: *another lost case for the Republic... not tough enough...the usual feebleness.* The Communists, meanwhile, expressed concern about their *proletarian brother Haarmann.* They hadn't heard him railing against them in the interrogation, Lahnstein thought. 'Takes a Red to do that,' he had said, referring to a wrecked car.

Enormous pupils, grey skin, dishevelled hair—Haarmann had indeed become a different man overnight. His cheeks were sunken, his face drawn and pinched, and he licked his lips constantly. A rank smell hung about him.

'Inspector,' he whined, 'they didn't let me sleep all night, kept waking me up an' sometimes someone came an' played the trumpet, right in my ear. Let me sleep, for heaven's sake, we can talk later.'

Lahnstein felt the same pity for him that he'd felt for a man with typhoid in the military hospital. He even looked a bit like him. Quickly, Lahnstein pulled the photos of the missing boys from his pocket and placed them on the table in front of him.

'We'll talk first, then you can sleep. It needn't take long.'

'Please!'

Haarmann folded his arms on the table, dropped his head into the hollow and closed his eyes.

The policeman who was watching over him yanked him up by the hair.

'Not so rough, please,' Lahnstein said. 'Haarmann, I'm going to show you the photos of the missing boys again and

I'd like you to tell me which of them you know and which of them you killed. After that I'll let you sleep.'

The door burst open. Müller came in, carrying a rubber hose. He sat down on the stool in the corner and laid the hose on the floor. Haarmann looked at him, confused and then imploring.

'Help me, Inspector Müller.'

No reaction.

'Let's get going,' Lahnstein said.

He pushed the first photograph towards Haarmann.

'Friedel Rothe,' he said.

Haarmann shook his head.

'Sure?'

'Yes.'

'Think about it.'

'I have.'

The next photograph.

'Adolf Hannappel.'

Again, Haarmann shook his head.

They went through all the photos and he shook his head at each one, his eyes growing wilder and wilder, his head moving faster and faster, until it was flying from side to side and looked as if it might come adrift.

'All right then, we'll go back to the beginning and start again. Maybe you'll remember something this time round. Take your time, give it some thought.'

Haarmann's head slumped into the hollow of his arms. The policeman put his hands on his temples and jerked it back up.

They went through the photos again, this time at a more leisurely pace. Haarmann's eyes drooped as he stared at the faces, and whenever he looked as if he was dropping off Lahnstein made a sign to the policeman who gave Haarmann a nudge. This sent a jolt through him and he'd stare at the picture again and shake his head, his eyes very big and then very small.

Most of the time, Lahnstein managed to see it as a normal interrogation—one of the hundreds he'd presided over, some of them gentle, others tougher, none of them violent. Once, he found himself boxing Haarmann's ears, but immediately regretted it and apologised. He ignored the sleep deprivation; he ignored the rubber hose that lay on the floor behind him, in full view of Haarmann. He put his questions, waited, probed. Routine police work.

When they were about to go through the pictures a third time, Haarmann said, 'I'm hungry. I had no tea an' no breakfast.'

Lahnstein turned to Müller who gave a slight shake of his head.

'We'll keep going,' Lahnstein said.

A howl went up from Haarmann; it sounded more like a sick wolf than a man. Lahnstein showed him the photograph of Friedel Rothe. Haarmann denied having harmed the boy.

The fourth time round, Lahnstein asked Haarmann for alibis. He asked for precise details, making no allowances for Haarmann's growing tiredness. He demanded accurate information, meticulous accounts of what happened when. Haarmann was increasingly exhausted by the questions. He was slow to reply and not always coherent or even intelligible.

His hand kept drifting to his forehead which he rubbed and rubbed. Once he cried out, 'No, no, no!' Another time, plaintively, 'But I love the boys.'

Again, his head slumped into the hollow of his arms. The policeman made to lift it, but Lahnstein signalled to him to wait. Thirty seconds later, he signalled again and Haarmann was jolted out of a deep sleep, confused and disoriented.

'Did Hans Grans incite you to these murders?'

Haarmann stared at him as if he hadn't understood—as if he were still in another world.

'Did Hans Grans incite you to these murders?'

Now he had the face of someone who was slowly returning to the world, seeing its horrors without really grasping what was going on. He swallowed, licked his lips.

'No.'

'Are you sure?'

A long stare. His hand shot to his forehead again; there was a patch of red from all the rubbing.

'Yes.'

'I see in the files that you were twice arrested together on suspicion of theft or fencing, but each time Grans got away while you ended up in prison. Do you realise he squealed on you to save his own skin?'

'That's rot.'

'It's not rot. It's here in the files.'

Which wasn't true.

Haarmann closed his eyes.

'Seeing as I didn't harm anyone, he can't have incited me, can he?'

They stopped for an hour and a half's break. A new policeman came on duty. Müller gave him strict instructions not to let Haarmann sleep.

Lahnstein went into the cafe opposite headquarters. He sat down with a newspaper and ordered roast beef and onions and a cup of coffee. After a while he noticed a man watching him. He resumed his reading and the next thing he knew, the man was standing at his table, asking if he might join him. Lahnstein was far from keen, but he gestured him to a chair. 'Please, sit down.'

Fine-drawn eyebrows, alert eyes, curling hair. A stray lock tumbled over his high forehead and a tapering beard pulled his chin into a point. For a man with such a narrow face, his nose was disconcertingly fleshy. He wore a high-collared shirt and a black suit.

'Theodor Lessing, how do you do.'

He extended a hand.

'How do you do. Robert Lahnstein.'

'I know, I know, you're the inspector who's trying to hunt the beast down.'

'And you are a journalist?'

'I am a philosopher, actually, but I do write the occasional piece for the *Prague Daily*. One of them was about your case; you may have read it.'

Lahnstein didn't reply.

'Might I ask if you are making progress?'

'I'm afraid I can't discuss the case.'

'I see, I see. Do you have a theory why Haarmann might

have done it—if indeed it was Haarmann?'

'I have no theory. I need a confession first.'

'In 1914, I treated a soldier in a military hospital who was famous for sneaking up to enemy guards and strangling them with his bare hands. For this he had been awarded the Iron Cross. Haarmann, meanwhile, unless I am much mistaken, has only the death sentence to look forward to. Circumstances are everything, are they not?'

'They certainly are. We are now living in more moderate times.'

'I can only hope you are right. What interests me is the motive. Why did he do it—if he did do it?'

'I can't answer that question.'

'Let me tell you another wartime story. The war, you see, lingers on. In the second year of the Great War, I worked in a military hospital of five hundred severely wounded patients, among them a number of Russian prisoners. A young Baltic man named Oskar had been engaged as an interpreter on the Russian ward. He was perhaps twenty years old— genial, affable, popular with patients, nurses and doctors, and much prized as a general factotum. After a while, we noticed that there were several unaccountable deaths among the Russians—deaths quite unrelated to the men's illnesses or injuries. When this sinister epidemic persisted, we began to suspect poison. The bodies were exhumed and, sure enough, arsenic was found in the dead men's stomachs. At the same time, we discovered that there were drugs missing from the drug cabinet in our laboratory. The head nurse was in charge of the key to this cabinet and had to apply to the senior physician for permission before handing it out. We recalled that we had sometimes sent Oskar to the head nurse to fetch things from the cabinet; it was not impossible that he was the thief.

'Almost as soon as we began investigations, Oskar went missing. The building was searched and, before long, an orderly came to us, white as a sheet, and reported that Oskar was hanging from the rafters in the attic. He was already dead; our investigations had to be abandoned. But there was no doubt in anyone's mind that this universally popular young man had, without purpose or motive—for he had never shown the slightest hostility towards the patients—slowly killed about twenty of his fellow countrymen by poisoning their food. People didn't bother their heads too much over such mysteries in the war. Most of them dismissed the affair with the word 'sadism', comparing Oskar to a naughty child who likes tormenting animals. Such children watch the agonies of their victims, half in terror, half in wary delight, driven to keep experimenting by horror and curiosity. Perhaps, too, the young man's shady pursuit was in part the result of that scientific self-importance that comes of playing with people's fates. But if I recall his modest vanity when praised, it seems to me more likely that it was the boy's displaced ambition that stirred his interest in mystery and the macabre, and made a mass murderer out of him.'

'I don't wish to be impolite,' said Lahnstein, 'but why are you telling me all this?'

'Just a few thoughts that occurred to me. Will you give me another five minutes of your time? I promise to leave you in peace after that. Of course, if lust is involved, that changes things again. Is lust involved? It seems more than likely.'

'We shall soon know,' Lahnstein said.

'I hope so, I do hope so. But not, I trust, at any price.'

'What do you mean?'

'One hears all kinds of things about the inner workings of our state—the authorities, the police. I would venture to suggest that there is some considerable delay in their adjustment to the practices of democracy and republic. I am not talking about you, Inspector Lahnstein. You are new here and, I am told, a man of social democratic conviction. Indeed, I am counting on you. For we have reached a critical point in the case—critical for the accused and the state, but most especially for the police. You say yourself that you need a confession and, given the threat of capital punishment, it would certainly be for the best if the possibility of error could be eliminated.

'But—one last point in conclusion, and please don't misapprehend me. I know that certain trends of thought have survived from the old times and the war—the notion, for example, that pain is a means of settling things. Pain is a hangover from the past and has no place in the present. Though in fact, of course, it was forbidden even under the ancien régime—banned by old Fred the Great. Not that he was particularly strict about it.'

Lahnstein raised his hands defensively.

'I know, know, I'm preaching to the choir. But over there on the other side of the road are men who know what a rubber hose can do to a person. They know the power of depriving a man of sleep or dunking his head in a bucket of water, and they know that the great convenience of these things is that they don't leave a single trace—not on the outside, at any rate; I have little doubt that they make their mark on the inside. Torture—that's what I'm talking about—the practice of using torture to extract a confession. It's still going on over there in the basement, I'm sure of it.'

The roast beef and onions arrived.

'Please begin. I'll soon leave off lecturing you and I do hope you'll forgive me for going on at such length. But no one should be tortured, ever. Of course, the threshold falls when a man has committed as many murders as Haarmann—is *suspected*, I should say, is *suspected* of committing as many murders (for I don't know for sure and nor, if I have read the signs correctly, do you). And when a man has led the police a dance for as long as Haarmann, feelings may run high and the threshold fall lower still. You know all this; I am sure you are a man of integrity, but please, suffer no exceptions. There can be no just-this-once with human rights. They must be taken as a whole; they apply at all times. Permit them to be violated only once and you prepare the ground for the next violation and the one after that. Human rights apply or they do not. There is no twilight zone.

'And another thing—if you will allow me one last remark before I leave you to your luncheon. You and your colleagues are hoping for results from your interrogations; you are hoping for a confession. That is understandable. But in a democracy, it isn't only the results that count, but the process. I am not talking about a court process; I mean the general process by which results are arrived at. A monarch or tyrant has only to show good results to legitimise his power to the people. The process by which he gets there is usually hidden from view and not open—or barely so—to moral judgment. In our fine republic, things are different. We expect process and results alike to conform to fundamental democratic principles. Our politicians in Berlin are not a shining example in this respect, but I should like *you* to be an example—to see to it that the process is a good one and that the interrogations are a credit to democracy. That is the best thing you can do for the well-being of our Republic. You know how sensitive our young democracy is—how much the opponents of the Republic are watching and waiting for her to slip up. Is the food good?'

'Not bad, thank you.'

'All right, now I really will leave you in peace.'

He stood up.

'One very last thing. What is a confession worth when it is obtained under duress? How much truth can it hold? Good day to you, Inspector Lahnstein. I wish you success.'

'The same to you, Mr Lessing. Goodbye.'

Glumly, Lahnstein chewed his beef and onions and drank his coffee. Then he paid the bill and returned to headquarters where he made straight for the interrogation cell.

Haarmann looked even more of a wreck than in the morning. His eyes drooped; he had to force them open. Lahnstein questioned him for another five hours, surrounded by a protective membrane that allowed him to forget almost completely what condition Haarmann was in and why.

Müller sat behind Lahnstein, the rubber hose at his feet, but Lahnstein didn't even turn his head.

That evening he waited until the last customer had left Emma's shop and then, just as she was about to lock up, he jumped out and asked to be let in. She refused; he pushed against the door until she relented. Inside, she retreated behind the counter and he sat down in one of the armchairs.

'I'm sorry, Emma, but I urgently need to talk to you.'

'I'd rather not.'

'I understand that you're angry, but it's about your brother this time.'

'It's always about my brother.'

'It isn't, but we won't go into that now. Your brother needs help and you're the only person who can give it to him.'

She was silent.

'He's the culprit, believe me; he's murdered an awful lot of boys. But we need him to confess.'

'If it's really true that he did it.'

'He did it all right; he only has to own up to it. Your brother would like to relieve his conscience, but he knows he must die if he does. Given the nature of the crimes, the death penalty is inevitable. One may or may not regret that, but there's no changing it.'

'You're asking me to help you send my brother to his death?'

'That's one way of looking at it. You could also look it like this: your brother has sinned heavily against those boys and their families; he has sinned against society. He is the worst serial killer that Germany has ever known. He is aware of the enormity of that fact; I can see how tormented he is. He has done great wrongs and there is no undoing them, but he can do his bit in helping society to make peace with itself by giving us his confession and accepting a fair trial and an appropriate punishment.'

'He can do his bit by dying—have I got that right?'

'Someone has to make him understand that he cannot continue to live in our society—that he has to die—but also that his family won't stop loving him, however awful the crimes he has committed, if he helps to shed light on those crimes, so that the victims' families know that their losses have been atoned for—that there is such a thing as justice.'

Emma stared at him for a long time. She looked fragile and translucent—thinner than he remembered and more sombre, too, as if she'd been pining a good deal. Her dress hung limply from her shoulders; it must have been a size too big. That's all your work, he told himself, but immediately suppressed the thought.

'You can forget it,' she said. 'Get out of here.'

She came around the side of the counter and went to open the door.

'Emma, I didn't want to say this, but I must: complicity in this affair would be no petty offence. And you knew about Friedel Rothe—or at least suspected something. We both know that. Rothe was the first. If you'd taken action then—'

She looked at him with cold contempt—and a trace of fear. 'Get. Out.'

—

The interrogation the following morning went no differently from the previous ones, except that Haarmann now looked like his own ghost, his eyes ringed with black, his cheeks hollow. He struggled with his speech and acted submissively and fawningly, arousing fierce displeasure in Lahnstein who wanted to remain inside his membrane of normality, and knew that interrogated men rarely behaved that way—not convincingly, at least. He sensed fear in Haarmann's obsequiousness, and a hope that they might be lenient to him after all. But deep down he remained defiant, refusing to relent, admitting nothing.

After three hours there was a knock at the door. Müller got up and went out, returning a moment later to ask Lahnstein to step outside for a minute, please.

Standing in the corridor, accompanied by a policeman, was Emma. She wore a navy-blue suit and, perched on her head, a navy-blue hat with a short lace veil that fell over her face.

'Can I speak to my brother?'

Lahnstein called Müller and the officer out of the cell and took Emma in to Haarmann. He didn't recognise her at first, but screwed up his eyes and stared at her, as if through a fog.

'Emma,' he said at length, feebly.

'Alone,' Emma said to Lahnstein, and in her eyes he saw her horror at Haarmann's state.

'You're not to let him sleep,' Lahnstein said and went out.

He paced the corridor nervously, keyed up with adrenaline. Now and then he looked through the spyhole and saw that Emma was holding her brother's hands. Haarmann was listening to her. Once, when it looked as if he'd fallen asleep,

Lahnstein sent the policeman in.

After an hour or so, he saw her saying goodbye, holding Haarmann, clasping him in her arms. He waited a moment before opening the door. They both had tears on their faces. Emma didn't look at Lahnstein, but stroked her brother's cheek and left. Haarmann and Lahnstein sat down; Müller and the policeman returned to their posts.

'Hans wanted me to kill Wittig, because he was keen to have Wittig's things, so he could sell 'em. He had such beautiful things. It's Hans's fault.'

'So you killed Franz Wittig?'

'Yes.'

'And the other boys?'

He shrugged. 'They were just dolly boys.'

'How many?'

'Lots.'

Lahnstein put a few more questions, then sent Haarmann back to his cell to sleep. He asked the examining magistrate for a detainer, which was granted immediately. It was plain sailing now; he had results. As for the process by which they had been arrived at, that was safe with him inside the protective membrane; he hadn't tortured Haarmann or beaten him or kicked him, and he hadn't personally deprived him of sleep—or only during the day, which didn't count. He went to a pub and got drunk for the first time in a long while, and in the morning he picked up a prostitute on the street to take back to his room. Nothing mattered anymore. He had made up his mind to resign; he would leave the city as soon as Haarmann had been executed. Maybe he'd go back to Bochum; the French were withdrawing and his dad would soon be needing help, the age he was. Or maybe he'd try Berlin.

He had deliberately chosen a prostitute of uncertain sex. It turned out to be a woman—but that was all right too.

Things remained tricky with Haarmann. He admitted nothing willingly; everything had to be wrested from him through persistent questioning. He was most forthcoming on the cases involving Grans—those of Franz Wittig and Adolf Hannappel. He remembered that Hannappel came from Düsseldorf and that Wittig had a withered arm.

'No use in bed, that right hand of his.' Haarmann laughed.

It was Hans, he said, who had introduced him to Wittig. The boy soon grew clingy, partly because he needed somewhere to stay, but Haarmann didn't love him the way he loved the other boys and kept sending him away. Wittig, however, kept coming back. 'I can't love that boy,' Haarmann told Grans, who replied, 'It's easier with someone you don't love.' Grans, it seemed, was after Wittig's suit.

One night, after being sent away, Wittig yelled from the street until Haarmann threw the front-door key down. Eventually, the boy managed to get work in Hamburg, but Grans waylaid him at the station; Haarmann was there and saw him. Then Grans took Haarmann aside. 'Haarmann, you idiot,' he said, 'that suit's just my size. Take the boy home with you. I've set my heart on his suit.' And so Haarmann took Wittig home again and killed him.

He recounted this in a light, easy manner, presenting himself as a reluctant, harried patriarch and Grans as a childish, greedy supplicant.

When he was chopping up the corpse the next morning, Grans called to collect the suit.

'I shoved the body under the bed; Hans won't have seen the blood.'

But he wanted to know what the stink was. Haarmann said he didn't know; he chuckled as he recalled the scene. 'Where's the stuff?' Grans asked. Haarmann told him that Wittig had gone. When Grans heard this, he wanted to start searching the flat, but Haarmann planted himself in front of the bed and gave him the key to Wittig's trunk.

'Hans pulled out the suit an' flung his arms round me saying, "Fritz, you're the best. I can always depend on you."'

Then Haarmann asked Grans for forty marks to cover the costs he had incurred buying food and drink and so on for Wittig. Grans gave him eight marks and they drew up a contract for the remaining sum.

Lahnstein went out and fetched an arrest warrant for Grans. He sent three men off with it and returned to the interrogation cell.

Most of the time, the interrogation went something like this: Lahnstein would show Haarmann a photograph of a boy and tell him that everything belonging to this boy— say, Hermann Spicker—had been found in the cupboard in his, Haarmann's, flat. Haarmann would study the picture.

'Pretty boy,' he'd say. 'But I can't remember him.'

'He had a glass eye.'

'I don't remember a glass eye.'

'So what were his things doing in your flat?'

'S'pose I must've killed him,' Haarmann said meekly.

He looked at the photo again.

'Maybe that's the boy that was lying dead in my arms when I woke in the night. I passed out when I saw him—or felt so faint I fell asleep again. In the morning, the body was lying next to me, all stiff an' cold an' blue—awful sick he looked. I pulled him out of bed by the hands, laid him on the floor an' chopped him up.'

'How did you kill your victims?'

'Oh, you know, a lot of the pretty boys from Cafe Köpcke like being "choked" or "throttled", a bit of pressure on their throats. They were always on at me for it, an' sometimes I got carried away an' bit their Adam's apples till they were dead. I couldn't stop an' they couldn't scream.'

Silence in the cell. Each man was frozen in his own shock. Haarmann looked from one to the other in bewilderment.

'Crikey, did I scare you that much?' He gave a shrill laugh, then broke off abruptly.

'I tried to protect the boys,' he said. 'When I'm in one of my moods, things happen. "Careful you don't make me wild," I'd tell 'em. But they couldn't keep their hands off of me, those pretty boys. Hans, now, he took care. He always pushed me away when I tried to kiss him, 'cause he knew I bit.'

'How did you chop up the corpses?'

He told them, coldly, matter-of-factly, in detail, as if he ran an abattoir and was instructing his new apprentices in the arts of his trade. He showed them how he positioned the knife, from what height he brought the cleaver down.

'The skulls we found,' Lahnstein said, 'were in one piece. But you say you chopped them up. Can you explain that?'

'Really? In one piece? Maybe I didn't chop 'em all up, I can't remember.'

'How many boys?'

'Dunno.'

A petulant face.

'We've found the thighbones of twenty-two boys in the Leine.'

'That many?'

He seemed genuinely astonished.

'Were there twenty-two boys?'

'A lot, anyway.'

'Let's take the last case, Erich de Vries. You must remember him.'

'I dumped Erich in the pond at the entrance to Palace Gardens. Had to make four trips. I transported the pieces in Friedrich's briefcase. He was the one before.'

He chuckled, looking about him with pride, as if he'd pulled off quite a coup.

'Friedrich Koch?'

'Dunno. Either I never knew the surnames or I forgot 'em. There were too many.'

Lahnstein let him have half an hour's rest, then he put him

in a car and drove with him to Palace Gardens. Officers in waders slopped through the pond, pulling body parts out of the water under Haarmann's directions. The skull was intact. Lahnstein vomited.

On the drive back he thought of what Lessing had said. Now they had more than a questionable confession; they had sound proof because Haarmann had known where the corpse was. Lahnstein leant back in his seat. When the driver stopped for a moment, Lahnstein saw an elderly gentleman in the car next to theirs, and thought he recognised Paul von Hindenburg.

—

I'm not going without my head. One of the guards told me it would stay here, but I need to take it with me—I won't let 'em chop it off otherwise. That's what I'll tell 'em—that they're to bury it with me, 'cause I'll be needing it up there—my eyes, so as I can see, an' my ears, so as I can hear.

I'll be with Mother up there an' I'm looking forward to it, can't wait to see her. She'll be pleased to see me an' all. I don't want to see Father, though.

Mother said there's a big garden up there, full of beautiful flowers an' trees; we can play nice games, an' there's music up there an' we can sing.

Everything up there's nicer than what it is down here.

They'll bury me, an' after that you get wings an' fly to heaven an' your head flies with you.

When I'm up there, the ones I killed'll be up there too. But they can't hurt me up there; they don't have heads. I smashed all the heads up, they won't find 'em again. The heads are off an' they're all broken. They can't see me; they've no eyes, no heads.

When I'm up there with my mum, no one'll hurt me, 'cause she'll take care of me.

My mum likes me. She was a beautiful woman. Beautiful little hands, she had, really little.

Before the execution I'll drink a nice cup of coffee, smoke a nice cigar an' eat a nice cheese sandwich.

The main thing is that the knife's good an' sharp, wouldn't want it making a nasty mess of my throat. Needs to be sharp, like my knives. Always sharpened 'em, I did.

I'd like people to say: Fritz Haarmann climbed the scaffold with colossal an' fearless military courage—an' I'll finish off with a little speech.

I've even made it to the pictures. I'm on the weekly newsreel in cinemas all over the world—China, Japan, even America. The people there all know me now, an' next they'll make a book an' everyone'll buy it.

It's a sin. I knew it was, but the boys were always after me.

It'll still be winter, a cold day, but the sun'll shine. An' then— off with my head.

After my execution, I'll haunt my brothers an' sisters, an' knock at the door every night, like my mum did. Oh, Emma.

An' they'll put up a gravestone to me in the cemetery, it's already paid for by death benefits, an' it'll say: Here lies Fritz Haarmann the mass murderer.

9

The thought that she shared something with this man was outrageous, almost unbearable, but although the circumstances could hardly have been more different, they both had a certain knowledge of Martin's body. Now he sat there, guarded by two policemen. She was right at the back of the court so she couldn't see his face—or only if she craned her neck, and she didn't want to do that too often in case people thought he held a particular interest for her. Which, of course, he did.

How childlike he seemed at times—and how cocky and pleased with himself at others. Monika was struck, too, by the harsh tones of the judge and the public prosecutor, and the apparent indifference of the counsel for the defence. She drank it all in. She couldn't follow everything that was discussed, but that only fired her determination to understand this world with its strange language and rituals. Her father had known what he was doing when he asked her to come with him to Hanover where Martin's parents were to make their witness statements. They all travelled together, going by the route that Martin had taken on his last day. His parents sat quietly, sighing occasionally. Once his mother said, 'I don't understand, I just don't understand.' That was hard for Monika to bear because she, of course, did understand; if nothing else, she knew why Martin had run away, and for a moment she was tempted to explain. It might have been some relief to his parents to know that in Martin's case it was the 'natural' as opposed to the 'unnatural' that had set off the fatal chain of events. The 'unnatural'—that was the blanket word used to denote what had driven this man. Always the same word; they seemed to have no other.

The 'natural', at any event, had been brought to an unnatural end. There were no complications and only a slight loss of blood; she was up and about again after two or three days in bed. She had it bad this month, she told her father and he suspected nothing and brought her tea with honey. He didn't probe into such matters.

Did I drive Martin to his death? That was her first thought when she heard that he'd been a victim of the man now referred to in the papers as 'the werewolf'. Bitten to death—it didn't bear thinking of, though she couldn't always stop herself. He didn't have to run away, she thought. It was his decision.

They were talking about Martin again and she felt her pulse quicken, suddenly afraid that he might have confessed to this man in his last hours—told him why it had become impossible for him to stay at home. But it seemed that he hadn't. His mother and father identified the clothes they were shown. They couldn't explain why their son had come to Hanover. 'I don't know, I just don't know,' his mother sobbed.

The man in the dock claimed not to remember Martin; he looked at the photo and shook his head. Then came a witness who had seen Martin leave the station with the accused that night. Martin's mother, who had returned to her seat next to Monika, wept.

'Then I s'pose that's what happened,' the accused said.

—

'How's your Latin?'

Theodor Lessing put the question to Lahnstein as they stood at the door smoking during a break in the proceedings on the ninth day.

'So-so.'

'Simia homo sine cauda, pedibus posticis ambulans, gregarius, omnivorus, inquietus cordis, mendax mentis. Furax, salax, pugnax...'

Lahnstein held up his hands, pleading ignorance.

'...at artium variorum capax. Animalium reliquorum terrae hostis, sui ipsius inimicus teterrimus.'

'I pass. Except for the odd word, of course: gregarious, omnivorous, heart, mind, earth. Help me out.'

'A tailless ape that walks on its hindlegs, is gregarious, omnivorous, unquiet of heart, lying-minded, thieving, lecherous, pugnacious, but a creature of many accomplishments. The enemy of all other earthly beings, and its own most redoubtable foe. That is the earliest description of primitive man.'

He smiled at Lahnstein, a little complacently perhaps, but with evident delight in the words.

'Isn't that exactly how Haarmann comes across? A fluid

character in whom childishness and imbecility, both feigned and genuine, are bizarrely superimposed. Driven exclusively by hunger and lust, he is intuitive and naive even when he's acting—primitive by nature, completely unused to being called to account. He has no dread of the things that every civilised person dreads—death, corpses, decay. But during a storm, he will hide away, trembling, like an animal, and begin faithlessly grovelling to God.'

Lahnstein felt overwhelmed by this flood of words, but he was fascinated nevertheless. Haarmann was just as Lessing said.

'Mr Grans,' Lessing went on, 'has shown himself to be a very different kind of person, tender but tough, obliging but robust, a genial type and yet as watchful as a fox in danger— on the lookout for any little hole in the devil's snare that might provide escape. He is also more familiar than Haarmann with the icy reaches of loneliness. Don't you agree?'

'You're quite right. And the relationship between the two of them—how do you see that?'

'Haarmann is bound to Grans by the old wolf's love for the young fox. Grans is bound to Haarmann by the parasite's gratefulness to its host, but also by a sort of pitying connivance: the man loves me—what would he be without me?'

'I suppose it'll be death for them both.'

'But it isn't a fair trial,' Lessing said. 'Especially for Grans.'

The usher called them back in; the proceedings were about to be resumed. From the first day Lahnstein had followed the trial in a state of anxiety and at times outright fear. Would Haarmann mention the interrogation methods? When

Lahnstein made his statement he was so nervous that his voice cracked several times and once it failed him altogether; the words stuck in his throat and wouldn't come out. The judge asked for a glass of water to be brought. Lahnstein tried not to look at Haarmann, but sometimes glanced at him in spite of himself, wanting to know how he was taking the statement and whether he felt provoked.

Lahnstein spoke matter-of-factly, avoiding the words that were being used in the press: werewolf, monster, bloodsucker, vampire. He made Haarmann out to be rather more intelligent than he judged him. Was he trying to flatter him? It was more than likely, but he didn't admit it to himself—or only fleetingly.

Soon he grew calmer, because neither Böckelmann the presiding judge, nor Roven the public prosecutor had reason to accuse him of errors—not even Siebling, the counsel for the defence. Lahnstein was asked to give an account of the investigations and his version was accepted. It wasn't incorrect—slightly abridged, perhaps, but you couldn't tell everything; there wasn't time. The trial, which had begun on 4 December, was to be over by Christmas.

By and large, Haarmann stuck to the statements he had made to Lahnstein, but the list had to be renumbered several times as new cases came to light. In the end, the public prosecutor brought twenty-seven murder charges. Haarmann confessed to nine and described twelve further cases as 'possible'; six he denied.

Lahnstein was afraid, but decided he'd been right. There was no denying that the Reichstag elections of 7 December, three days after the beginning of the trial, had turned out in the Republic's favour. The Social Democrats carried the day with 26 per cent; the extreme parties were the losers. The Communists lost 3.7 per cent, falling to single figures, and the National Socialist Freedom Party slumped to an insignificant 3 per cent. Hurrah! The Republic had another chance. The only blow was that the German Nationalist People's Party had again attained a fifth of the votes. It was hard to tell where their loyalties lay, but they were hardly likely to come down on the side of the Republic.

Perhaps, Lahnstein thought—very probably, in fact—it couldn't all be put down to Haarmann's conviction, but the case had made the headlines across the country, and no one could claim that it had been entirely without influence. The truth was, there was no way of knowing, and that left Lahnstein at liberty to assume at least some connection between the success of his investigations and the election results. Who said democracy was under threat? Safe and sound, my dear Lessing, safe and sound. Unemployment had fallen recently; that presumably played a part, too.

The Schiefer Case was next. Annabelle Schiefer, elegant in an expensive-looking black suit, entered the court and walked to the witness box, surrounded by an aura of immunity, as if nothing of what was going on touched her. Lahnstein leant forwards to get a better look, but couldn't see her expression. She didn't spare a glance for Haarmann.

She told the court of a harmonious, almost sublime family life, a symbiosis between parents and son, a shared love of science.

'We often discussed pharmaceutical matters at the dinner table.'

From his seat, Lahnstein could see Haarmann. He was staring at this woman with a mixture of astonishment and fascination, occasionally grinning salaciously.

'Do you have any idea why your son might have gone missing?' the judge asked. 'Is it possible that he had reason to leave home?'

'Certainly not. What are you insinuating?'

'Well, we've seen a number of cases where boys were driven to run away by a certain affliction.'

'I would ask you not to mention us in connection with such cases,' Annabelle Schiefer said. 'I assume that my son was kidnapped. There was definitely violence involved.'

'The woman's barmy,' Haarmann shouted.

Silence in the courtroom.

'Haarmann,' the judge said sharply. 'Keep your mouth shut when you're not being questioned.'

Not so harsh, Lahnstein thought. Don't provoke him. For God's sake, don't provoke him.

'But it's not true what she says. I remember Richard Schiefer. He had these fancy clothes. Hans had his eye on 'em. He was always on at me to get 'em for him.'

'Nonsense,' Grans shouted.

'I did not ask you to speak,' the presiding judge said.

'It was clearly murder and robbery,' said Mrs Schiefer.

'I met Richard in Cafe Köpcke,' Haarmann said. 'He came over to talk an' was keen to come home with me. So I took him. But I didn't want to 'cause I knew what might happen an' he wasn't one of those dolly boys—he was going to win the Nobel Prize.'

Laughter in the courtroom.

'Quiet,' Böckelmann shouted. 'What's this about the Nobel?' he asked Haarmann.

'It's something he told me when he was in bed with me—that his mother was set on him winning the Nobel Prize, for chemistry or something. Richard didn't give a toss. All he wanted was to be with me, polishing. Proper bad one, he was.'

He grinned.

Annabelle Schiefer was staring at a point above the judge's head.

'I sent him away, but he kept coming back. Stood at my door, begging to be let in. "Open up, Fritz. I want to see you, Fritz." In the end I took him in again. He didn't just want to polish; he wanted to suck an' all.'

In the witness box, Mrs Schiefer held herself straight as a rod.

'It is a disgrace that the man is allowed to speak here like this,' she said in a firm voice. 'I assume you don't believe a word of it.'

'He came round an' said he had to stay a few days. A customer in the chemist's shop had told his parents that he was always going to Cafe Köpcke an' the Queer Kettle, an' they'd asked him if it was true. An' Richard'd had enough of telling lies so he said yes, it was true an' it didn't stop him winning the Nobel Prize. Makes no difference to the Nobel Prize who you like kissing, does it?'

He looked about him slyly.

'Then they chucked Richard out.'

He broke off and looked up at the chandeliers. A gathering storm had turned the sky black, and the lights had gone on.

'Like a Christmas tree,' Haarmann sighed.

'Is that true?' the judge asked Mrs Schiefer.

'It's a revolting lie.'

'He came to stay with me,' Haarmann said, 'an' the second night I bit him till he was dead, I remember clearly. I couldn't help it; it just happened. I gave Hans his things.'

'Hans Grans was wearing them when he was arrested,' the public prosecutor said. 'The complete set.'

Lahnstein caught Haarmann looking at Grans. There was resentment in his gaze, but he was evidently still in love.

'Do you know these clothes?' the judge asked Mrs Schiefer, indicating a small pile on the table in front of him.

She shook her head.

'Please get up and step closer.'

She did as he asked.

'Do you know these things?'

The courtroom was silent.

Mrs Schiefer ran two fingers over the sleeve of a jacket.

'Yes.'

'You may go now.'

She went out. She was still straight as a rod, but her features were frozen and she moved stiffly, as if she were walking with sticks.

On Day Nine, the case of Adolf Hannappel came to trial. His parents had travelled up from Düsseldorf and told the court what they had told Lahnstein, though without mentioning the sausage. When they had finished, Haarmann was presented with a picture of Adolf Hannappel.

'I know him. Hans pointed him out to me.'

'That's not true,' said Grans. 'It was the other way round.'

'What rot.'

'He's lying.'

'Let us first hear what Mr Haarmann has to say,' said the judge.

'Hans said to me, "There's a pretty young boy sitting in the waiting room, why don't you go an' see? You might like the look of him."'

'Nonsense.'

'Quiet!'

'"He's sitting on a box in a nice pair of breeches," Hans said. "I'd like those breeches of his."'

Grans stood up but remained silent. A guard pushed him back onto the bench.

Grans, Haarmann said, had spoken to Hannappel. At first he'd been rebuffed, but then he had managed to persuade Hannappel to deposit his box at left luggage. From there they went to the station buffet where he bought the boy a beer, offered him a cigarette and promised to find him somewhere to sleep. He signalled to Haarmann to go on ahead and then followed with Hannappel. They staged a chance encounter in Schillerstrasse, and Grans asked Haarmann if he could put the young man up.

'And of course I could,' said Haarmann with a grin.

Lahnstein looked around at the boy's parents. They

were aghast.

'Did you fondle him?' the judge asked.

'Didn't I just.'

This time Lahnstein didn't dare look round.

In the morning Grans came to the flat; Hannappel was alive.

'Hans pulled me out onto the landing an' pitched into me 'cause I didn't have the breeches ready for him.'

'Liar.'

'Quiet!'

Three or four days later, Haarmann killed his guest. The following afternoon, Grans came to the flat again.

'I'd cleaned up by then,' Haarmann said.

They went to the station together and collected the box from left luggage.

Grans' version was that Haarmann had drawn his attention to a young man in the waiting room.

'Fritz said to me, "Take a look at him and tell me what you think. His breeches might fit you." I was eating in the buffet and Fritz went to speak to the boy while I finished my meal.'

'And you didn't help Adolf Hannappel take his box to left luggage?' the judge asked.

'Oh, yes, I offered to help. But I didn't go to the flat the next day to collect the breeches. It wasn't until a few days later that I saw Fritz again. I bumped into him on the street and he asked me to help him carry a box home from the station.'

A witness came forward who had seen what happened at

the station and confirmed Haarmann's version.

Grans and Haarmann also made contradictory statements concerning Wittig's case.

Grans said that Haarmann had told him of a young man he was 'stuck on'.

He said that Haarmann had approached Wittig.

That it was nothing to do with him that Wittig stayed at Haarmann's.

That he hadn't pressed Haarmann into getting Wittig's suit for him.

That he hadn't seen the corpse.

That, since he hadn't seen the corpse, he hadn't asked for the suit either.

Again, witnesses confirmed Haarmann's version.

On the eleventh day, the dispute between Böckelmann and Lessing escalated. Böckelmann, the presiding judge, was angered almost daily by Lessing's reports. Sometimes, after skimming through the latest newspapers brought by the court usher, he confronted Lessing directly.

'Yet more untruths.'

'What do you mean, *untruths?*' Lessing asked from the press seats.

Böckelmann ignored this and went back to questioning whoever was in the witness box. After a while, he turned to Lessing again. 'Allow me,' he said, 'to draw your attention to Paragraph 176 of the Judicature Act, which states that it is the judge's prerogative to allocate seats to the press. I will not suffer partial or untruthful journalism.'

'Oho, a threat!' cried Lessing.

Lahnstein read all of Lessing's articles with concern and fascination. Nobody wrote as concisely or trenchantly.

The sad small-town drama of aggrieved juridical ambition, medical self-righteousness and ministerial abuse.

The drama of a disturbed anthill, biting and squirting acid as it strives to remove the intruding foreign body.

The longer the proceedings go on, the harder it is to deny that one cannot judge a snake without also trying the swamp from which the snake draws its sustenance.

Haarmann, Lessing wrote, made all his statements under pressure from and at the mercy of the Hanover police. The main expert witnesses were partial. Legal medical counsellor Dr Brandt was the same expert witness who in 1908 had saved Haarmann from the lunatic asylum by declaring him sane. Were he now to reach a different verdict, it would be tantamount to complicity in all Haarmann's crimes; he could hardly be expected to come up with new findings. Nor was it in the interest of Dr Schackwitz—the pathologist who had failed to analyse properly the meat found in Haarmann's room—to bring the authorities into disrepute.

The man speaks true, Lahnstein thought.

On the twelfth day, the expert witnesses refused to give their reports in Lessing's presence. When the public prosecutor and counsel for the defence also aired complaints, the judge turned to Haarmann and asked if there were any truth in the accusations that he had not been well-treated by the authorities. Lahnstein held his breath.

'It's all lies what the fellow says,' Haarmann said.

The relief of it.

The judge spoke roughly to Lessing. 'You are admitted here as a reporter, not a novelist. We cannot have anyone engaging in psychology here in court.'

'I refuse to tolerate this attempt to influence my reporting,' Lessing said. 'The free press is a cornerstone of the democratic republic.'

He was sent from the courtroom.

Lahnstein had read Professor Schultze's psychological report in advance of the trial and barely listened. He was thinking of Emma, whom he hadn't seen since that day in the interrogation cell.

'According to the results of the tests,' Schultze said, 'Haarmann has the intelligence of a six- to eight-year-old. During my own examinations of him, however, I observed him give not only correct, but also prompt replies to many of the questions he had been unable to answer in the intelligence test proper. His writing, too, suggests that his knowledge was above average; some witnesses, indeed, consider him intellectually superior to Grans.'

A fake, Lahnstein thought. My impression exactly.

'I should also like to stress that in my many meetings with him I was struck time and again by his talent for observation, his quick-wittedness, the pertinence of his remarks, his unusual ability to adapt himself to a situation and his extraordinarily good memory.'

Half an hour later, Schultze came to the end of his speech. 'To conclude and sum up what I have said, I remain unconvinced that Haarmann suffers from imbecility in any clinical sense.'

On 19 December Böckelmann announced his verdict.

'Firstly: the accused, Mr Fritz Haarmann, trader, is sentenced to death twenty-four times on twenty-four counts of murder and acquitted on three further counts of murder; moreover, he is to be deprived of civil rights for life.

'Secondly: the accused, Mr Hans Grans, trader, is sentenced to death on one count of incitement to murder and to twelve years in a penitentiary for complicity; moreover, he is to be deprived of civil rights for life.

'With regard to the crimes themselves, Haarmann went to bed naked with each of the young men and they fondled and kissed each other. This excited Haarmann sexually and he sucked the young men's throats, biting them as he did so and thus killing them. He saw bite marks on the throats of all the young men he killed. It is also possible that in some cases he put his hands on the young men's throats and applied pressure to their Adam's apples. He did not, however, intend to kill the boys. There was never a struggle between him and the young men, although on one occasion he woke up the next morning with scratches on his hand and on another he thought he heard the boy cry out, "Help, Fritz," in a choked voice. He was unable to explain why he bit his victims' throats.'

The judge read in a monotone.

'The overall picture is that of a pathological personality, a man of considerable moral inferiority and extreme intellectual weakness. At the time of committing the killings, however, he was neither unaware of what he was doing, nor in a state of pathological mental disturbance such as would have prevented him from exercising free will.

'In light of this, the court considers Haarmann's statements concerning Grans' actions to be plausible and finds that Grans was aware not only of the killings of Friedel Rothe and Fritz Franke, but also of those of Haarmann's subsequent victims, and that in a number of cases he actually saw the corpses. Grans knew moreover that Haarmann killed the young men to excite himself sexually and to gain possession of their things after killing them. He made a deliberate decision to take advantage of this activity, namely to participate in the spoils or, in the defendants' own words, to "divvy up" with Haarmann.'

The two accused received the verdict with composure.

Lessing was waiting at the door and asked Lahnstein whether the sentences were as expected.

'They'll both end on the scaffold, if that's what you mean.'

'A mistake with Grans, a dreadful mistake. And in Haarmann's case, the wrong path to the verdict. An early fall from grace on the part of our republic. How are things to turn out well after getting off to such a bad start?'

Lahnstein said nothing.

'We've already discussed this, I know. May I accompany you a little way, even so?'

Lahnstein nodded. They lit up cigarillos and went out. It

was a fine, sunny day.

'I am going to make a suggestion to the authorities of Hanover,' Lessing said.

As he didn't go on, Lahnstein asked, 'What?'

'Did you know that in the old days, when people still knew what it was to feel a sense of common guilt, there was a tradition of communal expiation. Whenever bloodguilt lay over a city, the citizenry would atone with an act of public spirit, building a chapel or monastery, erecting a monument, planting a tree. The beautiful Nikolai Chapel—the oldest building in the city—is said to be the result of such an act of civic atonement.'

'I didn't know that.'

'In the present case, the sins against the national soul and honour—not least the lurid sins of sensational journalism— have been so great that those responsible for our nation's health—clergymen, doctors, teachers—must do their best to steer such ghastliness back onto the path of dignity and beauty. Children should be spoken to in school; adults in church. All the bells of the city should toll out a warning. And at the very hour of the guilty-innocent monster's death, we will lay the young men's sad remains in a common coffin, decorate it with flowers and bury it in our earth at the expense of our city—not hidden away in a churchyard, oh no, but in one of our big public squares. And all of us, an entire city, will follow behind: senators and magistrates, mayor, public officials, civil servants, teachers, clergymen, governor of the province, district president, chief of police—not to "pay our last respects", for that is beyond our power, but to take upon ourselves the burden of our common guilt. In common parenthood, we will walk behind the coffin of a youth which, through our own fault, has been prematurely cut down. Beside the house of murder where the children were sacrificed, lies a large tree-covered square, behind which stands a church, the resting place of Leibniz, the wisest man ever born to Hanover. Here on this square we will lay the coffin in the earth. We will fetch granite from our Harz Mountains—or, better still, a great primitive boulder from our heathland. This boulder shall serve as a memorial stone and on it posterity shall read three words only: "Our Common Fault".

'Now my question to you is, will you take part, will you join us?'

'I'll think about it,' Lahnstein said. They came to a crossroads and he wished Lessing goodbye, mumbling something about things to do.

For the last time he entered the office and sat down at his desk. Before him lay a thick, cream-coloured envelope, addressed to him by hand. Inside was a card with a single line:

Congratulations on your success with the case.
(signed) Comrade Gustav Noske

On the following day, 20 December, the papers had something else to talk about. Thanks to the intercession of the head prison warden, Adolf Hitler had been released from gaol after only a year. It seemed he had behaved himself. Lahnstein attached no great importance to the news.

—

337

Hanover, 5 February

The Confession of Fritz Haarmann the Murderer

As I will be driven by car in Person through the streets to drive to Police Head Quarters, I have the oportunity to give this letter to the Public.

I dont want these lines to fall into the hands of the Court or Police because I can only asume that they will Withhold my Confession from the Publick & bring an inocent man, Hans Grans, to death by the Executioner's blade. May the honest finder bestow God's blessing on his family & children for all eternity. That is the wish of Fritz Haarmann who is Doomed to die. However I will give my full Confession to the Reverent Hauptmann Court Prison. Wanting that document too to be seen by the Publick & not dissappear, I hence write this letter. Thus my lawyer Dr Lotze must request the document from the Reverent Hauptmann. I, Fritz Haarmann, have written this letter by my own hand, to proove the Truth that this is indeed my writing, my brother Adolf Haarmann-Fortmüller of No. 16 Asternstrasse is perfectly aquaintanced with my handwriting. My Conffesion. What I say here is the plain Truth, so help me God, & condemned man that I am, I dont desire to add to the burden on my conscience before God.

Hans Grans robbed & deceived me dreadfully over the years, but still I couldnt give him up because I had no one else in the world. Grans was to support me in my old age because I had always Provided for Grans & would have saved a tidy sum if Grans hadnt taken everything from me. Grans was not a bad man, but he was very reckless. Grans's reckless drinking and womanising went so far that I was nothing but a Milch Cow for him. Because of his debauched way of life, Grans was unaware of my doings with the young people. Grans didnt have the faintest idea that I murdered anyone, never saw a thing. All Grans knew was that I was perverse and harmonised with boys. When my affairs concerning murder was discovered by the local police I was compelled by force & violence to speak untruths, & for fear of wanting no further violence I afterwards said yes to everything & incrimminated Grans by telling untruths. My sister Emma & brother Adolf who I called for help when I see them coming, I said to them in the officer's presence, Emma, Adolf, here I am being beaten & compelled by force & violence to speak untruths. I asked Mrs Witzel to petition for me to make my statements to the Public Prosecutor, but sadly my request was not heeded. Then I lied & said incriminating things against Grans so that the police would leave me in peace. But when the police said that Grans had also said Very incrimminating things about me, I said to myself Grans had no right to do that because I was always so good to Grans, & the more lies I told about Grans, the more decently I was treated. As for withdrawing my statements in Court, I didnt want that either, I thought only of taking revenge on Grans & with the help of the police I did indeed succeed. Here I would like to mention that Grans knew nothing of my past life. Hans Grans didnt know I had ever been in a lunatic asylum, & nor did he ever blackmail me about it. Grans knew of no murder, never saw a thing had no idea. None of the statements made by Grans were believed, or else they were twisted to Incrimminate Grans. Hence Grans's words in Court that Haarmann confused Truth & Fiction until there was no telling them apart. I, Fr. Haarmann, call on Heaven as my witness that Grans has been wrongfully convicted. Grans isnt even guilty of recieving stolen goods from me. Grans never brought me a person whom was harmed by me & had Grans known that I Murdered, he would surely have prevented it. I cannot take this guilt with me to the grave & call on my Mother as witness, my Mother who is Holy to me & who is with God. Hans Grans has been wrongfully convicted through the fault of the police & because of my revenge on him, for Grans said such incrimminating things about me, though I had never been anything but good to him. Take my bit of life I do not fear death by the Executioner's blade it is a release for me, but put yourself in Hans Grans's place, he must Despair of God & Justice & all through my fault. I was believed though I lied, Grans went unheeded though he spoke the Truth. May Hans Grans forgive me my revenge & may humanity forgive my murders which I commited in a state of sickness. I gladly deliver my death & blood into God's arms & Justice in atonement.

(signed) Fritz Haarmann.

10

Haarmann was executed on 15 April 1925, in the penitentiary on Cellerstrasse which is surrounded by a red-brick wall. It was a fine, cold day. A small birch grew out of a corner of the wall, the only plant far and wide.

Lessing's suggestion had not been put into practice; Lahnstein wasn't even sure that he had filed it. And so he was spared the decision of whether or not to take part in the procession.

Grans' execution was suspended. A letter to his father, the bookseller Albert Grans, had been found on the street one day. It seemed that Haarmann had written it in his cell and later thrown it out of the car window as he was driven from prison to police headquarters. Grans would presumably be retried.

That was embarrassing, as was Haarmann's claim that he had been mistreated by the police. But the chief of police had assured Lahnstein that he had nothing to fear. Disciplinary action had been taken against two policemen suspected of having beaten Haarmann. Müller was not one of them.

The main thing, Lahnstein thought, was that the murders had come to an end. In future he would stay clean—he swore to God he would. He'd made an exception—there had been no other way—but it wouldn't happen again.

Haarmann was in good spirits, almost cheerful. He drank a cup of coffee, smoked a cigar and ate a cheese sandwich. The sandwich was so good that he asked for another and it was granted him. He thanked Lahnstein warmly for coming.

'Off to Mother now,' he said.

Lahnstein left the cell. Emma was waiting outside and slipped in after him without a glance. He didn't wait for her to come out, but went to find a cafe where he could have breakfast.

Acknowledgments

This novel is based on *Haarmann, the Story of a Werewolf* by Theodor Lessing and *Die Haarmann-Protokolle*, edited by Michael Farin and Christine Pozsár.

The passages on pp. 305–06, 322–23 and 336–37 are quoted from Lessing, slightly adapted in places (translations by Imogen Taylor). The quotations from the medical reports and trials also correspond largely to the originals. Haarmann's confession at the end of Chapter 9 is taken word for word from his letter.

I should like to thank Christer von Lindquist and Thomas Schühly for the many conversations about Fritz Haarmann. Schühly's film *Deathmaker* is a great work.